Carl Weber's Kingpins:

Brooklyn

Carl Weber Presents

Carl Weber's Kingpins: Brooklyn

Brooklyn

Carl Weber Presents

Brandie Davis

www.urbanbooks.net

Urban Books, LLC
300 Farmingdale Road, N.Y.-Route 109
Farmingdale, NY 11735

Carl Weber's Kingpins: Brooklyn
Copyright © 2022 Brandie Davis

ISBN 13: 978-1-64556-357-0
ISBN 10: 1-64556-357-X

First Trade Paperback Printing July 2022
Printed in the United States of America

10 9 8 7 6 5 4 3 2 1

*This is a work of fiction. Any references or similarities
to actual events, real people, living or dead, or to real
locales are intended to give the novel a sense of reality.
Any similarity in other names, characters, places, and
incidents is entirely coincidental.*

Distributed by Kensington Publishing Corp.
Submit orders to:
Customer Service
400 Hahn Road
Westminster, MD 21157-4627
Phone: 1-800-733-3000
Fax: 1-800-659-2436

Carl Weber's Kingpins:

Brooklyn

Carl Weber Presents

Brandie Davis

Chapter 1

Brooklyn, New York
March 1973

Wesley welcomed the cool air that danced along his forehead, books clutched to his chest as the spring breeze slid its way between his short, shiny charcoal 'fro. It shoved out the force needed to push his feet forward quicker. Mama timed his voyage from school to home, belt at hand and ready for takeoff whenever his trip resulted in delays. Wesley pushed himself down Brooklyn's concrete sidewalks that spit up sad attempts of greenery through their cracks faster with every person he passed by. He caught pieces of giggling schoolgirl conversations, and he couldn't help but wonder whose face they visualized and gawked over.

Like a vehicle in a movie's high-speed chase scene, Wesley made a sharp turn on the corner of Broadway and Hancock, where he temporarily stopped and caught his breath. School books still stapled to his chest, he stood erect and looked up at the sky. Mouth open, he breathed heavily in and out. The group of ponytail- and skirt-wearing girls he had outwalked minutes prior strolled past him. Not far in the lead, they looked behind themselves and snickered at what they labeled "dramatic breathing." Wesley lowered his head before making eye contact with the one who laughed the hardest. He smiled bashfully and listened to their giggles until they crossed the street, turned the corner, and made it out of sight.

"Wes! Wes!"

Wesley looked to his left at the person who had said his name. Ruby was dressed loud and rich as ever.

Wesley proceeded to walk. "Ruby, I can't wait around. Walk and talk."

Ruby jogged his way. The sound of his platforms banging against the ground was an unwelcomed, annoying distraction.

"I forgot Mrs. May want you in that house immediately." Ruby playfully slapped the back of Wesley's head.

Wesley felt around where Ruby had hit. His friend's strong hand, luckily, hadn't patted his hair down.

"That's Mrs. Evans to you. Now, you know Mama told you since you were seven to refer to her as Mrs. Evans."

Wesley looked across the street. He was approaching and noticed the traffic light had turned red the moment his eyes touched down on it.

"Dammit!" He slapped one of his hands on his left hip and faced Ruby. "Fooling with you, I done missed the light." He turned to the moving traffic and sucked his teeth.

"Man, you're the oldest young person I know. You're so serious down to how you dress." Ruby looked Wesley up and down. His chestnut face scrunched up, and his head moved from side to side. "Man, those threads are tired."

Wesley gave himself a once-over, starting with his pristine blue-and-white shell-toe sneakers only worn to school, bell bottom jeans, and ivory turtleneck. A wave of insecurity slammed down over him. The questionable feelings that took over and made him feel inferior in the clothing department led him to hear his father's voice. *Toughen up, boy. Don't let anyone talk to you any kinda way.*

Wesley ripped his eyes off his clothing and slammed them on Ruby's outfit. "Man, look who's talking. You look like a *Soul Train* reject."

Ruby gasped loudly just before he extended his right leg that was kept warm in black bell bottoms, folded his arms, and declared, "I look good!"

"You look like a fool." Wesley insulted Ruby without taking his eyes off the cars that slowed down. What felt like it was taking entirely too long only took seconds because the light changed, and he was permitted to walk across the street. Wesley's fast walking turned into a light jog. Ruby kept up with a few steps of his long legs.

"This is the style!" Ruby held open his purple beaded vest. The fringes on the bottom jumped in all directions. His silk long-sleeve purple button-down was set off with a wide, long collar.

"So!" Wesley spat. His arms tightened around his books that were now back on his chest.

"So? You jive turkey! Style is everything. Look at this!" Ruby grabbed Wesley by the shoulder, forcing him to stop walking and face him.

"Maann, if you don't stop slowing me down!"

"You see this, youngblood?" Ruby rustled a gold chain with a diamond and red ruby pendant out from his shirt and wiggled it in front of Wesley. "A ruby for a Ruby. Cool, right?" Ruby's large teeth took up almost half his face when he smiled. "You need to get you one of these, brotha. Then maybe I'll think you're stylin'." He looked down at the books glued to his friend and patted them. "Then get you a backpack, youngblood. Those days of bootstraps and book holding are long gone."

Wesley pushed his hand away. "Stop calling me young-blood. Youngblood, you're thirteen, one year older than me. And where'd you get the money for that? Last time you had big cash you were—" Wesley stopped talking. "Shit, man. You pushin'—"

"That heroin, soul brother." Ruby fixed his gigantic collar and spun around one full time.

A tall woman with afro puffs on each side of her head walked by hand in hand with a man whose size met hers.

"You working for JoJo?" Wesley asked.

"Yeah, man, who else?" Ruby continued walking.

"Rumors are going around that someone working for JoJo is stealing from him. A young head. Ruby, don't tell me you're—"

Three loud popping noises filled the streets.

The books Wesley had securely held on to slipped out of his grasp and met the city's concrete as soon as Ruby's blood and inner tissue splashed and soiled his face and turtleneck. In the midst of women hollering, school kids and neighborhood residents bolting for safety, Wesley's feet remained planted on the ground while urine raced down his legs. Gumball-sized teardrops tumbled down his cheeks and inside his slightly agape, trembling mouth.

With a slight pitch in his voice, the name Goldie slid from Wesley's tongue. His tears intensified, and his mouth momentarily ceased movement. Circuits between his head and his mouth must have malfunctioned. That was the only logical explanation for why a twelve-year-old, whose common sense surpassed a majority of adults, would voice the identity of a man who killed for pay.

Wesley reluctantly took in the sight of his friend sprawled out, submerged in blood, without the back of his head. The big, bad man, Brooklyn's monster, draped in a vest of gold chains that sat on top of a wide-collar black-and-gold silk shirt, looked Wesley's way. His leather cowboy hat hugged the left side of his head, allowing for his bald head to breathe on the right. He responded to the kid's slip of the tongue.

"Yeah, youngblood, it's me, the big bad wolf, Goldie." He gave a small, fast smile.

Right after the kindly jest, he looked down at his mark. "Aye, Ruby. Aye! JoJo has something he wants you to know. You're fired!"

Wesley's hands shook. He needed to hold on to something. He needed his books. He needed a sense of comfort.

"Aye! You hear me?" Goldie nudged at Ruby's leg, using the tip of his cowboy boot.

Ruby's body lightly rocked. The movement caused a loose chunk of cranium to detach and slither to the ground. Within Wesley's stomach, a race ensued as his lunch outran his breakfast and made it out his mouth. Brown and white moist chunks saturated the covers of his academic and recreational books. Wesley let out whatever his insides had left next to a tree.

Although his literature was destroyed by brain matter and vomit, a small voice inside his head held on to the belief that they could be salvaged. After he caught his breath and wiped his mouth off with the sleeve of his shirt, he went for the reads. Wesley held up his English book by the spine with his thumb and pointer finger. The once-crisp white pages now dripped with mucus and blood. The printed black words were a running blur.

"Aye! What's your name?"

Wesley's attention snapped to Goldie. "Wesley," he whispered.

"Speak up!" Goldie demanded.

"Wesley!" he loudly voiced. "Wesley!"

"Wesley, do me a favor and tell your friend what JoJo said."

Wesley sucked in his lips and looked at his friend's remains. Immediately, he cleared his throat and said out loud, "JoJo says you're fired, Ruby." He cleared his voice box once more, then looked at Goldie. The soiled book still lingered between his two fingers.

"Thank you, Wesley. You know, for some reason when I'm working, these guys never hear me. They seem to respond better to others."

"Well, Mr. Goldie."

"Just Goldie."

"Sorry, Goldie. Ruby's not in the best of shape to answer you right now."

Goldie kicked Ruby for the last time. "I guess you're right," he muttered. He slid his firearm in the back of his pants when he noticed the books at Wesley's feet. "Hey! What's with you fucking up Toni Morrison and Mario Puzo's work?"

This guy knows who Toni Morrison and Mario Puzo are?

Goldie picked up *The Godfather*, and with the palm of his gloved hand, cleaned off the cover. Witnessing its damage up close, he sucked his teeth and confiscated *The Bluest Eye* out of the body fluids. He pushed what fragments he could off of the piece of literature.

"This is a damn shame." Goldie pouted. "There's one thing the man can't take away from no brotha, and that's what's in here." Mario Puzo in hand, Goldie jammed his finger into the side of his head. He stared for a long time at Wesley. Wesley took a short step backward. Goldie tucked the ruined authors' works under his arm and dug inside his pocket.

"Here. Take this." He handed Wesley a fifty-dollar bill. Buy your books over and keep reading. A smart brotha is a strong brotha."

Wesley reached for the cash. His fingertips were coated in blood. When he touched the money, an unsettling, nerve-mounting sense of guilt invaded him.

"Thank you," he fought to say. Stuck in place alone on a street where bystanders had taken off, he did what he thought best. He kept talking. "Goldie. You killed Ruby in daylight on a busy street. You should go before the police get here."

"Youngblood, they're already here." Goldie nodded behind Wesley. The kid followed the killer's eyes to a cop car that sat on the corner of the last street Wesley had to cross to make it home.

"Crackers require a lot of money to look the other way. Tsk, tsk, tsk. But they're not my problem at the moment. Do you know what the problem of the day is, Wesley?"

Goldie's stare made Wesley's skin turn cold.

"No. I don't."

"JoJo's down a youngblood. Ruby's caused a glitch in the system. A glitch in need of quick repair."

"I'm sorry for your dilemma."

"I like you, Wesley. You're smart. You use words like *dilemma*." Goldie snickered. "You'd be an upgrade from Ruby, you know?"

No. Oh, no. He wants me to work for JoJo. Be what? The organization's blind spot? Kids are hard to connect to people like JoJo.

"I don't understand."

"You do. But just in case you don't, you now work for JoJo. Ruby made me look bad. I brought him in, and he made trouble. Now I must right that wrong." Goldie smiled and nodded. He had a tooth missing on the side of his mouth.

"Goldie, I—"

"Will do whatever the fuck I say, or I'll put a hole in your fucking brain."

Wesley thought he heard a heartbeat. He settled for believing the muscle racing like a track star belonged to him, because the dead, glazed-over look in Goldie's eyes proved he had no heart.

"Keep reading those books, youngblood. I'm sure they'll help you, but I'm your new career venture. I'll see you after school tomorrow." Goldie looked down at Ruby. "Nephew, you finally made me proud. Had you not been such a fuck up, I'd never have met Wesley." Goldie smiled.

Then he said, "Oh, look at this. Boy done went shopping." Goldie ripped Ruby's ruby from around his neck. He shoved his hand in his pocket, and then turned to leave with Wesley's two books and Ruby's chain in his possession. However, Goldie didn't allow his nephew's new purchase to fill the lining of his pocket for long before he took it right back out and tossed it to Wesley.

"Consider this a welcome gift, youngblood. You're our new Ruby."

Chapter 2

One week after Miles' aunt's divorce was finalized, she left behind all furnishings she had worked her fingers to the white meat to earn. The terrorizing carousel known as her marriage had finally shut down, which gave her the opportunity to uproot and start fresh in New York, where her family and friends were at their strongest.

Haddy had to rebuild her dream apartment out of the lack of sleep and double shifts she forced her body to take on, but it was worth it. Worth decorating a home that didn't house her jobless, junky husband. The sunshine walls and kitchen appliances represented her rainbow after the storm; the rich wooden cabinets, her strength; and the green-and-yellow vinyl flooring, her wild side. Haddy's home was the desired child her ex never allowed her body to have. It was all she had, all she trusted and loved, second to her nephew, Miles.

Miles was her older sister's son, whom Haddy had convinced her sister to keep despite his deafness. Haddy had bonded with Miles long before he accomplished any childhood milestones, and that love was what led her to allow him to house sit.

"Do not have anyone in my house, Miles," Haddy signed. "And water my plants. All of them."

Miles nodded profusely. Haddy had repeated the same thing every day leading up to her one-week vacation to Hawaii. The bothered look defining Miles' face made her drop her luggage and pull him in for a hug. Behind him, her eyes were closed, and she patted his back.

After she released, him she told him, "I'm sorry. I don't mean to act like your mother. I trust you."

Miles tried to turn his back, but Haddy grabbed him and held him in place by both shoulders. "Understand, besides you, this place is a big deal for me. I can finally rest without that junk stumbling in during all hours of the night and don't have to worry while at work if my valuables will be there when I got back or was lost in some damn bet."

Miles' grimace died down. The truth of his aunt's past twisted his heart with every mention of it. *I should have gone with her when she left New York. I could have protected her and kept her from marrying that wanker. I could have done better for myself.*

Miles threw his hands up. "I can dig it. Your pad is safe with me."

Haddy beamed. Seeing that he was watching her lips, she said. "Good! Now give me some skin."

Miles rolled his eyes and smiled. Their palms slapped against one another, followed by the backs of their hands. "You're one cool brotha. You know that, Miles?"

"Miles!"

Mayo waved his hand in front of Miles' face. The wind created by his heavy hand woke up Miles' nerves as he forced his sight on his friend.

"You cool?" Mayo sucked his teeth and repeated his question using sign. For ten years, the two had been friends, yet occasions still rose when Mayo slipped up and forgot his best friend was deaf.

Miles threw his hand up and slid his bony knees fully under the kitchen table. He grabbed the meat mallet and continued to crush the Hawaiian baby woodrose. *Wham! Wham!* He beat the light brown seeds harder than needed.

Mayo turned around and scanned the area for what hypnotized Miles. Nothing from the busy sunk-in living room stood out as reason enough to fixate. The dragon trees and humongous arrow mural stretching across the room were nothing new. And then he saw it—the photograph taken of Miles and his aunt during last year's Fourth of July block party. He remembered that party. Mrs. Watson had snapped the shot of the two engaged in giving one another some skin. Haddy had surprised everyone that day and made it known she was back in Queens for good. That picture was taken that day. Miles couldn't have ripped the smile off his face if he wanted to.

Good times, Mayo thought.

Slowly, he walked over to his friend. He wiped his hands on the small apron he had forced onto his heavy frame and slid on the cushioned kitchen chair across from Miles. Before he spoke, he wiggled around in the seat. If he hugged the left side of the chair, his right butt cheek hung over the side, and vice versa. So, he squirmed around in his seat in search of the most comfortable spot.

Although Mayo knew sign language, he could not help but speak in a hushed tone. "It's not what you think. He didn't do it. JoJo did not kill Ms. Haddy. Not everyone who dies in New York is at the hands of my brother." Mayo's beady hazel eyes pleaded with Miles to hear him out.

Miles banged the mallet down harder on the seeds. The table rumbled, and seed fragments hung in the air. Three pounds later, Miles dropped the small club.

"This is not right." Miles' hands raged. "What he's making us do in my aunt's apartment is not right. Had he loved her, I wouldn't be doing this, and this . . . experimenting wouldn't be done here." He turned his nose up at the small mountain of woodrose, then grimaced at the three food dehydrators drying pieces of mushrooms on the kitchen counters.

"You have to admit, Miles. Cooking here was a pretty good idea. I mean, we're in a good part of Queens away from Brooklyn, and a lot of people—"

The twitching in one of Miles' eyes and the hard grind of his teeth momentarily stopped Mayo from signing.

He started again. "Umm, I'm just saying if you—"

Miles stood out of his seat. The unpredictable, swift action made Mayo push his chair back instantly.

With every hand motion, Miles added an emphasis to every other word by pounding and banging his hands. "He may not have done it himself, because we all know who gets his hands dirty for him. But he did order it," he signed furiously. "It was no mugging gone wrong. Everyone in Queens loved her."

Mayo moved his seat back some more. "You heard what the police said. A junkie on a bad trip did it."

Miles shook his head. "Haddy knew that junkie. Gave him cash every time she saw him. He had no reason to rob and kill her."

Miles' hands moved so quickly that Mayo almost couldn't translate what he was saying. Mayo pointed to his lips. Slowly, he said, "Consciences and friendships don't exist for junkies."

Miles' hands replied, "Now read my hands. JoJo's responsible. He's the only one besides me who knew when Haddy was returning from her trip. Haddy was bigtime cautious because she didn't like the night. So, when she had to come home at night, she took a completely different way in comparison to the everyday Queens head. Her way took her out of the way, but it was safer. Nowhere near where junkies hang."

Miles paused. The emotions in his heart had worked their way up to his chest, passed his neck, and into his eyes. He blinked three long, hard times. When the pain tumbled back down into his soul where he kept it locked away, he spoke more calmly.

"Again. Besides me. JoJo knew this. He set her up. I know it." The veins in Miles' neck bulged out. The temperature in his skin raised, and he stood there numb.

Mayo slid his chubby hand down his butter-colored face. Dull and with a lack of energy in his hands, he asked, "Why would he kill his girlfriend, Miles?"

Miles slammed himself down in his chair. He removed his thick-brimmed glasses from his face and set them down. He dropped his face inside the palms of his hands, where he took several deep breaths. When he finished, he took his face out of hiding, looked into the eyes of his childhood friend, and sighed, "I don't know."

"Mayo, Miles, this is Hendrix. He'll be assisting in our projects. Extra hands are needed." Ruby grabbed Hendrix by the sleeve of his shirt and forced his left arm up, only to drop it when he finished speaking. Hendrix gave his arm and Ruby a look.

Miles locked the door behind Ruby and his guest, whose arms were riddled with muscles and whose wardrobe looked like it belonged to the Black Panthers.

"We don't need no help, Ruby." Mayo pulled his mother's knee highs he used as a stocking cap off his head. He walked farther into the foyer, where Ruby and the newbie stood. "We're on schedule. All that's needed is for you to give the word, and we'll start the process of syncing the woodrose with the heroin."

"That's good to hear."

Ruby moved the book he held from one hand to the other. The insides of both hands were roughened with calluses. His knuckles were dry and overwhelmed by tiny slits. "But we still need additional hands on board to cook the heroin. While you two primarily oversee the handling of the Amanita muscaria mushrooms and Hawaiian baby woodrose, he"— Ruby's thumb pointed at the new chief—"will cook up the heroin. Whether these ideas work or not, we still need to have our money train on track."

Mayo nodded.

"What language are you speaking, youngblood? What the hell is an Amanita muscaria mushroom? Just say mushroom," Hendrix said.

The room momentarily fell into a lull, until Mayo stepped forward and offered his hand. "What's happening, my man? You can call me Mayo."

Hendrix looked at Mayo's stained hand and sucked his teeth. He turned to Ruby. "That's where I'm cooking?" He pointed to the kitchen.

Head low, Mayo's small noggin swayed from left to right. "Ruby," he called out. Mayo used his head to guide Ruby in the direction that led out of the foyer. Ruby followed behind Mayo, and Miles behind him.

"Stay here," he ordered Hendrix.

Inside the living room, Mayo placed both hands at his sides and let out a long, exaggerated breath of air. "I don't like the cut of that boy's jib"

Ruby and Miles' eyes temporarily met. Ruby was tempted to repeat Mayo's statement, or if not, then laugh in sheer entertainment over his elderly choice of speech.

I think I heard my grandma say that before, Ruby thought.

Ruby's photogenic memory flipped through the files JoJo kept on each of his workers. Their government names, physical appearances, contact information, date of birth, and family tree acted as a sideshow in front of Ruby's eyes. His mind searched the Rolodex of employees until it came across Mayo's and gave a little insight into his word choice.

Name: Maynard Yao Li
- *Blasian (high yellow). Weight: Two hundred and fifty pounds. Height: 5 feet 10 inches. Facial Features: Dimples, one missing eyebrow.*
- *Born 2/10/1959 in West Virginia to mother Patty Marshal and father Yao Li.*
- *Address: 63rd Avenue W. Lives with mother Patty and stepfather, Harvey Pain.*
- *Family: Father deceased. Mother nurse at Coney Island Hospital. Stepfather Dennis Cooper USPS mailman. Only child. Raised by his grandparents until the age of twelve when he moved to New York with his mother following his father's death.*
- *Phone Number: 642-184-9971*

Ruby cleared his throat. It was the only choice of action he immediately thought of that would ward off his desire for laughter. The last thing he needed was to offend a loyal worker such as Mayo because he grew up with elderly influences.

"Please elaborate." Ruby placed his book down on the coffee table. Miles could not help but to place his attention on his aunt's cluttered, unorganized wall-mounted library. He'd always offered to help her organize her books. Ruby stared at Miles, whose attention was posted on the wall of books. He scooped his read back into his hand.

"I know him." Mayo peeked out from behind the wall into the foyer.

"Again, elaborate." Ruby demanded.

"He used to hang with Jerry and his gang a couple of years back. Learned the ins and outs of his whole operation and took it all right from underneath him. Jerry didn't leave NY voluntarily. He was pushed out, and by that sucka."

Ruby looked from behind the wall at Hendrix, who had migrated from the foyer into the kitchen. Hands tucked behind his back, he bent over and inspected the cooking and creation of the hallucinogenic mushrooms and woodrose. *JoJo mentioned nothing about this to me*, he thought.

Ruby used his photogenetic memory to do his bidding once more. No file based on Hendrix was retrieved. *How could I have missed that?*

Ruby turned to Miles and pointed to his lips. "What do you think?" he slowly mouthed.

Miles looked to his friend and nodded twice.

"Okay, then. Let's get to work." Ruby stepped forward, and Mayo jumped ahead of him.

"You're going to let him stay?" His voice was more quiet this time.

"Precisely. If this man is who you say and does what you say he does, then he'll dig his own grave. All you two have to do is watch while he's executed."

The sound of keys chattering inside the lock turned all three of the young men's heads and drew them near. With every step each boy took, Ruby kept his hand on the firearm tucked behind him. He released his hold when Sammy, whom they all referred to as Ruby's Goldie, slid in.

"Sam the man. You were this close, my brotha." Mayo held up his pointer finger and thumb with a small space between the two. "This close to having that bone head of yours blown off." Mayo high-fived Sammy.

"Oh, really? You young boys were finnin' to take me out, huh?" Sammy removed his oversized newsboy hat and hung it on the coat rack. Afterward, he slapped his hands down on his knees and slowly seated himself on the chair beside the door. His suit pants rose a little at the ankles and showed off his black dress socks. "I'd like to see y'all try," he huffed. He leaned over the side of the chair and grabbed the day-old newspaper he'd left behind from underneath the seat.

Miles gave his back to the man whose personality resembled his late father's. The smile that grew across his face was hidden.

"Don't I know it!" Mayo shouted.

Two hours into cooking, no words were exchanged between any of the five. Each was devoted to his job. The absence of communication was, in Ruby's opinion, the perfect work environment, especially when reading *The Art of War*.

Hendrix backed away from the table that housed kilos worth of heroin and pulled down his face mask. "Hey, youngblood, I have a question." His heavy voice boomed throughout the front of the apartment.

Although at a distance, he faced Ruby, who sat in between the tight nook between the fridge and the kitchen archway, his face nestled inside his read.

"Hey, youngblood!"

Ruby peered up from his book and pointed at himself.

"Yeah, you," Hendrix confirmed.

Ruby dropped his eyes back into the pages. "That's not my name."

"What?"

Ruby turned a page. "That's not my name."

"You see this, youngblood? A ruby for a Ruby. Cool, right? You need to get you one of these, brotha. Then maybe I'll think you're stylin'."

"Consider this a welcome gift, youngblood. You're our new Ruby."

Ruby coughed into his fist. Hendrix took a couple of steps forward. He pushed his neck out a little, moved his head from side to side, and looked intently at Ruby.

"Wait a minute. You're little Wesley. You live over by the junction. Well, ain't this a bitch. You done grown up, a working man!" Hendrix antagonized him. "How's your daddy, boy? I heard he off in Vietnam." He folded his arms.

"That's not my name."

"Huh? Speak up, boy!" Hendrix freed his arms and slapped his hand on the back of a chair.

Sammy waltzed inside the kitchen and positioned himself next to Ruby just as Miles shook his head. Without hesitation, Mayo stopped what he was doing to distance himself from Hendrix.

Ruby slammed the book shut. "Wesley's not my name, and *boy* is not my name. You will call me Ruby, the name I introduced myself as when my driver and I picked you up from your rat- infested home."

"I can dig it," Hendrix slowly replied. "I can dig it, but I do have a question, youngblood— I mean Wesley. I mean Ruby."

"What's that?"

"Why are we in here working like slaves in a cotton field while you're sitting there reading like you's a free nigger?"

Ruby held his hand up when, out of the corner of his eye, he saw Sammy inch for the pistol on his hip.

"Fair question. So, you want to know why I'm sitting here reading like some free . . . what's the word you used?"

Hendrix stepped closer. Had he taken one more step, he'd tower over Ruby like a giant to an infant. "Nigger."

"Oh, shit," Mayo let out.

"Nah, Mayo, it's cool, man. After all, it's only a question." Ruby chuckled while he got up. He laid his book down behind him on the chair, then looked up at Hendrix. "Yeah . . . nigger." Ruby allowed the word to marinate and hang over the room. "I just wanted to make sure I heard correctly." He smiled. Then, without breaking eye contact, he snatched the gun Sammy had left exposed off his hip, jabbed it into Hendrix's chest, and shot three times.

Hendrix fell to the yellow-and-green-colored floor, but not before he left behind blood splatter on Ruby's and Sammy's button-down shirts.

"Why am I allowed to read while you work?" Ruby jammed his hand inside his pocket, where he pulled out a handkerchief and wiped down the weapon. Pistol concealed inside the fabric, he handed it over to Sammy and then began to unbutton his filthy top. "Because I'm Ruby, motherfucker. And when JoJo's not around, Ruby runs shit. And if Ruby wants to read while you make me money for me, the brains behind all this shit, then dammit, Ruby's going to read." He took off his shirt, folded it, and dropped it into the bag Sammy held open for him.

Ruby looked down at the stained tips of his Oxford shoes. "Chump done fucked up my shoes. Look at this shit."

Sammy shook his head in disapproval.

From afar, Mayo yelled out, "Fuckin' popsicle!"

Miles signed, "Head in the bathroom and get yourself cleaned up. We'll take care of this mess out here."

Ruby took heed to Miles' suggestion. So as not to track blood on the bright, soulful floors, he removed his shoes and went for the restroom.

"Nigger. Who the hell did he think he was calling a nigger?" Ruby aggressively washed his hands. The aggression and frustration were still fresh in his veins. "I'm tired of these old cats taking my age for a weakness." Ruby lathered his hands with soap and applied it to his face.

After he rinsed himself off, he looked in the mirror. Water lines surged down his forehead and cheeks. "Wesley died long ago, but not before I promised to do us all a favor and get revenge for the real Ruby."

Ruby touched the stone that hung from around his neck. "Your death will not be in vain, Ruby. I'll see to it." Water tracked below Ruby's eyes, and he quickly wiped it away.

Chapter 3

Paradise Island, Bahamas
2021

"Good afternoon, Mr. Evans. I'm sorry to show up at your home unannounced. It's just that I have something really important to discuss with you." Terrance paused his speech and smiled. "No, no, don't smile. Every time you smile when you're nervous, they say you look like the Joker," he told himself.

Terrance walked a short distance back and forth along the long trail of stones that led from the entrance of the greenhouse to the acre of land that had been transformed into a luxury, upscale garden. On school trips, Bajan children visited the massive garden set in the back yard of one of the Bahamas' wealthiest residents. It was the segregation implemented within the placement of the flowers and plants. Their detailed descriptions, stabbed inside the ground and plastered on marble walls, along with experienced gardeners and man-made waterfalls, made the experience educational.

Terrance stopped wearing out the walkway with his constant pacing and stood in place. He turned and looked toward the biggest home he had ever seen. "Damn. Must even his home be intimidating?" He turned back to the greenhouse. "Two fifty-five. Five more minutes." An average-sized American family could live and read the time on his wristwatch, which had cost the equivalent of some people's yearly salary.

Terrance balled up his lips and fist. "Why didn't I listen to Pop Pop and practice what I'd say at home? This man is going to think I'm a joke. He doesn't care if I come from money or I'm American. You can't impress with what someone's done better than you, faster than you."

Terrance could feel each chamber of his heart beating recklessly. Of course, it had to be that moment when it was brought to his attention that he had forgotten his inhaler.

"Fuck it. I'm not doing it. I'm kidding myself!"

A text message hit his phone. Thankful for the distraction, Terrance unclipped his cell phone from his belt buckle and dove into the notification.

Don't second guess yourself. Mr. Evans would be proud and lucky to have you as his son-in-law. All you have to do is ask.

Pop Pop always knows when to come through. Terrance clasped his phone with both hands, closed his eyes, and bowed his head.

"Dear Lord, please remove all nerves and negativity from my mind and heart. Please guide me, and if this decision is the right one, please grant me access into this next stage of life. Amen."

Terrance opened his eyes, held his up, and took a deep breath. *You got this.*

"Mr. Evans," he said out loud, this time with confidence. "From the countless dinners and celebrations I've attended at your home these last two years, I believe it's safe to say that I have picked up on a few of your personality traits. One being, you say what you mean, and mean what you say."

"Damn right."

Terrance spun around. "Good afternoon, Mr. Ev . . ." His voice faded out.

Embarrassed by the fast pitfall in confidence, Terrance slammed his fist into his chest while he cleared his throat. "Sorry about that. Good afternoon, Mr. Evans. I didn't hear you coming."

Terrance extended his hand. He hoped that when the elderly man took hold, he would fail to witness how it slightly shook. Ruby shook his hand with strength and a hint of dictatorship.

"Not a problem, young man. I prefer it that way. Glad to know I still got it." Ruby chuckled, then released the grasp of the gentleman in his mid-twenties.

"I'm sorry for showing up unannounced, but I really was hoping to speak with you. It's highly important." Terrance slid his hand through the back of his four-day-old haircut.

Ruby took a couple of light steps in the direction of the anthuriums and amaranthus. "Take a walk around the garden with me. I have to put in some steps."

As the two walked, Terrance bounced around his open statement in his mind some more, while Ruby approached the flowers designed by his wife.

"Mr. Evans, I admire you. You're very business-oriented. You've built yourself up in the US, then came here and capitalized further. I respect that. I've learned and earned a lot just from the breadcrumbs of advice you've thrown my way. Something my father never bothered to do. When you met me, I was a young, thought-he-knew-it-all, spoiled rich kid. I look up to my grandfather, he's my mentor, but not even he could help me see past my nose. Yet you did, and I appreciate that. Pop Pop appreciates that."

They walked past the anthodiums section. A large, jagged rock sat in the center of the path. Ruby bent down and chucked it back into the bushes.

"You have it all. I admire it all, and I want it all."

"But . . ." Ruby pushed into Terrance's speech.

And there it is. That challenge, that push. That New Yorker way of life, I presume, Terrance thought.

"There's one thing that you have that I have yet to acquire." Terrance paused. His hands slid deeply inside the pockets of his slacks.

Ruby stopped walking. They stood in between two motivational signs on the outside of the path that read: TEACHERS PLANT THE SEEDS OF KNOWLEDGE THAT GROWS FOREVER and EVERY PLANT HAS THEIR OWN REQUIREMENTS IN ORDER TO GROW . . . AND SO DO PEOPLE.

He sized Terrance up. However, his eyes had become preoccupied by the placement of his hands. Terrance looked down. Immediately, he snatched his hands out of his pockets.

Ruby picked his head up and smiled. "I guess you can take the man out of the hood, but you can't take the hood out of the man," he declared.

However forced it was, Terrance managed to pull out a small laugh.

"What do you want, Terrance?"

"I want a family. I want to marry Whitney."

When Ruby said nothing but continued to walk, Terrance went into survival mode.

"I'm ready. I'm ready to be a family man, and I only see that happening with your daughter."

Still nothing.

"She's everything I want. In fact, she surpasses that which, in actuality, I never thought was possible. Not many women these days want you purely for you. She holds herself down without either of us." Terrance darted his eyes to whom he hoped would become his father-in-law.

"She's so down to earth. You'd never think she had money unless she told you. And a major plus, she's all-natural! No weaves, no body enhancements. Just her. Just how God intended." Terrance smirked.

When he was yet again met without a response, he looked ahead of him and did what his grandfather had always told him to do. *Talk like no one's listening. And that's when the world hears you.*

"Whitney doesn't laugh at me."

It took every ounce of strength that transmitted from the bones in Terrance's toes to the nerves in his nail beds not to tear up. What he felt, what he was about to admit, he'd told no one. Not even Pop Pop. And that's because their bond surpassed verbal communication. Pop Pop knew his grandson well enough to know his feelings before they were even felt.

"I'm always laughed at. By everyone. Everyone except my employees and business associates, who see me as a lottery ticket. My family, especially my father, finds everything that I feel and do comical. I've been their live-in comedy show since the age of six. My drive and egotistic behavior stem from me first trying to gain their approval, which transformed into me trying to impress them, and eventually grew into me trying to outdo them." Terrance rubbed his nose. An extremely short break, but a needed one.

"So, when I made by first million at the age of nineteen, three years ahead of them all, I thought things had changed. But they didn't. The only thing that changed was that they now had something to pick and poke at. A new comedy routine based on every flaw in my million-dollar app. Outside of my grandfather, who entertained all of my ideas and backed me in all of my early failing business ventures, I had no one. Then, I met Whitney, and when I told her my ideas to expand my app, she didn't laugh." The shock in that fact still made Terrance laugh.

"After every sentence I said, I waited for a smirk, an insult, a let-down. I waited for what I had been given for years. Belittlement. Yet she wouldn't give it to me. In fact, she refused to."

Two of the estate's gardeners passed by the men, but not before they greeted their employer.

"I was so used to criticism that when Whitney gave none, I started to give some of my own. Man, did she light my ass up for that!" Terrance chuckled so loudly that birds resting inside the trees flew out. "She hit me with so much reassurance and positivity, negativity no longer had a place in my life. It doesn't matter who tries to give it. She created some kind of cool anti-negativity force field around me that never seems to need a tune-up." Terrance looked out in front of him with a light in his eyes that only a woman could ignite.

"I thought she had magical powers. What other reason could there be, without the use of medication and therapy? Then it hit me, after us being together for our first year. It wasn't magic. It was her. I loved her so much that my love for her made me love myself, and once I loved myself, no one else's bullshit and thoughts of me mattered."

He felt it. Terrance felt the moisture well in his eyes and fill them to the brim.

Talk like no one's listening.

"I love her. She's literally my better half. My challenge, my partner, my heart, and I need you, Mr. Evans." Terrance stopped underneath the purple wisteria tree. "I need you to grant me her hand. I can't go back to life without her."

When Ruby looked Terrance in the eye and puffed out his chest, the tears that dangled within the bottom of Terrance's eyes fell. Ruby held his hand out. Without removing the wet streaks on his cheeks, he took Ruby's hand, and they shook.

"You have my blessing."

Terrance smiled. It was a smile that hit not just his lips, but his eyes. Profusely, he shook Ruby's hand, and when he tried to let go, Ruby held on.

"You keep that same love and the same honesty toward yourself and my daughter, and I'll see to it no one ever laughs at you again."

Terrance balled his lips inside his mouth. His legs trembled. Its vibration traveled up his body to his hands and rattled Ruby's. Ruby pulled him in and held him in a tight embrace. Every son needs a hug from their father, but Terrance had never collected from his own. Terrance's body went weak and fell into Ruby's. Mouth wide open, no soul-piercing cry escaped until seconds later, and when it did, it roared and cracked like thunder. It purged his soul of everything that had once bottled him down.

Ruby patted his back. "Let it out, young brother. Let it out."

"Wesley, I'm scared for when Terrance proposes." Sherry rubbed cocoa butter lotion into her face, arms, and hands.

"Why?"

"I was at her house today and found a homemade wedding planner."

"Homemade wedding planner?"

"Yup." Sherry covered her wrapped hair, held in place by bobby pins, with a floral silk scarf. "Instead of buying one where all you have to do is fill it out, she went and brought a binder, dividers, and cut out pictures and made her own." Sherry chuckled. "I'm scared for us all. As soon as he pops the question, wedding planning begins. None of us is safe. She's already told me we'll all be assigned jobs."

Bare foot and covered by a long night shirt with the words *My Bed is Calling & I Must Go*, Sherry rushed from her beauty station in the corner of their bedroom and flopped into bed. Energetic and childlike, her body bounced from side to side and her feet kicked into the air in a dramatic attempt to get under the covers. Ruby's body rocked. His paperback slid out of his hands and shut just as his glasses fell down his face. He turned to his wife, who was out of breath; however, finally under the blankets.

"You good?" he quizzed.

Sherry nodded her head. Her face stretched and placed on exhibit her straight, ivory teeth. For a moment, Ruby looked at her, makeup free, smiling, and in the comfort of her oversized shirts and head scarves—her M.O., which dated back to their teenage years.

I love the fuck out of this woman.

Still nothing but a face full of teeth. Ruby smiled back at her.

"Does she know he's doing to propose?"

"One day, yes. Anytime soon, no. She said she started that book after they discussed marriage for the first time, which was last year." Sherry rolled her eyes. "Whenever it happens, she claims she wants to be ready."

"I don't understand the female mind," Ruby admitted.

"Female mind? Now you know good and well that's not how I thought at her age. I was too worried about school and getting the hell out of my parents' house. I have no time to put together a *just in case* collage." Sherry threw her right arm over her head and closed her eyes. "But I did tell her if she was going to do it, at least create a board on Pinterest. That way no one can find it and think she's crazy like I now do."

Ruby let out a deep laugh.

"Be real with me, Wes. You really fine with Whitney marrying Terrance, or are you being a supportive daddy that doesn't want to stand in the way of his daughter's happiness?" She cracked open her eyes and looked at her husband.

Ruby returned her stare. His eyes were dull and lips were pushed to the side. The look said only one thing: *You shittin' me, right?*

"If I didn't approve of him, he would have never gotten close enough to even consider proposing." Ruby took his book and eyeglasses off his lap and set them down on the nightstand.

"Fair enough. Just making sure."

"He's a good kid. Just misunderstood and in need of some guidance. Nothing this family can't give him."

Sherry opened her eyes fully and turned her head fully in Ruby's direction. "Where's all of this coming from? I know you've never had a problem with Terrance, but you've never gone this deep in analyzing him."

"I've had my thoughts, and today he's confirmed them. He's lacking a father figure. Yes, he has his grandfather, and Sinclair Rids is a stand-up guy, but he's not his father. From what I've collected on their family, he doesn't have a good relationship with his own son, Terrance's dad."

"So here you are thinking that since you don't have a son of your own, and Terrance practically without a dad, you two can become a second version of what you and your dad was?"

Ruby's face hardened. "Would there be something wrong with that?"

Sherry lowered her arm and shuffled closer to Ruby. She laid her hand on his thigh. "Of course not. I'm just trying to put the pieces together and understand where you're coming from."

"Had you remembered today's date, that wouldn't be hard for you to do." Ruby moved her hand off him.

Sherry's face twisted. *Today's date? What does today's date have to do with anything?* Then her mouth opened, and her hands immediately covered it. Before the words could form, her mouth opened and closed several times.

"Wesley, I'm so sorry." She grabbed Ruby by the shoulders to turn him in her direction. "Look at me. I am so sorry. I don't know how I forgot today."

He shook himself out of her hold.

Pained by her forgetfulness and unwilling for her husband to think less of her, she straddled him and with both hands on either side of his face, made him look at her.

"I fucked up. I fucked up bad, and I'm woman enough to admit that, but don't shut me out. That does nothing for none of us." Sherry's brown, slightly wrinkled eyes repeated the words she just said a hundred times over.

Ruby wrapped his arms around her and pulled her in closer. He rested his head underneath her chin. "I miss them both."

Sherry laid her cheek down on his head. "I'm so sorry. I know I never got the chance to meet your father or Ruby, but the pain this day gives you makes me wonder if I've subconsciously meant to forget. To lose two people on the same day and watch you relive those days every year breaks my soul. I'm sorry, but it does." She squeezed him.

For a moment, they didn't speak. They didn't want to speak, which worked out in their favor because they found themselves physically unable to. Sherry covered her husband's face with kisses then got off him. She sat close to him with her legs crossed. Ruby straightened his back and laid his head back against the black wooden headboard.

"What are you thinking?" Sherry dreaded the response, yet she had to know.

"Exactly what you said. Reliving when Goldie killed Ruby on the street like a dog. Then two years later, coming home to a house full of family trying to console my mother, hours after getting notice of my father's passing."

Sherry rubbed over his cocoa-colored hand. Every year she'd been with Ruby, she examined his hands, and every year, she hoped they'd magically transform into healthy, youthful hands, but they never did. The longer he worked the streets of Brooklyn, the more callous, scarred, and hindered his hands became, which mirrored his attitude toward all except her. His hands told the story of his life that she wished would heal.

"Wesley, I'd like to ask you something."

"Anything."

"How did JoJo die?"

Ruby slid his fingers between hers. "Like everyone else, you know how JoJo died. He was stabbed to death." He brought her hand up to his lips and kissed her.

"Yes, I know that, but . . . Wesley, how did you do it?"

Ruby kissed the top of her petite hand once more before he placed it in his own. "Remember, we agreed to never the discuss the details of my Brooklyn days."

"We agreed never to discuss those days while you were still in it. When you got out is up for grabs."

"Why do you want to know?"

"I've always wanted to know."

"Why?" Ruby pushed.

"Because JoJo was stabbed to death in broad daylight in a crowded area by at least eight different types of knives, which means more than one person is responsible. Yet no one saw anything, and the murder goes unsolved? How? I know Ruby's death happened in a public area as well, God rest his soul, but this is a whole 'nother ballpark." Sherry's face softened, and the tips of her fingers tapped away in Ruby's hold.

"How did you know the knives were different? JoJo had but a paragraph in the newspapers."

Sherry cocked her head to the right.

"Oooooh, I forgot. Chief Asher to the rescue."

Sherry used her free hand to point at her husband. "Don't start. Daddy only told me the details because he was trying to warn me about the evils of dating a drug dealer. Not that it helped." Sherry took her hands back, folded them together, and sat her chin on top of them.

"Please." She poked her lip out. "Tell me."

Chapter 4

Brooklyn, NY
March 1975

"You sure Mrs. Evans cool with me coming over? I'm not going to get a pot of grits thrown on me, right?" Miles quickly signed before Ruby pushed open the door to his Brooklyn apartment.

"Cool down, man. It's all good. Mama's asked to meet you." Ruby turned the key to the left, and when he heard the lock click, he pushed the door open. He waved Miles inside.

When inside, Ruby instantly felt unsettled. The short hallway that led from the front door to the living room was as dark as night, and the television volume, which his mother never went an afternoon without blasting, went unheard. Ruby's hand eased inside the inner pocket of his denim jacket. He held on to the grip of the gun, turned around, and held his finger up to his lips.

Both he and Miles slowly made it down the end of the hall. Ruby peeked inside the family room, and to his surprise, took in an eyeful of just that—his family. Aunts, uncles, cousins, and his grandparents on his father's side sat scattered around the front of his mother's orange-and-brown apartment. Platters of fried chicken, arrays of fruit, macaroni and cheese, and beans and rice sat untouched on the kitchen counters and living room coffee tables. The only thing consumed by them all were the bottles of red wine and liter of vodka. Silently, family members Ruby had seen every Sunday, on special holidays, and periodically just because, drank from flower-decorated glasses. Grandma Rose sat in the middle of the sofa. Her stocking-covered legs shook, and she used both of her puffy hands to lift the glass up to her mouth. Her naked lips trembled every time the wine left her.

Ruby let go of his weapon and instructed Miles to do the same. They stepped out of the shadows, and every watery eye landed on Ruby.

"Hello, everyone." Ruby waved at them all. Mentally, he took a swift count of how many members of the Evans clan filled his home. "What's happening?"

Miles positioned himself beside his friend.

From the back of the apartment, Ruby's Aunt Joan, his mother's sister, scurried out. Her voice hoarse, Aunt Joan called out to Wesley. The first thing he noticed about his aunt was her empty face. No makeup, no jewelry, no nothing. For the first time, she was a plain Jane. She used the back of her hand to clean away the wetness and snot from her face. Then she took both of Wesley's hands into hers.

"Wesley, baby." Aunt Joan's body swayed from left to right, and she kept licking the top of her upper lip. "We have some bad news, baby. Some really bad news." She squeezed his hands so hard her nails cut into the skin above the knuckles of each his middle fingers.

Grandpa Paul banged his half-full glass down onto the end table. With his cane by his side, he hobbled away. Not long after his departure, the front door slammed shut, followed by the building's staircase door.

"Wesley Senior, your daddy . . . he's . . . he died, sweetheart." Paired with a running nose, Aunt Joan's mouth sank low, and sobs were released. She hugged Wesley. His face plunged inside her gigantic breast.

He pushed himself out of her hold. He circled around where he stood.

"Bullshit. Where's Mama?"

His mother's elderly sister laid her hand over her heart and pretended to look out the window.

"Where's Mama!"

"She's in her room, Wesley!" Aunt Joan hollered in a pain-stricken tone.

Ruby hurriedly headed for his mother's bedroom.

"Wesley, baby, she's in no good shape. She doesn't want you to see her like this."

Before her legs could take off after her nephew, the door to her sister's room slammed shut.

"Mama?"

Mrs. Evans sat on top of her tight, perfectly made bed, clothed in her short-sleeve, mustard-hue jumpsuit. The shades were drawn. The darkness of the room covered his mother's face.

"Mama, why are you in bed in your street clothes?"

"Junior, come sit down."

"Okay, let me change out of my street clothes." Ruby moved to leave.

"Wesley, please come here."

Head low, Ruby trudged himself over to his mother's bed. He stood at her feet. "I'd rather stand." Ruby tucked his hands inside his pockets.

Mrs. Evans eased out of the darkness and peered down at Ruby's hands. Her face was a replica of her sister's, with thick, long eyebrows and full bottom lips. Beauty marks touched on the corner of her mouth and earlobe. Even that day, Ruby saw the beauty of his mother. Sadly, it wasn't strong enough to mask the light blown out in her eyes, the cold flesh he felt when he accidentally brushed against her foot, and the loss of melanin, replaced by paleness.

"Didn't your father say never trust a man who hides his hands in his pockets while speaking? Is there a reason I shouldn't trust you, Junior?"

Ruby ripped out his hands. "No, ma'am."

Mrs. Evans dropped her head and scratched her bushy eyebrow with the tip of her chipped nail. "What Joan told you. It's true. We got word today by mail."

Ruby didn't mean to, but he crashed down on the bed. "How did it happen? Do you know?" Ruby could feel the temperature of his skin decrease and race to meet his mother's.

"That's not important. What we must focus on is—"

"He was my dad, Mama. Don't nothing get more important than that." He looked up at the ceiling and swallowed what felt like a boulder.

"You are your father's son, yet I wouldn't have it another way." Mrs. Evans swung her feet off the bed and rubbed her temple with two of her fingers. "He overdosed, Junior. Heroin." She spit out the words, fast and raw. The truth was a nauseating thing she couldn't hold down.

"Daddy did drugs?"

"Not until he was sent to Vietnam. Lots of soldiers turn to something, anything to help cope with what they're seeing and doing." She patted his leg. "But this doesn't take away from who your father was. He was a good man, ya hear me? A God-fearing man who wanted nothing more than to support his family and raise you into the best man you can be." She poked him in his chest.

"But drugs, Mama? Drugs? Daddy always spoke against all drugs. Look how he downed Uncle Leon for being a drunk, and he runs and does heroin when things got tough?"

Mrs. Evans grabbed him by the shoulders and shook him one good time. "Now, you listen here! Only God can judge! Was he wrong for all he's said about his brother?

Yes! But dammit, we all make mistakes, all talk about things we know nothing about, and I'm sure before he died, he regretted his words because he found out what it was like to walk in those shoes." She stopped talking and swallowed, pulling one of her hands off him and pointing in his face. "You never know what's going on in someone's mind, someone's soul. Sometimes decisions are made outside of someone's character because of pain."

Ruby blinked slowly. *I should know. I've spent two years transforming into a criminal just so I could learn JoJo's operation, gain his trust, then give him the ultimate fuck-you right before I take everything.*

Ruby laid his head on his mother's lap. "You're right. Sometimes we do things others shun when in our minds, we're fully justified. I'm sorry. I'll never fix my mouth to speak on what I don't understand ever again."

Mrs. Evans could feel the wet spot on her thigh grow by the second. She reached down and kissed her son on the top of his head, then wiped away his tears.

"I'm your mother. I'll always forgive you."

Ruby opened his eyes and found himself lying next to his mother. Her small, soft snores disrupted the tranquility of the room. He sat up, and when he looked down at their feet, he noticed Aunt Joan sprawled out across the foot of the bed. Her face was snuggled inside her arms. Her snores were in sync with her sister's.

Ruby slid out of the bed and dragged himself into the living room. The television played, minus the volume. All of the food was put away, and no one who Ruby had seen earlier had stuck around, except for Miles. Ruby sat in his father's favorite chair.

"Sorry for your loss," Miles forced and pushed out of his throat.

His words were hard to distinguish but clear enough for Ruby to understand.

"Thank you," Ruby signed. "Me too."

It was his first time hearing anything come out of Miles' mouth. Under normal circumstances, it wouldn't have startled him, but made him a little proud. Sadly, today was anything but normal, and Ruby could not think of anything outside of his father.

"Your family's good people." Miles was back to using his hands.

"Thanks."

A knock hit the front door like a bag of bricks falling out a second-floor window.

"Shit. Motherfuckers going to wake my mama and auntie." Ruby jogged to the door and flung it open before another hit could be made. There, standing on two feet, just a little wobbly, Uncle Leon held onto a paper bag in each hand. His dungarees held one large brown stain at the knee, and his checkered long-sleeve silk shirt was untucked and wrinkled. The only thing Leon wore that remotely appeared presentable was the newsboy hat.

"Uncle Leon, kind of late, don't you think?"

"Wesley Junior, my favorite nephew." He licked his cracked lips and held a paper bag out in front of him. "I couldn't show up empty handed. Here. This is yours."

He jammed one of the bags into Ruby's chest, then pushed his way past him and through the front door. Ruby hadn't noticed the short, undernourished man that stood behind Leon until he followed his friend inside.

Before he stepped over the doorstep, the dingy-clothed man removed his hat, exposed his bald head, and told Ruby. "My condolences, young brotha."

Ruby nodded. "Thanks." He held his breath at the smell of stale liquor covering Leon's comrade.

Leon sat where Ruby previously had. "That's Bert. He's a good friend of mine," Leon quickly mentioned. "Where's your mama?" He popped open the bottle of gin he kept for himself and took a swig.

Ruby sat on the arm of the sofa Miles had claimed for the last hour and a half. "Her and Aunt Joan are in the back, sleeping. It's been a long day for everyone."

"Joan is here? Hot damn." Leon turned over to his friend, who found a seat on a kitchen chair left behind in the living room. "Wait till you lay eyes on that one. Prime real estate, I tell ya!"

"Uncle Leon, focus." There was much more Ruby could have said to redirect his attention on why he had visited, but he settled for something simple. There was no energy left inside him for speeches.

Leon took another swig. "So, my baby brother's gone. War's no place for the black man." He took in a little more gin. "I blame the white man just as much as the man who Wesley got that shit from, but there's a JoJo everywhere, selling that shit and killing motherfuckers."

With the next swig, he consumed more than the last. "You folks are ashamed of me, embarrassed because of my boozing, but hell, least my shit is legal and I'm killing no one but myself."

Wesley Senior had had lots to say about his brother; however, one thing Ruby forgot he had mentioned until now was that some drunks spoke the truth, and Leon was one of those drunks.

"I'm late because I didn't feel like being the topic of discussion. This day here is about my brother. The day which we got the telegram, March fourth, is when he actually died."

"I hear that," Leon's friend chimed in.

"Junior, pass me those glasses over there, and you two have a drink. I know you need one."

Ruby looked to the back of the apartment. When he felt a sense of long-term freedom, he grabbed the glasses and handed them to his uncle to fill. He and Miles chugged it. Both coughed and grabbed their throats.

Leon and his friend laughed in unison.

"How you holding up, nephew?"

"I don't know," Ruby answered. His voice was a little dry. "I don't think it's really hit me yet. I mean, I'm sad, but I'm still in disbelief."

"I can believe that."

Leon's friend nodded.

Leon crossed one of his pole-like legs over the other, his scuffed platforms in the air. "What's happening, young brotha?" Leon asked Miles, who didn't respond. "I said, what's happening?" Leon looked to his nephew. "What's wrong with him? Ain't his mama teach him manners?"

"Miles is deaf, Uncle Leon."

"Deaf?" Leon snapped his fingers. "You's . . . what's her name's nephew?" Leon snapped his fingers two additional times, until his short friend lent a helping hand.

"Haddy."

"Haddy! That's her name!" Leon uncrossed his legs and slammed his platform down on the floor.

"How you knew my aunt?" Miles asked. Although he signed facing Leon, Ruby knew to translate.

"I'm Leon, baby. I know everyone. Haddy. That there was a good woman. Never judged no one for none of their sins. She kept it classy and never trashy." His long mouth turned upside down. His frowny face added to his already depressing appearance. "That motherfucker JoJo is out of control," he spit out.

"Ain't that right," Leon's friend confirmed.

Ruby and Miles shared a glance. "What does JoJo have to do with anything, Uncle Leon?"

"Everything!" Leon belted out. "JoJo's the reason that boy's auntie is gone!"

Miles jumped up. Loud and strained, he asked, "What are you saying? What happened?"

Miles' unpredictable reaction caused Leon to push back his chair and spill drops of liquor out of the bottle. "I thought that boy was deaf. How he know what I said?"

Also on his feet, Ruby explained. "He can read lips. He's not great at it, but sometimes he catches on."

"Tell me!" Miles shouted.

Leon kicked back a mouth full of gin, closed his eyes when he swallowed, then came back to reality, replenished and clear-minded. "That man killed Haddy. You see, people think drunks don't pay attention and what they do hear, they don't remember. Jokes on them turkeys, because I pay attention and remember everything." Leon held the bottle high. "This here liquor is what keeps me alert."

"Let me get a taste." Leon's friend grabbed the bottle and partook in the liquid poison. He wiped his mouth with the back of his hand and gave it back.

"A few weeks before Haddy was killed, I seen them at that Hawaiian-themed bar, you know the one on Broadway. They were seated next to me at the bar, and I heard him tell her he needed her place to cook up that stuff. Said her neighborhood was the perfect spot to keep a low profile. Even mentioned her doing a couple of things in the business herself."

Miles focused hard on his lips. To ensure he missed nothing, Ruby signed after every breath taken by his uncle.

"She refused. Refused to have herself or her place be associated with that shit. She specifically told him, 'It's a stretch that I'm seeing you. I'm not stepping further into your world.' For twenty minutes, they sat without saying a word to one another." Leon scratched the gray hairs that covered his chin. "That is till JoJo offered her a trip to Hawaii. Wanted to make it up to his old lady for angering her. Three weeks later, on her way home from her trip, she's dead, and you two cooking that shit out her apartment." He pointed at Miles. "Makes you think he kept this one around just to keep up appearance."

Miles pounded his fist on top of his knees, and Ruby stopped signing. "What you talkin' about, Uncle Leon?"

"Don't play dumb, youngin'. I know all about your business with JoJo, *Mr. Ruby.*"

Ruby sat back down. "Uncle Leon—"

"Your secret's safe with me, Junior. I'm not the one you owe, but let me pick your brain. What are *you* going to do about all of this?"

"Me?"

"Yeah, you. You done made a name for yourself out in Brooklyn. Would be a shame if you didn't use it for good and get that sucka for killing your friend and now your new friend's auntie. If that buster's not stopped, you're gonna be all out of friends, nephew."

Leon shook the bottle of gin. When he felt its emptiness, he searched for the bottle he had given Ruby. Ruby handed it over. He had kept it close, already aware it was never truly his.

Leon cracked open the drink and went for the kill. He opened his mouth wide and stuck out his tongue. The burn was strong but mesmerizing. "Like I was saying, what you gonna do about it? Seems to me like you're in the perfect seat to make some moves that can bring down Brooklyn's king."

Ruby looked over at Miles, who had mentally dropped out of the conversation soon after hearing his assumptions were valid. He was staring into space, his face periodically twitching.

Leon pointed at a zoned-out Miles. "You see, this young brotha's too emotionally invested. If he makes a move against JoJo, he'll get himself killed."

"Damn right," Leon's yes-man co-signed.

"Don't I know it," Leon added.

Ruby turned up his facial expression. "I may have a few things in the works."

"If you're anything like your daddy, whatever you're planning, you're in it alone, and that's all well good, but that boy's directly affected by this shit. Use his anger to your advantage and bring him in on your plans. There's nothing more loyal than two friends with a common enemy."

If Uncle Leon's brain works like this when drunk, imagine how'd he be if he was sober.

"Keep talking, Uncle Leon, and don't forget to have a little more to drink."

"Don't mind if I do." When Leon took his face out of the bottle, he stretched his legs out and rested his feet on the edge of the sofa. His folded his hands in his lap.

"You know, there's a lot of folks out there wanting a piece of JoJo. You two aren't the only ones. Would be epic if everyone, and I do mean everyone, can get a little payback too."

"I'm not interested in letting any rival dealers in on this, Uncle Leon. Too many chiefs and not enough Indians is never good."

"Not if you play your cards right. There's a few dirty pigs and workers of JoJo's whose palms are long overdue for a grease. Not to mention the friends and families of those such as yourselves, who JoJo's responsible for killing. All of these people either can't or won't talk, but if only approached the right way . . ."

"Your mind is remarkable!" Bert complemented him.

"Uncle Leon, with all due respect, you're a grimy motherfucker."

Leon joined in on a smile with Ruby. The colors yellow and brown were a permanent fixture on his teeth.

Miles jumped up and made a beeline for the door.

"Get your right-hand, nephew. That's your guaranteed friend till the end."

Ruby took off and caught up with Miles just as he hit the stairwell. Ruby slammed the door shut the second Miles opened it.

Miles faced his friend and said, "I'm going to kill him!" After that short sentence, he resorted to sign language. "And if you stand in my way, friend or no friend, I'll kill you."

Miles tried to open the door, and Ruby closed it again.

"I won't stand in your way. Only beside you."

Miles' scared eyebrows collapsed.

"He had my friend killed in front of me, and his henchmen named me after him. I've wanted him dead since the first day I was forced to work for him."

"So, you're not gonna try and stop me or tell JoJo?" Miles still appeared puzzled.

"No. Not if you do this right—and by right, I mean we do this together. I have a better idea of how we're gonna take this sucka out. Courtesy of Uncle Leon."

Lines of tables bombarded with merchandise from clothing to jewelry to home appliances sat stationed in the cut-off streets of Downtown Brooklyn. Sellers stood behind their items and shouted their best sale pitches, while some flirted with browsers in hopes of sealing a deal, and others sliced down price after price. The annual spring flea market brought New Yorkers out of their homes into the crowded streets with the intent to shop second-hand and eat at low prices.

In need of space and air to breathe, JoJo nudged Goldie in the ribs and slid out of the crowd he found himself swallowed into when he entered the market. He approached a table selling handmade colorful wood and metal jewelry.

"I remember when my mama used to come out for this. She was all focused and on the hunt for a good deal on shoes and clothes for me and my sisters." He fingered a beaded bracelet. "But now that I'm me, I refuse for her to be caught dead buying second hand."

People behind JoJo shifted from side to side and stood on their tiptoes, attempting to see past the mammoth of a man whose two afro puffs on either side of his head blocked their view. He pulled his hand off the bracelet and moved on from the setup. Mixed in with a new group of penny pinchers, he could hear Goldie speak from behind him.

"I see no problems with a flea market." Goldie rammed the hot dog he had purchased four tables back inside of his mouth. "Just everyday people trying to make an honest living." Relish flew out of his mouth and landed on the back of JoJo's neck.

"Hey, man!" JoJo's mouth curled up as he plucked the vegetable off him. "Why are you eating in this crowd anyway? It's pure mayhem!" JoJo shouted. The gold chains that hung off his neck moved violently with every step he took.

"It's to be expected, my man. You know how this flea market shit goes!" Goldie smiled at a group of women that squeezed past the group they were forced to be a part of.

"I know, but this shit is crazy! Is it me, or is it more people here than usual?"

"It's a hell of a lot more people here this year," a middle-aged brother responded to JoJo. The two were shoulder to shoulder. "There was talk of live entertainment by a surprise celebrity, so everyone made sure to come out."

JoJo's head moved up and down. "Wish I knew that before I came."

After JoJo's short comment to the stranger, he felt himself being pushed forward. Three kids shoved and pushed their way past. Their giggles were lost in the crowd of people.

"You little bastards! Where's your mamas?" JoJo's skyscraper height allowed him to watch the unsupervised children plow their way through anyone in their way, which was everyone. "Little bastards," he repeated. "Goldie, I'm done! I'm blowing this joint. If Ruby wants to meet up, it can't be here."

JoJo aggressively pushed past people that blocked him from freedom of space. During his struggle, he looked behind him for Goldie. Goldie's hand swayed in the air like a flag. There was a group of people in-between the two giants.

"Meet me at the car!" JoJo hollered.

Goldie chewed on the last of his dog and threw his thumb up.

"This is bullshit," JoJo complained.

"Hell, yeah, you right on that one!"

JoJo turned to the voice that belonged to the man he had spoken to minutes ago.

"Fuck, man. You Houdini or something?" JoJo laughed.

The stranger followed suit and laughed along with him. "Nah, man. The Grim Reaper." The stranger held JoJo in place by his belt buckle and stabbed him with his pocketknife.

JoJo stumbled. Mouth agape, he bumped into a woman with long pigtails.

"Are you okay?" she asked.

JoJo looked down at his hand pasted to his side. When the woman saw the blood, her breath caught in her chest.

"Oh, my goodness. Careful not to touch the wound," she told him. "Let me help you." She took his hand and placed her other hand on his lower back.

JoJo hunched and leaned over. She attempted to guide him through the crowd. Two steps in, she stopped and voiced, "There's no way you're going to get through this crowd like this."

JoJo leaned into her. "Please help me."

She looked him in the eyes. "Like you helped my father?"

Without blinking, without allowing herself to miss a second of this moment, she plunged the box cutter straight into his belly button. JoJo collapsed. His tall frame fell over into two people who caught him. JoJo's vision became blurry, yet he still managed to clearly see Miles' face before he again felt the burning, painful, breathtaking sensations return.

In and out of consciousness, JoJo managed to notice that his curved body was being held up and dragged forward by both arms. When he fought to focus, he made out the faces that surrounded him and kept him trapped inside their center of death. These were faces to whom he owed money, who had begged him not to kill a loved one, and who he had once loved yet deceived and abandoned.

How the fuck am I just now noticing them?

Blood seeped out of his mouth. His eyes closed, and when they finally opened, he saw Ruby push into their well-guarded circle.

"Rubyyy." The words seeped out of JoJo's mouth.

Ruby grabbed JoJo by the back of his head, drew him near, and made his voice the last one he'd hear. "You made this monster. Made this sweet kid . . . you." Ruby sank the utility knife into JoJo's chest. For good measure and reassurance of his death, he twisted the knife as much as his fourteen-year-old strength would allow.

Confident in his work, Ruby pulled out the weapon and walked out of the intimate circle—away from where JoJo's body was dragged and dropped for people to walk over. Those denied entrance into the stabbing spree, however, were paid off to keep watch and act as a barrier. They patted Ruby on the back as he exited the market.

Ruby got into the back seat of the car where Sam sat behind the wheel. They were three blocks from the flea market when Sam informed Ruby of his two-minute warning.

"Is he in the abandoned parking lot?"

"Yup. I found him waiting on JoJo. Told him you found JoJo at the market and that he wants Goldie to meet him at the abandoned lot for y'all meeting. Said JoJo complained the market was too crowded."

"You sure he's there alone? I want no casualties." Ruby looked at his shirt, spotted with blood. He removed it and sat bare chested.

"Positive."

At a red light, they heard a loud, booming noise.

"Goldie," Ruby said out loud. "You're fired."

Chapter 5

Paradise Island, Bahamas
2021

"Wesley, I was at that flea market. There had to have been hundreds of people there. There's no way you could have pulled that off. I'm just not seeing how. Someone would have talked." Sherry sat on her knees. The firm mattress made it so that she barely sank in.

Ruby's two fingers walked up her thigh. "Anything is possible. It's all about how you plan and manipulate the situation. The market hit was all about the setup, the crowd's blueprint. You keep outsiders out and the insiders in." Ruby's fingers walked up her stomach, past her chest, to her lips. "Revenge goes a long way when the heart is involved, and money shuts mouths when it's needed. JoJo did a lot of wrongs. His sins are what brought it all together, and him letting me inside the fold is what sealed the deal." He slowly outlined her lips.

"Let me find out Leon was some sort of mastermind. Sounds like he has a hand in it."

Ruby thought for a second before answering, a light smile on his face. "Yeah, he was something special. Right until he overdosed." His smile evaporated.

Sherry turned the discussion in a different direction. "You must have really known JoJo and Goldie. Anything could have gone wrong that day." She kissed his fingers.

"I know. That's why it's important to take your time and know your enemies. To do your research and throw yourself into the task." Ruby leaned over and kissed her neck. "I fully invest myself in what I find to be important." Gently, he pushed Sherry off her knees, onto her back, and climbed on top of her, kissing her lips repeatedly.

"Then tell me something about myself."

He kissed her again. "You're fuckin' gorgeous. From your dimples down to your cesarean scar."

She wrapped her legs around his waist and kissed him back. "No. Tell me something about myself you've learned that I would have never noticed you picked up. Use your observational skills on me, mister gangsta." She lifted her torso upward and rubbed the back of his sprinkled gray head.

He pulled himself up a little. "That's a challenge. We've been married for over thirty years. You know everything I know about you."

She held his face in place with both her hands. "Do I?"

Her stare seemed to leak inside and pull at his soul. It was her magical power, the specialty Terrance spoke of Whitney having. Whitney had inherited from her mother, right along with her habit of challenging those they loved.

Ruby got off of her. "You always were inquisitive."

Sherry sat up and laid her head on his shoulder. She fiddled with his fingers. "Talk."

"I know I never really courted you, but you courted me."

Sherry stopped playing with his fingers. "What? Man, you're bugging." She playfully slapped his leg.

"It took a long time for me to figure out, but for years, you have literally been my shadow. From you laughing at me with your friends when I used to rush home after school, to the market. Which, by the way, I knew you were at." He took her hand into his.

She laughed. "You figured out that was me laughing at you portraying Speed Racer. Your short ass stopped to catch your breath after every block." She laughed harder and grabbed a hold of his arm.

"In my defense, I couldn't always notice you. I had to get my ass home before I got it kicked."

"Your moms didn't play. I miss that about her."

"Me too. I remember Mayo was arguing with this girl named Bethany outside of my building, and as soon as he called her a bitch, my moms stepped out."

"Oooooh, no, please no!"

Ruby smiled a deep-hearted, genuine smile. "Yes, yes, yes! She lit his ass up in front of everybody. My moms couldn't stand that word and never tolerated anyone in her presence saying it."

He jumped on the train that led him down memory lane. "She went off on him bad. Mayo tried so hard to plead his case, but all he got out was, 'But, Moms, you don't know what she called me.'"

"Let me guess," Sherry interjected. "She cut him off and yelled."

The couple screamed in unison. "I don't care what she called you. You don't you call her a bitch!"

Sherry fell over into her husband's lap. She kicked at the air, while Ruby clapped his hands.

"Yo, every black mom says that!" she managed to get out in-between laughs.

"Moms must have gone on for two minutes straight. Then Mayo's girl started feeling herself, and in between my mom's rant, said, 'Yeah, nigga, don't you ever call me out my name!' Sherry, no lie, the whole block got quiet. Everyone knew my moms despised the word *nigga* in all its forms way more than the word bitch."

Sherry sat up.

"Moms stopped screaming at Mayo and asked the girl what she said. When the girl repeated herself, Mayo's seven-point-zero earthquake became that girl's ten.

Mama went so hard Mayo literally had to throw her over his shoulder and bring her back into the building."

"Damn."

"Mayo must have told me at least twenty times he believed that had he not removed Mama, she would have laid hands on the girl."

"Now, that's the exact reason I don't use the word *bitch* or the N-word. I remember just the look your mama gave me when I slipped up and said them around her. Never again."

"Since I was a kid, she installed in me that words held power. So, to berate an already verbally abused group of people such as the African American community made me just as ignorant as those who labeled us *niggers*." Ruby sarcastically laughed. "I was already poisoning my people. No use speaking ill of them too."

Sherry kept quiet. In fact, she took herself back in time to when Mrs. Evans had told her she was a queen and to accept nothing less. That day, Mrs. Evans found her alone in the park, crying over her rebound guy, who had cheated. It was during one of the many times she and Ruby had broken up as teenagers. That day, Sherry the woman was born.

"As crazy as that day was for Mayo and me, I have to admit, it was one of the best days of my life," he said.

"Why?"

"Because that's the day we officially met."

Brooklyn, NY
1981

"She would have killed that girl."

"No shit, Sherlock." Mayo pouted.

Ruby pulled up in front of Kings Grocery corner store and backed into a spot. The car rocked and pushed Mayo's husky frame forward. His hands slammed against the glove compartment that shot open just as the back window fell as Ruby turned off the engine.

"When the fuck are you going to get rid of that piece of shit?" he barked.

"When she dies on me," Ruby nonchalantly replied.

"When she dies on you!" Mayo's seat reclined all the way back and trapped him inside. His legs kicked and his arms swam in the air in an attempt to sit up. Out of breath, he puffed. "The broad's on life support!"

"But she ain't dead."

"Makes no sense. A damn kingpin buying a used hooptie" Mayo straightened out the jacket to his tracksuit and checked around his head to ensure his Jheri curls hadn't flattened. "Open up your wallet, man."

"Nah, I'm good."

"Getting a new ride won't put you on the po-po's radar."

Ruby looked up and down the block. His sight settled on the navy-blue baseball cap embroidered with the initials USPS on the head of the man bopping up and down the street, delivering mail.

"Your step-pops keeping his hands to himself?" Ruby asked.

"Yes, sir. He don't want to see New York City upside down from a twenty-five-story high building no more."

"Good."

Along the crosswalk in front of Ruby's car walked a female dressed in high-waisted jeans, a yellow crop top, and matching fanny pack.

Without removing his stare, Ruby asked his friend, "Son, you know her?"

Mayo squinted. His head followed the girl inside Kings Grocery. Her crinkly, bushy ponytail bobbing around was the last thing he saw.

"Yeah, I know her. You don't want that." Mayo frowned and shook his head.

"Why not?"

"Because she the daughter of a cop. Plus, I hear she uptight and bougie."

"Man, don't nobody care what mofos gotta say. Only tell me facts. Back when I met you, all dudes had to say was how you was JoJo's naive, ass-kissing fat boy. Now look at you, my savvy, street-smart, take-no-shit homie." Ruby exaggerated his smile. He stretched his mouth and exposed his teeth.

Mayo adjusted his square-shaped shades. "A'ight, a'ight." Mayo sucked his teeth. "She's quiet, keeps to herself. Only chills with Deck's sisters, Stacey and Ramona, but her being a cop's daughter . . . I was real on that one."

"Hang tight. I'll be back."

With the help of his shoulder, Ruby pushed the car door open.

"Whoa, whoa, whoa! Where you going?"

"Where you think? 'Bout to play my hand."

Mayo stretched across the driver's seat and grabbed the back of Ruby's sweatshirt. "Rube, she's the daughter of a cop. Hell you doin'?"

"I'm trying to talk to her, not her daddy." Ruby snatched himself out of his friend's hold.

"So you can drive around in a death trap to stay under the radar, but trying to sex the po-po's daughter is cool? You buggin'!" Mayo yelled out the car window.

Ruby jogged on the sidewalk, putting his middle finger up at Mayo, and entered the store.

Mayo mumbled to himself, "Motherfucker will do anything to get some." He hit the button on the radio; however, all that came through the speakers was static. "Bullshit!" he hollered.

As soon as Ruby pushed open the bodega door, he saw her standing at the counter. A carton of milk, stick of gum, and cat food sat in front of her, waiting to be rung up. Never looking at her, he slid beside her.

"What's going on, Papi?" he said.

The middle-aged, pale-faced Latino store owner turned around from collecting a number of scratch-offs. After he laid eyes on Ruby, his face lit up and arms stretched out.

"Ruby! My main man! Long time no see. Where you been, my friend?" Papi's heavy accent surged around the petite store.

"I've been around."

Papi looked to the girl, who still waited on her scratch-offs and three small items to be rung up. "Mami, I sorry, but give me one moment. Just one moment. This man here is a saint!"

She turned to Ruby. Her dark browns worked their way from his sneakers to his face. "A saint?" she asked.

"Yes, mami, I no lie. This man here, let me tell you what he do." Papi folded his arms across his chest and stood behind the counter in a wide stance. "Mi madre was very, very sick. Doctors tell us without a surgery, she die. No if, ands, or buts. We have no money and insurance no cover it. I come to work a mess. This man right here asks me what the matter. I tell him, and you know what he do? You know what he do?" Papi passionately slammed his hands down on the counter.

"What he do?"

"He pay for the surgery. No questions asked. And he want no money back!"

"Why?" she questioned Ruby. Her eyes switched from left to right. Her mind in search of answers.

"Why not? Papi needed help. I was able to help." Ruby placed his attention on to Papi. "How is your moms holding up?"

"She good! She good! She back to cooking. She happy."

"Good. Tell her I'll come by later this week. I've been a little busy and had to miss some of our visits, but I ain't forget about her."

"I tell her. You come, we eat, we drink. Now, what can I get you, my friend?"

Ruby dug inside his jeans pocket. "Let me get a Bluntville and a pack of Now and Laters." He opened his wallet. "And whatever beautiful over here's getting. I like her patience."

"You don't have to do that," she insisted. "I really don't mind waiting. You did a good thing." She went inside her fanny pack for her cash and pushed a twenty-dollar bill over to Papi. "Papi, ring us both up. I'm paying."

"Hold up. No woman is going to pay my way," Ruby objected. He continued to draw cash out of his wallet. "My moms always taught me a real man pays." He pushed her twenty to the side and placed his in front of Papi.

The crinkly-haired girl placed two of her holographic nails on top of Ruby's green. She pushed it back over to him, snatched her bill up, and rammed it inside Papi's hand. "And my pops taught me real women know when to show appreciation."

Ruby reached for his money, but she blocked his efforts.

"You better be reaching to take back your money because you're not paying." Her movements jiggled her large earrings and the bangles on her wrist.

Ruby was loaded with a snarky, snappy comeback when the bodega door shot open. Two teenage boys, along with heavy screams outside, came rushing in.

"Did you see that shit?" The skinnier of the two teens stuck his upper body inside the refrigerator and came out with two quarter waters in hand.

In between chuckles, his friend in the chip aisle loudly joked, "Just say no!"

The arguing outside increased in volume, which made each voice involved become more distinct and familiar.

"Here we go," Papi murmured. "Triggerz at his shit again. When will the man learn if he gon' do his dirt, do his dirt quiet?" Papi rang up both parties' items together.

"Triggerz cause problems over here, Papi?" Ruby curiously asked.

Papi bagged their items separately. He used the dead president stuffed in his hand to cover the fees.

"All the time! It's always something. He argues with the crack heads. He probably arguing with one now."

"Triggerz is crazy, man!" The teen squeezed himself in between Ruby and the girl and dumped small bags of chips on the counter. "Last month, he beat some guy down for shorting him fifty cents at the park. Cops rolled up, but Triggerz booked it and hopped the gate. Dude's a loose cannon. I'on' fuck with Triggerz."

"Word up," his friend cosigned.

"Umm," Ruby let out. "Y'all scared of Triggerz?"

"I wouldn't say scared," the teen holding juices replied. "We just know not to fuck with him. I ain't trying to end up on the back of no milk carton."

"Same here."

Ruby was young once—young and fearful of Goldie, who had been bigger and badder than him—so he knew that what the teens spoke on came from fear.

Mayo popped his head in. "Ruby, I think you should come out here, man."

Ruby acknowledged his friend with a bop of the head. "I see you later, Papi. And little men, fear no man. You hear me?"

Ruby was halfway out the door when he looked back at the reason he had entered. "You ain't slick, beautiful. I'm going to give you your money back. This ain't over."

"You can try, but I ain't takin' it." She grabbed their bags. She handed Ruby his things and told him to have a nice day. As she slid past him, she tried to avoid touching; however, her breast pressed against him.

Outside the store and officially amongst the warfare, Ruby inquired, "What's your name?" before she got too far to hear him.

"Sherry."

Sherry left in the same direction she had come from.

Just as it had been described, Triggerz was outside in broad daylight, hooting and hollering with a pregnant woman and an elderly lady. "I'ma tell you one last fuckin' time, bitch. Give me my shit!" Triggerz reached for the old lady's wrinkled fist that she held above her head.

"Ms. Wendy, please, please give him his stuff and go home. I'm okay, I promise," the golden-haired woman holding her belly urged the older woman.

"You're not okay! You out here buying crack and you're seven months pregnant. I'm not allowing it, Rochelle! I promised your mama before she died that I'ma watch over you."

Triggerz went for Ms. Wendy's closed hand yet again. This time, she backed up. "Go on, boy! If you plan on giving this woman who's carrying life this poison, I'm not giving it up!"

"Fuck this shit!" Triggerz growled.

Hand still high, Ms. Wendy backed herself against the brick wall of the store. Triggerz grabbed a fist full of her blouse in his hand and yanked her forward. With his other hand, he grabbed her wrist.

Ms. Wendy yelped in pain. "You monster! Get off of me!"

Triggerz released her wrist and cocked back his fist. Before it took flight, he was restricted by Ruby's hold. Triggerz followed the hand that covered his until he discovered the identity of the person holding him.

Triggerz dropped his arm. "Yo, Ruby, it's cool, man. I'm handling this."

"You handling this?" Ruby tore Triggerz off Ms. Wendy and pushed him a couple of feet away from her.

"Mayo!" he called out.

"What's happening?"

"Bring Ms. Wendy home and walk her upstairs to make sure she gets there safe."

Shaken but still clutching the baggie of crack, Ms. Wendy eased over to Mayo and allowed him to walk her home.

Rochelle wobbled closer to Ruby. "Ruby. I'm glad you're here."

"Go home, Rochelle."

Even from a short distance, Ruby continuously sized up Triggerz. "I need a hit, that's all, and I'll be on my way." Rochelle swayed from side to side. She bit down on her lip and alternated between rubbing her belly and patting it.

"Rochelle, you ain't getting none of my shit from any of my homes as long as you carrying. Now, get your ass on!"

"Ruby, please!"

"Now!" Ruby roared.

The bass in his voice and rage in his eyes sent a wave of chills throughout Rochelle's body. Her addiction told her to protest, but the terror inside her redirected her to her common sense. With her stomach poked out and her hand supporting her lower back, Rochelle walked through the crowd Ms. Wendy and Triggerz had brought in.

"Ruby, man, you ain't have to do all that. I had everything under control," Triggerz spoke with his hands. His gold name ring stretched across his knuckles.

"You out here hollering at women and about to put your hands on an old lady is handling it?" Ruby's laced-up shell toes inched closer to Triggerz.

"Yeah, man. How else they gon' learn?"

Ruby searched his surroundings. The number of faces that closed the two in belonged to past classmates, neighbors, and those Ruby had set up with work. Ruby spoke out to the crowd.

"Y'all ain't seen nothing, and y'all ain't see what's about to go down, right?"

Numerous responses were given.

"You're secret's safe with me"

"I ain't see shit!"

"I'm Stevie Wonder, man!"

With three long steps, Ruby was inside Triggerz's personal space. His hands wrapped coldly around his neck. "Your pops teach you that shit? Huh? Thought you was gonna come here to Brooklyn after your mama kicked you out and bring that negative shit over here?"

Triggerz didn't reply, so Ruby tightened his hold.

"Answer me, little fucker. You a woman beater like your daddy?"

Triggerz shook his head as much as he could. His hands pulled at Ruby's.

"He about to turn blue," someone in the crowd pointed out.

"Yes, you are. Heard you stood by and laughed when your pops hit Mayo's mom. You think that's funny? Then you gonna really laugh at this."

Ruby let Triggerz go. He fell to his knees, holding his neck where Ruby had gripped it.

Ruby searched the crowd for the two biggest men. "Yo, fellas! You two old G's in the back. Feel like handing out an ass whooping on this piece of shit down here for two hundred skins?"

"Hell yeah!" Both six-foot, muscular bodies stepped out from the crowd.

The biggest man removed his shirt and tucked it into the back of his pants to hang out.

"Triggerz, let's laugh! You about to get your ass beat while all these nice people stand and watch. Everyone! Let's laugh at this woman beater who sells crack to pregnant women. He's bringing the neighborhood down. He's instilling fear in our community."

Fists waved in the air and cheers, accompanied by constant agreements, piled around the bodybuilders who beat on Triggerz.

"Don't forget to laugh, everyone. Let's laugh at this clown."

On cue, the group of people broke into a storm of laughter. Their entertainment drowned out Triggerz's cries. After what Ruby timed as being two minutes, he called off his men for hire and handed them their pay. He stood over Triggerz and examined the beat down given to him. His eyes were swollen shut, lips busted. His nose was crooked and stationed to the left. On the ground with his arms wrapped around his torso, Triggerz groaned, coughed, and spit out blood.

"No selling to pregnant women and no disrespecting the elderly, Triggerz. We have a new set of rules in place. Don't break them."

Ruby got into his car. He slapped the glove compartment twice, and it popped open. He pulled out the pen and pad and quickly wrote out his thoughts.

Next Meeting, Establish New Rules

1) *Do not sell to pregnant women.*
2) *Do not sell to kids thirteen and under.*
3) *Respect the neighborhood elders.*
4) *Give back to the community twice a year.*
   Those who can't or won't follow will be subject to punishment

Ruby tossed the pad and pen back into the glove compartment. When the engine purred and the car finally moved, a large cloud of black smoke blew out the back. The car bounced, stopped, and for the rest of the day, worked just as well as a car driven off the lot.

Chapter 6

Brooklyn, NY
1982

The shabby two-family home with boarded windows sat in the center of weeds and dead plants surrounded by discarded paper bags, wrappers, and soda cans. A trail made up of holes plunged inside the ground. They were once filled with bricks and made up a walkway. When desperate times came around, dope boys tossed their stash inside the dirt and found their way back to it when night turned to day.

Three years ago, the home was alive. It sheltered newlyweds new to the United States in need of a fresh start, and it made for the perfect backdrop in photos sent home. They'd painted the front door red; the rest of the house, eggshell white. The lawn had an abundance of flowers and towering trees. It was homey. A comfortable, small, love-filled home. Then the couple moved. The house never sold and was eventually forgotten about by the State of New York. No one wanted it. No one cared to be bothered with it, and that was why Ruby had converted it into a stash house.

Down in the basement, the draft pushed each of the ten men in attendance to show up covered in either a jacket or sweater. Every meeting took place down in that room. During its abandonment, that space had held up well in comparison to all the other chambers. The floors were firm, the walls clean, and the smell of mold and mildew nonexistent.

"Effective immediately, some additional rules will be implemented." Ruby looked into the faces of each man who worked the corners and the businesses that acted as fronts for his drug dealing ways ever since he had taken JoJo's place.

His stare sat on Triggerz longer than anyone else. The young boy's black eyes, broken nose, and arm made him the topic of private conversations amongst the group of men. Emergency room visits never came and went quickly; however, fortunately, on that day, medical professionals had Triggerz in and out and in attendance for the meeting his behavior had inspired.

"Rule number one, no selling to pregnant women." As expected, the murmurs, questions, and concerns trickled out. Ruby raised his voice over the voices and disapproval.

"Rule number one, no selling to pregnant women." The rise in tone and annoyed look sprayed onto Ruby's face lowered their complaints and eventually caused his worker's opinions to conclude. "We're done with the belief that all money is good money. Pregnant woman, pregnant junkies; I don't give a fuck how deep their addictions fall. If they're pregnant, they're off-limits."

Behind Ruby, Mayo and Miles sat stone-faced.

"Rule number two, no selling to kids thirteen and under. I'm actually surprised some of you motherfuckers against birth control don't already have a problem with this. Good parenting, fellas. Rule number three, no disrespecting the neighborhood elders. I don't give a damn if Mrs. Tyler kicks you in the balls. You don't disrespect her. And by disrespect, I mean no verbal or physical abuse. Only pussies need to lay hands on and disrespect the elderly, along with women and kids, and I don't associate with pussies, so pick a side."

Ruby took a seat. "And last but not least, we give back to the community twice a year." Faces scrunched up. "I'm talking the whole giving-out-turkeys, playing-San-ta-Claus gig. We do it all, and if one year I feel like upping the ante and giving back more than twice a year, then so be it." He stopped speaking and allowed the silence supplied to help everyone formulate and make sense of their thoughts.

Ruby would have a lot of push back when it came to these new rules. He'd prepared himself for it. Greed was a sin many had fallen victim to, and his men sat in the thick of it.

After minutes of quietness, Ruby turned to his second and third in command.

Mayo's loud voice boomed. "Y'all got anything to say or ask, do it now!"

Rex raised his hand.

"Homeboy, we ain't in school. Speak your mind, man," Mayo instructed.

"Ruby, these rules, with the exception of giving back and respecting the community's elders, fucks with our money. We're isolating customers, taking out of our pockets."

A wave of "hell yeah" and "for real" traveled throughout the room.

"Rex, ain't your girl and sister pregnant now?"

"Yeah."

"So, if they was up, getting that monkey on they back, you'd be cool with Shed over there selling to them?"

Before Rex could respond, Mayo butted in. "Don't you have a ten-year-old little brother? I heard you beat the fuck out of one of Tone's boys in Queens who sold to him."

Rex threw up his hands. "A'ight! A'ight. I get y'all point."

Tony's squeaky voice joined in on the conversation. "No disrespect, but my girl ain't pregnant, and I ain't got no family, so I'm down to sell to whoever as long as they got that green, if you know what I mean." Tony gave a pound to Sammy, who sat next to him on the couch.

"If we don't sell to them, they'll get it elsewhere. So why not just pocket the profit?" Sammy added.

"Then they go elsewhere. Slavery is over, along with my refusal to be the white man's mule. I won't be a slave to the green. We all know what we're doing is fucked up on many levels. Let's at least have some damn integrity about us."

Slam stood up from the back of the room. "I'ma be real. I get the whole not selling to kids and pregnant women bids, but what's with the whole giving back and respect the elderly shit? What's that got to do with the business?"

"Everything," Mayo answered.

"Please explain it to me, because I'm Stevie Wonder, and I just don't see it." The group of men joined Slam in a fit of laughter.

"You treat the community good, the community will treat you good. It's a game of respect, an unsaid verbal contract of you scratch my back, I'll scratch yours. JoJo didn't have that agreement, and y'all seen how he went out. He was taken out in broad daylight amongst damn near all of Brooklyn, and no one said or did shit. They feared him. They didn't respect him. So, to have him dethroned was a thorn the community considered plucked out their side." Ruby got up and worked the room. "They can't fear us. The people of Brooklyn cannot view us as a threat. They must embrace us. To embrace us is to love us, and what do you do for those you love?" Ruby looked around for someone to answer.

Slam, who still stood, replied, "Those you love, you have their back. Make sure they cool."

Ruby snapped his fingers and pointed to Slam. "Exactly. You have their back. Our people are not stupid. They know what we do, but if we give them some good things for them to know about us, it rubs out a little of the bad, making it a little more acceptable. You know what I'm saying?"

Some of the men nodded their heads.

"I'm listening." Slam took his seat.

"We make the community feel comfortable and safe, and they'll keep us comfortable and safe when needed. They'll be more likely to turn a blind eye when one of you fools fuck up." Ruby snorted. "And some of you mother-fuckers will fuck up. Police are big on witnesses, but why would little old Mr. Cole want to help put us away when we saved him from getting mugged or helped him with his groceries? He has no family. We're his family. And what about Papi? Without his comradery, where will we hide out at and sell out of for such a small-ass fee? Papi cut that price real quick after I paid for his moms' surgery. Good deeds go a long way, man, and that price cut will make up for the loss of cutting pregnant women and kids out of the market."

"You think if we do good enough, maybe some other business owners will be willing to fuck with us like Papi?" Bill Boy asked.

"That's the goal. We just have to make it worth their while. Mayo over here is working on taking over Kaypeg's blocks over in Coney Island and Prospect Heights. Dude got a stronghold on them areas, and I want them."

"But Kaypeg used to work for JoJo back in the day, so he moves like JoJo moves, and the streets fear and hate him. We offer those parts of towns protection and security, and I'm sure we can take the cake," Mayo reassuringly stated. "We find a few holes in Kaypeg's ship, his bitch ass is going down."

Ruby pointed to his third in charge. "You see that. We over here growing. Making up and then somewhat we're taking away."

Slouched over in the wooden chair, Doover spoke out. "I don't know, man. Those pregnant chicks love the whole mushroom and woodrose concoction you got us selling. We fucked up trying to use those to enhance heroin, but selling them in the form of tea and shit really made the dollars. We're gonna take a hit if we get rid of the pregnant ones."

"Don't worry about the mushrooms and woodrose. Profits are about to increase. I locked down their market, found out where a bulk of Northern Europeans and Central Asians frequent in BK. They are ready and willing for a taste."

"If that's the case, then I'm good," said Doover.

"What if we have a problem with these new rules?" That was Triggerz's question. His busted lip made it a little troublesome for Ruby and his men to understand.

Miles smiled. With his hands behind his head, he got comfortable.

"You do what you want, but not under my command. So, you leave with what you came in with . . . shit. If I find out you fuck with my customers, business associates, or push products remotely similar to mine, you're dead. End of story."

"Triggerz, you need to shut the fuck up. Your ass is the reason for the change of shit anyway," Slam said.

Cosigning Slam's statement, Rex yelled out, "Word up!"

"Man, fuck you!" Spit flew out of Triggerz's mouth.

"Nah, fuck you, you crippled motherfucker!"

The room could not contain their laughter.

"This bitch gonna ask *after* he gets his ass beat what will happen if you don't like how shit's run. You out of all people should know. You're gonna get your ass beat, but in your case . . ." Slam went on to further insult.

Ruby allowed for the men's bashing of Triggerz to continue longer than necessary. Triggerz was everything Ruby stood against and despised. He just needed a little more time before he could officially declare his time was up.

"You're not bonded to this shit. We ain't the mob. You want out, get out, but you leave behind all of my shit, including my train of thoughts. You erase your fuckin' time with me. I'm dead to you. You don't do that shit and see what happens." Ruby took his firearm out of his waistline and set it on the small table. "You choose to stay in this with me and apply these rules, I will guarantee you what you desire most. Money, no jail time, and staying alive. Who's in?"

Heads turned and glares were delivered and shared. Taking on the role of the group's spokesman, Tony forced himself up. His hand rubbed his lower back.

"I think I speak on everyone's behalf when I say that some of us still have reservations. But your ass is book smart and shit, so we're willing to see what and if you can deliver. But at the first sign of shit going south, we're jumping ship."

Each man in the room, except for Miles and Mayo, agreed with all that Tony said.

"Triggerz, you got anything you want to say?" Mayo walked over to his stepfather's son. His wide frame blocked everyone's view of the skinny, battered man.

Triggerz looked up at him. His mouth was empty, so he swallowed nothing but spit. The marble in his throat slid down, slow and noticeable, the human replica of a python during mealtime.

"No, Mayo. I have nothing to say."

Mayo patted him on the back aggressively. The force he placed on Triggerz activated the pain from the day's earlier events. Triggerz's eyes slammed shut and his mouth sealed tight, the natural need to react to such agony restrained.

"Good boy." Mayo demeaned him. "Good boy."

"Everything's accounted for," Miles informed Ruby.

"Did you triple-check the numbers and product?" Ruby's hands asked.

"Yes."

Sitting behind his desk that reminded anyone who had seen it of high school, a board filled with notes stationed behind him, Ruby glanced down at his watch. His leg was feeling cramped, so he moved around in his seat behind the desk. "The postmen get here yet?"

Miles shook his head. Ruby sucked his teeth and temporarily placed his focus back down on the notebooks and textbooks in front of him. He flipped through a few of the science text pages, jotted down some notes, then closed the books. Underneath the hardcovers, Brooklyn building histories and blueprints lay flat.

Miles flicked through the prints. "Why do you have these?" his hands swiftly quizzed.

"We're taking over Brooklyn," Ruby signed. "All of Brooklyn. What we have is no longer enough. We're going to expand, illegally and legally. It's time we read clean on paper. We will legally tap into a couple of properties Kaypeg's working off and have the law do our dirty work. Make a few calls, give a few anonymous tips, and the rest we hit ourselves, take their product, cash, and weapons."

Miles pulled up a chair and studied the papers. "This is good, real good. And the science books, any new formulas?"

Ruby turned to Miles and spoke slowly. "Not yet, but the wheels are turning. This night school shit is helping."

Ruby heard footsteps descending from the top of the house. They rapidly drew nearer to the basement that Ruby and Miles still occupied two hours after their meeting had concluded. Ruby piled the books on top of the prints and instructed Miles to head behind the only other folding table in the room that was equipped with a bill counting machine. The creaky door forewarned that the men's visitors had arrived.

In walked three U.S. Postal Service letter carriers. Each donned a navy blue uniform and baseball cap although they were inside a roof-covered home. In an orderly fashion, two of the carriers lined up where Miles sat. The only female of the trio was the first to plop her mailbag on the table and remove manila envelopes full of money.

"Ruby, can I talk to you?" The overweight, lazy-eyed man approached Ruby. Like every other time Ruby had found himself around the middle-aged man, he asked himself, *What the hell does Mayo's mom see in him?*

Ruby removed his glasses. "After Miles counts you in."

"That's what I'd like to talk to you about. I'm short."

The bill counter screamed while it flipped through and accounted for every dead president's presence.

"Now, this I must hear."

"I had to leave work early today. You know." Dennis looked at him, his head slightly nodding and eyes wide.

"No. I don't know."

"My son, you beat him up pretty bad, so I left work to check on him."

"That's touching, Mr. Cooper. You're a good father. But I didn't touch your son."

Dennis touched the top of his head. "You didn't literally touch him, but you did put the word out." His voice lowered some, and his hands fidgeted.

Ruby placed his open hand against his chest. "Me? I put out the word to have your son's ass beat? Oh, no way.

Doesn't sound like me at all. Perhaps you have a witness to support this allegation?"

Dennis coughed inside of his fist. "Maybe I've been misinformed."

"Maybe."

"I'm sure you can understand why the job couldn't get done. I was scheduled for foot patrol, so that alone slowed my process."

"Oh, yes, I understand."

Dennis released stale air out of his mouth. "Thank you. Thank you very much."

"You now owe me what you've lost, plus what's regularly due. And on top of that, I want two grand for my being inconvenienced."

"Waaait, what?" Dennis stammered. "You just said you understand."

The bill counter stopped. Ruby looked over at Miles, who gave him a thumbs up.

"I understand, but you're not exempt." He corrected Dennis without meeting his eye. "Carrie, the post office got any overtime coming up?"

Carrie answered Ruby; however, her focus remained fixated on Miles, who loaded her carrier with ten manila envelopes. Each one was addressed to Brooklyn residents on her route. Her eye kept steady on Miles' actions, the fear of a possible error blamed on her not an option.

"Hell, yeah. We lost three carriers this month, so it's overtime out the ass right now."

Ruby turned to Dennis. "Sign up for the overtime and make me back my shit fast."

"I, I don't mind doing overtime, but the additional two thousand, are you talking out of pocket?"

"It doesn't have to be out of pocket. Out of your wallet is just fine."

Unexpectedly, Dennis burped. "Excuse me." Two more burps followed. "Ruby, I don't have two thousand to spare. Can't I work it off? Or at least have some time?" His bottom lip trembled.

"You have two days to give me my money, Mr. Cooper." Ruby held up two fingers, and when he knew the timeliness had sunk into Dennis's head, he lowered his hand. "I can't go around excusing errors and supplying significant amounts of time to right your wrongs. People will start thinking I'm playing favorites, with you being Mayo's stepfather and all."

"Good night, Ruby. See you next week!" Carrie gave Ruby the peace sign and made it out of the basement.

"I don't know what I'm going to do," Dennis said.

"Consider asking your son for the money. He is the reason you're in this mess. Now, please stand behind Herbert and wait for Miles to count in what you do have."

Dennis didn't move. Inside his mind, he felt himself sinking in quicksand. Oblivious to Dennis's state of shock, Ruby led him by the shoulders to stand behind his post office colleague.

Ruby slapped down on his shoulder and spoke directly into his ear. "In two days, I want what you owe me. Then and only then will we be even." He tapped his shoulder, then removed himself from Dennis's space.

Chapter 7

In one day, Dennis's 48-hour deadline would end. He pushed his cart slowly down one of the many Brooklyn neighborhoods he'd serviced repetitively for more than twenty years. Like a robot, he went in and out of mailboxes and delivered birthday cards with cash tucked inside, bills, and small, overly-Scotch-Taped packages. Then there were Ruby's customers. The same protocol applied, except Dennis either picked up payment housed in their mailboxes, or he slid product inside the small boxes for their daily pick-me-ups.

Dennis stood in front of the home of his route's top customer. Because of the home's appearance and the amount of crack and sometimes heroin the occupant purchased every other week, Dennis could only conclude that this addict was loaded.

Junkie bastard over here living it up. Got a damn-near-perfect repaved driveway and a house repainted for the second time in three years, and here I am struggling to scrape together two Gs to pay another rich piece of shit.

Dennis zeroed in on the open latch. Many gates that surrounded New York homes went unlocked, but the visual of this lack of protection sent Dennis's mind wondering, plotting.

I wonder if he keeps money in the house. I bet he lives alone. I should rob his ass.

When his thoughts took a break, a head peeked from the gap in between the dark curtains that shielded the living room windows. Unlike he did in every other transaction, Dennis met the gaze of this well-off junkie. The curtains shut and broke their silent conversation.

Pussy.

Dennis delivered the poison that made the pained and lost worlds go round. Sluggish and more defeated than before, Dennis moved on to the next house. His distressed thoughts occasionally fell out of his mouth and into the wind.

"Pops!" Triggerz pulled up and blocked a driveway covered in chalk. "Get in real quick. I have to talk to you."

Dennis waved him off. "Nah, boy. I got to figure out how I'm going to come up with the rest of this money. I gotta keep walking. I think better when I walk." Dennis moved his cart past an elderly woman pushing a shopping cart filled with groceries.

"That's what I'm trying to talk to you about," Triggerz said.

Dennis stopped his cart. "You're not bullshittin' me?"

"No bullshit," Triggerz promised.

Dennis tucked his cart inside the back seat of his son's truck. With his hand on his bad knee, he hopped into the passenger's seat.

"Did you scrape up something for me?" Dennis's hopeful eyes and the hip he leaned down on acted as the knife that plunged inside Triggerz's heart.

"Nah, Pops. I got nothing. Should have listened to Moms all these years and put away some."

"Then why do you have me sitting in this debt collector of yours instead of me pounding the pavement? What you got to tell me?"

The twitch in Dennis's lazy eye told on him. It told his son loud and clear that he feared the repercussions of not coming up with fifteen hundred out of two thousand he still had to get.

"We take that engagement ring and diamond bracelet Mayo's father gave Patty and pawn it," Triggerz suggested.

"Can't. I used that to put off my debt to Hershel."

"The bookie?"

"Yup."

"Dammit," Triggerz spit out. He wiped his face with his hand, and with his pointer finger and thumb, he pressed down on his eyelids. He pulled his hand off his face. "We got to do something, Pops. You're already on Ruby's bad side from hitting on Patty, and with my shit that went down, there's no way we're getting out of this without that money."

"Rodger, don't you think I know that? Boy, you wasting my time! Don't bother me again unless you can help me. God rest his soul, but if your brother Marvin was still here, he'd have come up with something to help me out of this mess. He had the brains out of the two of you, and he obviously took it with him!" Dennis flung the door open and swung one leg out of the vehicle.

Triggerz swallowed. Nervously and uncontrollably, his eyes darted all around him. His father had finally made it out of the car and was unloading his cart from the back when Triggerz turned and stuttered, "I–I–I–I got an idea!"

Halfway inside of the car, Dennis demanded his son speak clearly.

"I got an idea. I know where we can get the money."

"Where?"

"Mayo."

Dennis huffed. "That fat fuck ain't giving us shit." Dennis lowered his mail mobile to the ground.

"We don't ask. We take."

Dennis stared at his son before he responded. "You serious, aren't you?"

"As a heart attack."

The door opened, and with the cart beside the car, Dennis got back into the passenger's side. "Well, whatcha got? How can we make this happen?"

Triggerz took a few moments to mull over different possibilities.

"Patty got a spare key to his crib. We house that shit and rob him. I got word on when he'll be seeing that new movie that came out." Triggerz snapped his fingers. "*Porky's Two*. Tonight."

"Mayo's many things, but the fucker ain't dumb. What if he doesn't keep his money in the house, or it's in some safe or something?"

"Then we take something else of value. There gotta be something we can take that'll add up to fifteen hundred. I don't give a fuck if I gotta take his clothes and sell 'em down on Fulton or somewhere."

Dennis slapped his hands together. "Fine. I'm off at six. Meet me at my house. I'll find the key, and we'll leave from there. Patty thinks she can hide shit, but I always find it."

Dennis climbed back out of the car and pushed the mail transporter to the back of the truck. He paused and walked back over to the passenger's window and knocked on it. Triggerz lowered the window.

"Don't let me down, boy. Remember you still owe me for not whooping fat-ass when he found out about me beating on his mama and damn near killed me."

"I won't let you down, Pops. We'll get the money, and I'll make up for that and more."

"Good, because Marvin always took care of shit."

***

Ruby couldn't seem to remove himself from the mirror. He scanned his wardrobe for anything off-putting and out of place.

"Man, would you stop acting like some female and get out of the mirror?" Mayo smothered jelly onto a peanut butter-loaded piece of bread. "Act like you never chilled with a female before."

"None like her. Sherry's got her head on straight and goals she's working toward. She's about something. She goes to NYU." Ruby brushed his goatee. Afterward, he stepped back and tied his shell toes.

"Met her pops yet?" Mayo smiled in-between chewing.

"Nah. We ain't serious like that."

"A'ight, just let me know when you do so I can have the bail money ready."

With a smile on his face, Miles slid on a gold pinky ring with a diamond in the middle. Ruby tapped the ring with his pointer finger.

"Not to the movies," he signed. "You're making yourself an easy target for the police and stick-up kids."

"When are you picking up the future Mrs. Evans? The movie starts in an hour." Mayo threw out the left-over crust from his sandwich and wiped his hands on his jeans.

"She's meeting me there."

"Translation, she ain't trying to been seen in your broke-down car," Mayo said.

Mayo and Miles high-fived one another.

"Ha, ha, ha. At least I'm going to see this flick with a woman and not with Miles." Ruby emptied a piece of gum out of its foil covering.

Miles gave him the middle finger. "Joke's on you, my man," his hands spoke. "I ain't going. Got a few runs to make."

"What runs?"

Ruby sat next to his friend on Miles's leather sofa. Over the years, while working beside Ruby, Miles's lip-reading skills had matured significantly. It was his daily assigned homework in an attempt to decrease the use of a sign in front of outsiders as much as possible. The less anyone knew about them, the safer.

"The Chief, Laundromat City, and Barley's Liquor," Miles told him.

"Fuck. How the fuck did I forget that? Who's going with you?" Ruby asked.

He said to Mayo, "You gotta sit this flick out, son. I need you to copilot with Miles."

Miles shook his head vigorously. "It's cool. Jean and Heavy will be there."

Mayo's landline rang. The sudden sharp jingle internally alarmed Ruby.

"Hello? Hold on a minute. Hold on." Mayo put the receiver down on the kitchen counter. "Y'all figure it out. I gotta take this. It's my moms. Hang up the phone when I get in my room." Mayo's heavy-duty frame wiggled and wobbled down the short hallway to his bedroom.

"Hang it up!" he hollered.

Ruby did as his friend asked, then sat back down, where he automatically resumed their conversation.

"Jean and Heavy are cool and all, but I still think Mayo should go."

Miles sarcastically smiled while his head waved from left to right. "Why? Because I'm deaf?" Miles forced the words out of his voice box.

"You're deaf?" Mouth open, Ruby placed closed hands over his heart.

"I'm serious," Miles's hands verbalized.

"Cut all that noise, Miles. You being deaf ain't got shit to do with shit. If it did, you wouldn't be my right hand, but these are all important runs done back-to-back. You need more experience and muscle with you." Ruby's hands spoke as swiftly as possible.

"Mayo's the major general in our camp. It still won't work. Remember, you treat this shit like the government. The president and vice president never ride together, but in this case, it's your lieutenant and major general."

Ruby just stared, long and hard.

Miles threw his hands up. "Hey, don't shoot the messenger. I'm just reiterating what you said." He shrugged his shoulders and smiled. "So, checkmate. Big boy and his big-ass mouth will be in the same theater as you, laughing it up."

Ruby tried to contain his smile. However, it still came out halfway. "Fuck you, motherfucker. I'ma need earplugs for when his ass laughs." Both men chuckled.

"It's cool. I'ma be in and out. Get the latest updates on who's on the NYPD's radar, when and where their next raids will be, then pay the man. After that, head on over to the Italians and Arabs make the drop-off, and boom, we done." Miles clapped his hands together after his rundown, emphasizing the ease of it all.

"Page me after every run so I know things ran smoothly. If I don't hear from you within the customary meet time, I'm kicking down doors." Ruby's hands repeated his promise.

"Yeah, yeah," Miles signed.

Ruby eyed the clock above Mayo's kitchen sink. "Let's head out. Neither one of us can afford to be late."

Both men stood and felt themselves over for all the necessary protection.

"Yo, son! We out! You coming?" Ruby yelled to the back of the apartment.

"Nah! I'ma go visit mom dukes real quick! If I don't make the movie, I'll see you at the diner."

"A'ight! Be safe, brother!"

"Always. Do me a favor and lock the door behind you."

Seconds after Mayo made his request, he heard the front door slam and keys rattle.

"Mom, calm down. Dennis is a clown. He ain't gonna do shit. If he's acting different, it's probably because he's on that stuff again," Mayo said to his mother on the phone.

"Maynard, something seems different this time. I don't feel safe." Patty's voice periodically jumped then fell. "I'm telling you something ain't right."

"So, he came in and started an argument. Did you leave the house when he started?" Mayo stood in front of his window. He opened his blinds and looked down on the cats on the basketball court after dark.

"You damn right I did. I don't need his shit."

"Exactly. They probably wanted the place to themselves, so he started an argument."

"But when I came back, all of my stuff in my old hiding spots was out of place, and he was gone. What if he found the rent money and used it to buy that stuff? He could come home tonight ready to start some more junk. Maynard, I'm getting too old for this. I'm not used to this. Your daddy was a good man. He never brought my heart or body pain like this one. I don't know why I ain't leave this fool yet."

Mayo sat at the foot of his bed. "I don't know why neither, Mom, but if you're scared he'll mess with you tonight, you can spend the night at my place. I'll come and get you now."

"You're a good man, Maynard, just like Luke, your daddy. Just promise me one thing—you won't hurt him like you did before. I'm leaving him real soon, I promise. I can't take no more of this."

Mayo's eyes rolled and rid his face of the tears that had accumulated with the collar of his shirt.

You always say that.

"Be ready. I'll be there in twenty minutes. Love you, Mama."

"I love you too."

Mayo dropped the phone on its base and lay back. His hands covered his face and muffled the violent screams he let out on the king-sized bed. His stomach rose and fell. His heart kicked him from inside his chest, and his sneakers tapped against the wooden floors. He lay there and allowed the emotions, which he only gave life to when he was alone, run rampant out of his system until he felt less tormented. Mayo wiped away the evidence of pain that lingered on his cheeks.

Upward, he rested his palms on his knees as support to stand. When he caught a glimpse of himself in the full-length mirror nailed to the back of his bedroom door, he saw the overly fancy, diamond-encrusted gold link bracelet with the matching necklace that he wore. He moved over to his safe to secure his new purchase inside, but then thought against it. Instead, he tucked his necklace inside his shirt and covered his bracelet with the sleeve of his thin jacket. His hand touched the bedroom knob just as his bladder spoke to him.

"Fuck. I gotta piss again."

Mayo grabbed his crotch and jogged to the bathroom just outside his bedroom. Legs apart, Mayo held himself in front of the toilet and watched as his apple juice–colored urine flowed inside the bowl.

"Damn, I gotta drink more water."

After a good shake, Mayo found himself humming show tunes in the midst of toilet flushing and hand washing. He turned off the faucet, did a little fancy spin, and reached for the doorknob. He'd yet to grasp the brass when his front door closed, followed by multiple heavy steps. He heard voices.

"Shhh."

"Pops, no one's here. I told you. I spoke with my boys. They all said they're meeting Mayo at the movies and catching the eleven p.m. show."

"These motherfuckers," Mayo whispered.

Mayo dug way back inside the cabinet underneath the sink and pulled out his pistol. Reassured it was loaded, he turned the light off and cracked open the door. The small opening made all the rummaging done by the father and son in the front of the house sound loud and clear. He remained hidden in the dark, nestled behind the door. The noises that emanated from the front of his apartment were enough for Mayo to imagine where they searched: the freezer, the television stand, the kitchen cabinets, and the coat closet.

Light steps approached the bathroom. Mayo stepped against the toilet and raised his gun. The door opened halfway, the tip of a boot peeked inside, and a hand patted around the wall. Not long after the light switch was found and flicked on, Mayo lowered his weapon.

"Watch your step, motherfucker." He let off one shot into the footwear that dared to walk into his home.

Immediately, the trespasser collapsed outside of the restroom door.

"Fuckkk! Pops, run!"

Mayo stepped out of hiding and fired twice into Triggerz's chest. The deafening sound of bullets being fired locked Dennis in place. He told himself not to, begged himself not to, but still, he looked at his son, gunned down by one of the two men he despised most on earth.

Triggerz fought to breathe. Sadly, his hands tried to apply pressure on the wounds that sucked the life out his body. Mayo raised his pistol at Triggerz's head that dropped in the direction where his father stood.

"Run," was all Triggerz could say. All he wanted to say.

Mayo followed Triggerz's stare. His lips managed to sink inside his mouth and become thin, frail lines. The men connected visually, neither capable of turning away. Mayo squeezed down on the trigger and let go. The blood that erupted and landed on Mayo's clothing as well as Dennis's was enough motivation for Mayo to shoot again. This time, he stared into the eyes of his kill.

Not again, not again. Dennis's thoughts repeated. His shaking hand inched to where he carried the small gun that he armed always himself with but never used. He pointed it at Mayo. His quivering hand waved the gun up and down and from side to side.

"You pussy, you can't shoot even if—"

Bullets sprinted in several directions. Some hit the ceiling, some the floor and walls. Although he repeatedly pulled the trigger, Dennis was unaware that he had closed his eyes—until his eyes opened and took in Mayo's body on top of his son.

"Oh, shit," Dennis spat. He took long backward steps, his empty hand over his heart. He stumbled over the couch cushions he'd previously flung to the floor.

"What have I done?" His lips trembled recklessly. His cheeks inflated like a blowfish, and when they were filled, he vomited. Dennis released that day's food consumption in watery clumps. Slobber rolled down the corners of his mouth. "What have I done?"

He stood with his legs spread wide and his back hunched. Dennis's heavy tears mixed in with the blood and vomit that coated his skin and clothing.

"What have I done?"

Without one blink of an eye, Dennis lifted his arm and trained the gun against his temple.

"What have I done?"

The small firearm detonated. Dennis's soulless body joined his son's and stepson's on the floor.

The apartment was left in a peaceful silence for only ten minutes before Mayo's beeper went off. His mother was contacting her son in an attempt to discover where he was.

Chapter 8

Paradise Island, Bahamas
2021

Ruby stopped talking, and when he did, his glazed-over, glossy eyes kept focused on the scenery in front of him—the bedroom door.

"Wesley?" Sherry put her face in front of her husband's. "Wesley?" Slowly, from side to side, she waved her hand in front of his face.

Calmly and with a twitch of the eye followed by spontaneous lip jumping, Sherry rubbed his cheek firmly.

"Wesley, it's okay to be hurt by the past. You don't have to hide it."

He searched her eyes for more of the ease and comfort she supplied.

"Whenever I think about that day . . . our day . . ." Ruby used his thumb to play with Sherry's bottom lip. When she smiled, he stopped. "The story of Mayo's death is never far behind. The beginning of our love story is tainted." He took back his thumb.

Sherry rested her forehead against his. "Let's work on separating the two. When you feel Mayo's death seeping inside our beginning, stop and push on to another memory of ours. Keep on until it actually is a fairy tale memory."

"I don't know if I can." His voice cracked. "They're now a yin to the other's yang. A beautiful disaster made into one."

She kissed his lips again and again. "You'll never know until you try. It's time to disconnect the Siamese twins, Wesley."

"I despise that name," he hissed under his breath.

"What was that?"

Sherry's cell phone sang the song she dedicated to their daughter. "That's Whitney." She scrambled over to her side of the bed.

"Whitney, it's midnight. Are you okay?"

Ears pasted to the device, Sherry sat on her knees. Her inner voice prayed this was not one of those a.m. calls that would later require the family to dress in black, then drink heavily as they reminisced about the good old days and made promises to keep in touch.

"Yes. I'm sitting down. Whitney, you're scaring me. What is this about?" Sherry's well-endowed chest pumped in and out. She leaned forward a little, covered her face with her hand. When she pulled it away, a deep, cheek-rising, dimple-pierced beam brightened her face.

She patted her husband's knee. "Dollface, congratulations! Tell me everything. How did he propose? Where? Dammit, what does the ring look like?" She threw her husband a wink of her eye. His weak response pulled Sherry back to her husband's reality.

"You know what? Don't tell me a lick. I need to hear all of this in person. Tomorrow, you come over, and I'll have cocktails and every wedding magazine known to man waiting for you." She listened intently.

Her gaze fell on Ruby. "He wasn't feeling well today, so he turned in early this evening." Sherry cleared her throat. "Dollface, calm down. He's just been complaining about a headache. He took some aspirin, and I'm sure with some rest, he'll be fine tomorrow. Which will be the perfect time for you to tell him. Tomorrow and in-person. You know your father's no fan of the phone. He needs to read you." She chuckled and winked at her husband.

"Uh-huh, uh-huh. Really? If that's when he wants to tell his parents, that's his choice." Sherry's eyes crossed. "I understand, but you already know what you're dealing with. Right. Uh-huh. Dollface, let's not focus on this now. Everything will work out. Just live in the moment. You're engaged." She paused. "Noon is fine. I promise apple martinis will be on deck. Okay, I love you too. Good night."

Sherry fell face-first into the pillows. "Wesley, you know Dollface is my world, but she sure can talk."

"Why didn't you give me the phone? I could have spoke."

Sherry sat up. "Yes, but you wouldn't have been sincere. That's a moment where a father needs to be all in, not partial." She manhandled Wesley into laying in her lap. The tips of her fingers walked across his forehead.

"Now, let me tell you what I remember about the day we met."

Ruby tried not to smile.

"I walked by your beat-up hooptie, looking fly as ever, when you ran out, tripped over the curb, and bust your ass right in front of Papi's."

"That's it," Ruby growled. He got up and threw his wife under him and tickled her. Her shirt rose up, and her body wiggled relentlessly.

"Stop! Stop! Please, stop! I can't take it!" she pushed out in-between laughter and shortness of breath.

"Say you'll stop telling that bullshit story!"

"Never!" Sherry's legs buckled.

"Have it your way."

Ruby flipped her over, pulled down her shorts and underwear, and slapped her behind hard three times.

Despite her skin turning red, she continued with her laughing spree and pleas for him to stop.

"Say you'll never tell that story again."

Sherry locked her lips when he turned her face up.

"Okay." He lifted her off the bed.

"Okay! Okay! The story's dead! Buried and gone! I promise!"

Ruby lifted her higher. "You bullshittin' me?"

"No! No!" She chuckled. Her throat was raw from all the screaming.

He released her, and she plunged inside the fluffy mattress. Ass out, arms above her head, she worked on catching her breath.

"I can't stand you."

He plucked her nose. "Feeling's mutual."

Sherry elevated her torso and pulled up her bottoms. "I know I was gung-ho on leaving Brooklyn for years, but in all honesty, if it's one thing I could have taken with us, it would have been Papi's store. He made you feel like family when you stepped in there. Treated you like he knew you for years even when you met him only five minutes ago."

Ruby rested against the headboard. "I hear you. That was Papi's gift."

Sherry rolled on her side. "I heard he passed. Do you know whatever became of the store?"

"Yeah. His kids took over, kept it in the family."

"That's good to hear. I wonder how it's going. I hope not much has changed."

Brooklyn, NY
2021

Clouds of smoke created a fog so thick it was impossible for Grim to see Central, who sat next to him in the driver's seat. Central extended the blunt out to Grim.

"Nah, I'm good."

"Fuck you mean you good?" Central shoved the rolled Dutch closer into Grim's space. Grim pulled his head back and pushed Central's hand away. Ashes twinkled down on the gear shift.

"I'm good, C. Get that shit outta my face."

"Get that shit outta my face," Central mocked in a childish tone. "Bitch-ass motherfucker, more for me. I was tryna give you a hit of this new shit Boss got me tryin' out. Shit hella good. I give it an A plus plus plus." Central inhaled before he released the smoke into the already foggy car. He trapped it inside his chest and let it sit for as long as he could.

"You his guinea pig now?"

Central let the air out of his lungs. His voice was raw. "I'm whatever the fuck he wants me to be for free shit."

"Until your ass dies from the shit. Why is he trying out new shit anyway? What's wrong with what we have?"

"New supplier."

Grim repositioned himself. "What happened to House? We've been fucking with duke for years."

"Boss making changes. Said it's time for that new new."

Grim grunted, "Here we go with another change."

Central blew out smoke that moved the green and red little trees that dangled off the rear-view mirror. "Fuck is wrong with you? If shit ain't changing the cash coming your way, fuck you care?"

"It's ways of doing shit," Grim said. "We ain't running shit because we got lucky. It took a lot of time leveling up to win over New York. A lot of greased palms and earned respect. Know your history."

"I'm not interested in the *then*. I'm interested in the *now*, and now the money flow is tight and right." Central's voice gave out, and he fell into a coughing fit. His body rocked, and the small twist that covered his head rattled.

He beat himself in his chest and pressed the little button that let down the window. Central gathered a wad of saliva and spit it out the window.

"You're new," Grim told him. "Money was better before Straw, and it came faster and easier. He's fucking up the flow of shit, unnecessarily flexing for more clout. That's the type of shit that gets you caught up."

Central rolled the window up and rubbed his runny nose. "Man, all I know is I'm doing better with Straw than back in Philly."

"Yeah, that's what I heard from all you new guys," Grim shared.

Motherfucker done went out and got cheap labor. Let go of our runners and brought in these out-of-town cats. Disrespect at its best.

"I guess what I'm saying is falling on deaf ears then. Can't miss what you never had." Grim took out his phone and scrolled down his social media page.

"True story." Central was on the verge of rolling a new blunt when his phone went off. "That's boss right now."

Grim turned up the heat and sank his head deeper inside his winter coat.

"What's good, boss?" Central held the cell phone in between his cheek and shoulder. His hands were free to empty, crush, and distribute the weed inside the wrapper.

"You sure? Because I'll do that shit, real talk." Central licked the leaf wrapping.

Grim could hear Straw's irritating, boastful voice seep out of the phone.

"Bet. I'll do it now. I'm sitting in front the joint now. A'ight then." Central tossed his phone on the dashboard and started to roll his smoke.

"Fuck he say, man?" Grim questioned. He was irritated that he had to ask at all.

"Oh, Carlos time ran out. If he doesn't agree on us lowering the price for using his spot for distro, boss gave me the green light to handle it."

Central held the weed-filled leaf out in front of him. "Now, that's how you roll a motherfucker." He chuckled. "Watch out." Central reached over Grim and chucked his smoke inside the glove compartment.

"He wants Carlos to drop the price? We're already paying damn near nothing."

"Guess Straw wants him to pay nothing then."

"Fuck his ass doing? We been rockin' wit' Kings Grocery since the eighties when Carlos pops was in charge. This spot is all love."

"That's the problem with you old heads. Don't know when to let go. If Carlos don't go for the new offer, he'll be resting with his papi, ya dig?" Central hurled open the car door. He paused and looked back at Grim from over his shoulder. "You comin'?"

"Hell no, I ain't coming. I'm not gonna be a part of this shit."

"Don't try to play all innocent. Your ass is guilty by association."

Central had one foot out of the car before Grim held him back by the shoulder. "What you gonna do if he doesn't go for it?"

Central snatched his shoulder away. "I don't know. I'll think of something when the time comes. In the meantime, why'on't you and your bleeding heart sit tight and hope for the best." He slammed the door behind him. What smoke remained went out with him.

Walking across the street, Central made his burned fingers, torched in a fire two years ago, take on the shape of a gun. He pointed Grim's way.

"You wish, you punk motherfucker," Grim hissed. "Fuck around and I'll finish what dudes in Philly couldn't." Grim kept his gaze set on Central.

The first day Grim had met him, he didn't like him. He had no morals, no values, and showed no sense of self-control. Central reminded Grim of Triggerz, a gangsta all the young neighborhood kids feared back in the day.

Central disappeared inside the store. Grim's phone started to holler.

"Yo."

"Grim, real quick, where you get your new boots from?"

"Over in Chinatown."

"A'ight bet. Good looking."

"Yo, Dell, hold up. There's some shit about to go down that I ain't feeling. These young bucks reckless, messing up a good thing."

"What you talkin' about?"

Grim could tell he was on Dell's car speakerphone.

"Straw wants Carlos to lower his price, and if he doesn't, he put Central on it to handle."

"Oh, those motherfuckers. I told your ass get out when Straw came in. Dude's grimy. He's only out for self."

"I'm not feeling this whole Carlos takedown, fam."

"There's a lot of things you're not going to be feeling working under Straw. I know you got a feeling about him adding pregnant women to the clientele list."

"Of course I do. Nicole's pregnant with my first grand-kid. How am I supposed to feel if one day she decides to get lit and all she has to do is link up with any Brooklyn dealer?"

"I understand. Those giving-back-to-the-community events we used to hold, I fucked with hard. I never told anyone, but those events done by the hustlers back in the day is why my family was able to have Thanksgiving and Christmas. Without it, we couldn't afford to. Those turkey and toy giveaways helped. So when Straw stopped that, I had to get the fuck out."

"I hear you. I don't know about you, but I know the shit we do is wrong and only contributes to the stereotypes, but those little things right there like the food, toys, and clothes giveaways made me feel like less of a scum bucket. Actually gave me something positive to tell my kids I was doing when they were coming up."

The corner store's door banged against the wall and customers fled out. Screams and glass breaking could be heard every time the door opened.

"Get out now," Dell said. "Running with Straw is going to land you in some heavy shit, whether with the law or by the streets. The old Gs hasn't forgotten about that youngin' handing them their walking papers. They're not taking that laying down."

Grim eyed Central through the bodega's glass. With his back against the store's door, he waved his arms in all directions.

"As soon as he feels content enough to ensure that he knows everything there is and is left in the dark about nothing, he's done with you. Get out before he puts you out, or worse."

Central stormed out of Kings. His steps were loaded with rage and accompanied by a racecar driver's speed. His sneakers stomped in a small puddle lodged inside a hole inside the street.

"Grim, you there?"

"I'll hit you back." Grim ended his call. He watched Central head straight for the trunk of the car. Through the rearview mirror, he watched an irritated Central pull out a red gasoline can. Central lugged the can toward the store.

Grim got out of the car. "Fuck you doing?" he shouted, his arms opened. "Who the hell drives around with a can of gasoline in the trunk?"

Central turned around. He unscrewed the container. "I do! And I'ma have this fire put in some work. It'll get the job done. Trust me, I know." He jogged back to the store, dug inside his pocket, and pulled out a set of keys he immediately used to lock up the store.

Grim looked up and down the empty, still streets. The sidewalks were just as lifeless. Grim pulled his coat hood over his head and took off down the block in the opposite direction of Kings. His breathing erratic, he made it to the crosswalk just as a pregnant woman wobbled his way. Her attempt at transporting her precious cargo reminded him of his daughter and the few good deeds he had left to tell her about his life.

"Fuck! I can't go out like this," he muttered. Grim ran as fast as his short, middle-aged legs allowed him to, back to where tire streaks lay in the wake of Central's car exiting. Kings Grocery was covered in golden flames that traveled from the sides of the building to the roof. Small flames that were scattered about the foot of the front door and the store's display window threatened to grow.

Grim ran up to the entrance. The smoke that smothered the building cleared long enough for Grim to make out Carlos, his sister, and someone whom Grim assumed to be a customer screaming and waving from the other side of the door. He stepped closer; however, the heat from the flames denied him up close and personal access to the chaos and forced him back.

From the corner of his eye, Grim caught sight of the unbolted metal garbage can the city had never replaced. Tapping into his strength and determination not to have any more blood on his hands, he catapulted the can through the window. Once the garbage can made contact, shattered glass rained down on the concrete. Clouds of black smoke rushed out the exit wound.

"Get out! Get out!" Grim yelled. Coughing uncontrollably, he waved his hand in front of his face and backed himself farther away from Kings. Frantically, Grim searched the smoke for Carlos. He was seconds away from falling to his knees when Carlos and the others who had been locked inside rushed out.

Carlos ran to Grim and collapsed into him. "It was Central." His smoke-filled lungs coughed. "He took my keys and locked us in there!"

An explosion heard from the back of the store enraged the fire.

"Get back!" Grim warned the women by Carlos's side. When they all made it across the street, Carlos was dragged out of harm's way by Grim as the bodega exploded. What the windows and garbage can didn't blow out, the gas did. Shards of glass, wooden panels, and bars of metal flew into the street, creating piles of rubble.

The force knocked everyone down onto garbage bags piled outside of homes. Grim rolled Carlos's body from on top of him. On his back, he coughed some more and beat his chest.

Lost in the stars, he asked, "Is everyone all right?" When he heard a total of three yeses, regardless of how low and dry they were, he breathed a sigh of relief. "Good. Because I'm done with this shit."

Chapter 9

Brooklyn, NY
2021

Two out of the three duffle bags on the bed were filled. It took a lot of elbow grease, but Grim got them both zipped. What room the last duffle had Grim loaded with his two favorite devices, his tablet and blood pressure machine. The front pocket carried his passport and all other personal documentation needed to start his life anew outside of the United States. He did a full sweep of his bedroom when he validated all necessities were confined within the restraints of the synthetic fabric. He slung one bag across his chest and grabbed a hold of the other two by the handles.

He made it to the front door, where he gently placed down his bags and took the opportunity to send out a much-needed text.

What happened tonight was your pet's call. I'm out.

Grim turned off the phone. Inside the building's hallway, he disposed of it. Out of his back pocket, he pulled four envelopes, each blank on the front and back. Grim stopped at each one of his neighbors' doors and slid the cash underneath. Things had changed in Brooklyn. Neighbors now feared one another instead of becoming friends and having each other's backs, and the whole concept of being a community had been dismantled. The

strong display of unity by almost every Brooklyn resident, including those with whom Grim shared the tenth
floor, had died. Straw had obliterated what made home,
home. Since his reign started, Grim hardly, if ever, saw
his neighbors anymore. Leaving the safety of one's home
was a risk taken only if heading to work or school.

Pushing himself up, he let out a groan. The stiffness
in his legs was a loud and clear reminder that had things
been the same, he'd still have some form of youth left.
Using his knuckle, Grim called for the elevator. The large
circular button lit up in its center. It didn't take long for
the doors to open and for Grim's neighbor, Mr. Simmons,
to dash out. His head and eyes fixed on the tiles, he went
straight for his home. Not once had he bothered to look
around and see who was near.

Grim lugged his bags inside. After he hit the lobby
button, he leaned himself against the shiny walls and
handrail for the last time. As he was riding down to his
destination, the elevator stopped and opened its doors on
the eighth floor. Four people Grim couldn't recall seeing
before quickly stepped inside without displaying the
etiquette to speak. In silence, the five people rode down.
Every eye except for Grim's was glued to the numbers
that lit up and died out as they passed by each floor.

The elevator slowed and landed on the number four.
When Grim's phone vibrated, he wiggled it out of his
pocket and read the message sent to his social media
page.

Dad, hurry up. We can't miss this flight.

"Excuse me. Can you all move in just a little so my
friend and I could get on? It's much appreciated." The
two men squeezed in. "Thank you. Wow. I like that shirt.
Where did you get it from?"

"It was a gift," a resident of floor number eight answered.

"Well, whoever got it for you has great taste."

The conversation led by the newcomer sounded all too fake, snobbish, and familiar.

Grim looked up and met Straw's stare. Straw loomed over everyone in the elevator. His gaze traveled across Grim's chest, down to the duffels at his sides.

Without breaking his glare, Grim replied to his daughter.

Leave without me. Now. I love you.

"Ralph, are we going on vacation?" Straw asked.

Grim didn't answer; however, he did find it amusing that Straw had referred to him by his name. Straw was pulling rank, reminding him who was in control. Grim felt the eyes of the innocent bystanders land on him, awaiting his reply.

"Perry, do you remember me giving Ralph off? Did I say he could go on vacation?"

Dressed in army fatigues, Straw's companion, who stood three inches shorter than him, carried a face plastered with circular burn marks and free of eyebrows.

"Did I?" Straw asked again.

Perry shook his head no.

"Excuse me, handsome." Straw politely moved the baggy-clothes-wearing twenty-something-year-old away from the keypad. He punched the emergency stop button, and everyone inside rocked and fought to maintain their balance.

"I'm disappointed in you, Ralph. What happened tonight?" Straw asked.

"Whatever it is that's happening, I want no part of it. Can you please let us out?" the young girl whose two-toned hair fell in twists verbalized.

"Oh, suga, this won't take long." Straw dropped his smile when he looked back at Grim.

"I don't know what you're talking about," Grim said.

"Sure you do. Central handled a situation for me that you were there for. Now, you not helping a fellow comrade out is one thing. But to save someone who was meant to die is a whole other thing."

The four people who separated Grim from Straw huddled closer to one another and hugged one side of the elevator as much as possible.

"That's very disrespectful. Did you not like the call I made? Did you have a problem with it?"

"Do what you have to do. I'm an old school fool. I'm not here for all the yackety-yack. I did what I did," Grim said.

"You sure did," Straw verified. "And because you did what you did, Perry over here had to go and clean up your mess. Finish what Central started. Perry doesn't like to be woken up. He's an old school fool just like you. He's in the bed by eight o'clock every night. Now you done made me interrupt this man's sleep. Had to make him get up and kill Papi's nice family. Now, that ain't right."

The same girl who had asked to be released let out a cry. Her boyfriend pulled her into him to muffle her pain.

"I feel your pain, pretty lady. It's such a shame." Straw reached out and took one of her twists in between his fingers. He slightly pulled it and watched it bounce back into place.

"See what you did, Ralph? You made this girl over here cry. Say you're sorry."

Grim didn't move. Not his lips, not his body.

Perry exposed his firearm and aimed it at Grim.

"Say you're sorry," Straw ordered from behind clenched teeth.

The young girl cried out louder. When Grim's mouth remained in place, she begged.

"Please, please just say you're sorry, sir." She hid her face back into her boyfriend's snot- and tear-stained shirt. In that moment, Grim noticed that the girl bore an undeniable resemblance to his daughter. The guy Straw had referred to as handsome pleaded with Grim using nothing but his eyes.

"I'm sorry, my young sista."

"See? Now, was that hard?" Straw hit the button for the elevator to continue its journey down to the lobby. The seconds it took to touch down were mistaken for hours by the group stuck to one another.

Finally, the doors opened. Perry stepped back in-between the door's sensors and opened fire. He shot in every vital organ of Grim and the four young adults. Perry didn't stop until his clip was emptied.

"Damn. Overkill much?" Straw joked. He laid his arm across his hitman's shoulders and walked through the small crowd of people that had been waiting for their lift to their homes. "I think you guys may want to catch the next one. It's a mess in there." Straw's thumb pointed behind him.

At the entrance, Perry pulled an additional gun out of his hip holster and fired two bullets into the skull of every witness. The fallen bodies created a line that led from the lobby into the elevator.

"Damn, you're sexy when you kill."

Perry's hardboiled tone told Straw, "Don't."

Straw threw up his hands. "It's a joke, ha ha. Now, let's get you home, sir. You know how you get when you don't get your eight hours."

Chapter 10

Paradise Island, Bahamas
2021

"Dammit," Ruby muttered.

Sherry put herself in front of her husband and held her hair around her neck. "Zip me, please." Once her back was no longer exposed in the cherry red, knee-length sleeveless dress, she gave herself a look over in the full-length mirror her husband had been standing in. She turned around and made it her business to ensure the tightness of her behind and calves. "What's wrong? Who pissed in your Cheerios?"

"Gray grew back in my beard. I just dyed it. The girl just got engaged two weeks ago. Couldn't you have waited to throw this engagement party?"

After she blew a kiss at her reflection and ignored Ruby's disapproval of timing, Sherry shifted his face from side to side. "Yeah, you're right. Stop using that brand. It sucks."

"I'm over here looking like Uncle Ben." Ruby was back in the mirror. The more he searched, the more grays he counted. "Five hairs! Bullshit! Makes you look five years younger my ass."

Sherry set her chin on Ruby's shoulder. With the tip of her nail, she touched up her edges. "Stop it. You look fine. Your grays make you look sophisticated."

"They make me look old."

While Sherry remained gawking at herself, Ruby fake sulked.

"You're not old. You're mature," she told him.

"I'm sixty."

Sherry got serious. Suddenly, the lipstick on her teeth no longer concerned her. "You're alive. In your line of work, not a lot of people see sixty. You're blessed."

Ruby gave himself one more look. What Sherry shared with him was beyond truthful. It was what he had strived for while in the world of drugs. He willingly took the responsibility of ensuring money, freedom, and life for him and his team. That alone, without the added stress of losing his mother, his third in charge, and being given countless ultimatums by Sherry, his then girlfriend, had taken a heavy toll on him mentally and physically. For years, depression was a dominant issue in his life.

Although Ruby had won the battle, he had lost the war. Stress made its way out and showed itself through his skin, hair, and eyes. He remembered when he first noticed the decline in his appearance. It was the night Mayo was found in the Hudson River. Ruby drank himself into a light coma that night and avoided mirrors for the entire next month.

What Ruby had failed to plug into his life plan was the unavoidable fact that outside of the business, he held no control over the personal lives of his team. He could choke and control everything he wanted regarding his organization, but at night, when they all went home, they weren't his responsibility. He had no say over how they lived. Every wrinkle on his face told the story of old age and stress. Physically, he had made it out of the game, but mentally, he was forever a prisoner. A prisoner desperately trying to bandage the wounds left behind on his soul from years ago. Wounds that refused to heal and seemed to grow with every day that passed.

"Wesley. Do you hear me?"

"Yeah. I hear you."

She spoke to him through their reflection. "You're fine. *We're* fine, Wesley. You're retired and living out your golden years stress-free in the Bahamas. This is what you wanted, what *we* wanted." She gave her mouth a break and examined the sad expression that covered her husband's face. "You are happy right, Wesley?"

He mulled over the query. For all the years he'd been out of the game and settled in the islands of the Bahamas, life was good. Life was safe, without the concerns and stress of the streets and what it took to stay alive. However, lately and without reason, his comfort seemed to have shifted and left him in a world of confusion. Was he happy? Was he okay, or had his depression returned?

"Wesley?" Sherry called.

Ruby rubbed his eyes and stepped away from his reflection. "Can you do me a favor, Sherry?" He avoided the question, "Unless we're in front of people, can you hold off calling me Wesley for a while?" He sat down on the bed and slid his gold-toe socks inside his loafers.

"Huh? I've called you by your government name since we were teenagers. What's this sudden suggestion all about?" Sherry's hands sat on her hips.

"Can you just do that for me? I'm not saying forever, just for a little while."

"But why?"

Ruby bypassed her. Inside their walk-in closet, he grabbed the jacket to his suit and completed his look. "One of the things I had to give up to achieve this life was myself, and the first thing I had to get rid of to survive was my name, but every time you call me that, I'm reminded of what I've sacrificed. I need a break from it." He fixed his collar.

"Where is this all coming from, Wesley?" Sherry's voice softened. "What are you saying? You telling me you'd rather surround yourself with the life of Ruby, the name forced on you, the face of all your problems, instead of starting fresh like we agreed we would when we moved here? Nowhere in our deal was the exclusion of Wesley during any moment mentioned."

"Then I'm updating our agreement. This need of mine is nothing new. I just never asked this of you because I didn't want to take him away after all those years of you fighting to have him. But now, I need you to give me time without him. Excuse me." Ruby touched the arm of his wife as she occupied the doorway of their bedroom closet.

"You've had time without him since the day you started to work for JoJo. Years, as a matter of fact. Do you remember our conversation we had the other night about what you've been through? So, why are you now trying to act like he never existed entirely?"

"For a little while, yes." Ruby held the door open to their room. "You need to respect my wishes, Sherry. I don't ask you for much. Now, let's go. Our guests will be arriving shortly."

Sherry stomped her way over to her husband. "I don't know if you're undergoing an identity crisis or something, but I don't have to respect shit!" She slammed the door shut. "You've never asked me for much my ass! You asked me to go against everything I stood for and believed in when you refused to let go of that part of your life when I asked you to. For me to remain in your life, I had to give up mine." One of Sherry's legs shook. "I stood by you while you lived that god-awful persona for five years before I gave you an ultimatum, and still you did your dirt. I've earned the right to call you Wesley whenever I please, because you robbed me and the world of him when you choose that life."

She bent down. Her shoes for the night were next to the door. Sherry grabbed one by the straps. "You know what?" She grabbed hold of Ruby's shoulder and used him to keep her balance while she put on her shoes. "I'm not doing this shit with you. You want me to call you Ruby? Fine. So be it. I'll give you a few days of make pretend after tonight, because tonight is about Whitney and Terrance's engagement celebration, which means your ass is going to be Wesley to the fullest."

After both shoes were on. Sherry rubbed out the wrinkle or two at the bottom of her dress, touched on her hair, and finished off her rant with a couple more jabs. "You done lost your mind if you think you haven't asked me for much. You're not the only one who had to let go of themselves for reasons they deemed important. But honey, I do know one thing, and that is if you subconsciously miss that life and this is some sick way of getting back into it, then you have another thing coming. I've been there and rode that road with you already, and I'm not doing it again." She flung open the door she had moments ago declined to walk through. "I'll see you downstairs!" she snapped over her shoulder.

Ruby stepped out into the hallway before he was reminded of the help he had sought out two months ago. Quickly, he traveled back inside his room to his nightstand, where he used the palm of his hand to push down and open the white top to the prescription bottle.

Sherry had mentioned Ruby losing his mind. For quite some time, he wondered if he had. In an attempt to organize his thoughts and live with the past, he had turned to anti-depressants to help ease the journey. Although he had given up that life, the memories by far hadn't given up on him. He chased the two white pills with a bottle of water.

If you subconsciously miss that life and this is your sick way of getting it back somehow, then you have another thing coming. Over everything, that line sat front and center in Ruby's mind.

Is she on to something? Do I miss the past? He cupped the pills, asking himself the question again. Before he could genuinely answer, the intercom to his bedroom went off.

"Hello, Betty."

"Hello, Mr. Evans. Mrs. Evans asked for me to notify you that the guests have started to arrive."

"Thank you, Betty. I'll be down shortly."

Ruby returned the pills back where they belonged. He bypassed the mirror, the object at fault for that evening's trauma. Before he could search his own eyes and into his soul, he punched the mirror. Large and small shards separated from one another. Slits on his knuckles and fingers gave an exit for blood to escape. Quickly, Ruby made it to the intercom and buzzed Betty.

"Is everything okay, Mr. Evans?"

"No. I fell into the mirror, Betty. Old folks lack of balance," he joked. "Can you please bring me the first aid kit? Please do tell Mrs. Evans I'm working on getting down there."

"Right away, Mr. Evans."

Chapter 11

The master bedroom door opened and, upon her entrance, closed with enough intensity for her presence to be heard. The short chrome nails clung to the first aid kit.

"Betty! I'm in the bathroom. Come on in!"

The cotton candy mirrored-toe heels covered in rhinestones carried her from the bedroom, through the walk-in closet, and inside the bathroom. There, Ruby stood with his tattered hand under the stream of cold water.

"Mr. Evans, you hurting yourself is not going to stop Whitney from getting married. It's time she leaves the nest, flies the coop, says bon voyage, adios, see ya later, peace out, see-ya-wouldn't-wanna-be-ya, toodle loo, so long," Whitney joked, insinuating her father's wound was an attempt at sabotaging her wedding.

"Okay, okay." Ruby broke into a head-shaking grin. "I get it. My attempt at keeping you an Evans failed miserably. I'll be sure to arrange my next scheme with more diligence and creativity."

"Good. Because I'm saying, the 'I'm hurt' ploy is weak." Whitley playful punched her father in the shoulder. Gently, she took his hand from underneath the water and gave it a once over.

"Your mother send you up here?"

"Yup. She caught Betty trying to sneak away. She pulled her right on back and made her confess where she was going. That old lady folded like a cheap lawn chair."

Ruby's head dropped backward.

"Sooo, Mommy told her she wasn't going nowhere to help you and that if you needed help, it wasn't going to be from anyone with experience in the medical field. That's when she ordered me up here."

Ruby closed his eyes and dropped his head forward.

"Little does she know that CPR class that I took also taught us first aid. So, ha, ha, you're in good hands, my friend."

"My girl!"

Whitney led her father over to the circular table partnered with two chairs in the center of the his-and-her bathroom. She pulled out the first aid kit and went to work.

"You punch something after you and Mommy's argument?"

"What argument?"

"Humph." Whitney studied his hand just as intently as she studied the recipes she prayed would wow her professors in culinary school. "Daddy, I'm not a kid anymore. You can let up on the *everything's okay* act."

"Everything is okay."

"So Mommy's not mad at you for you wanting her to call you Ruby instead of Westley?"

Ruby withdrew his hand. "Why are you listening to our conversation, Whitney? That's not cool."

"I was walking by your room and my nosiness got the best of me. I'm sorry." Whitney didn't try to dress her mistake in a bow. She did what she did and admitted to her mistakes. Although she didn't voice it, her full face said, *What can I say? Sue me.*

"Mind your manners. We taught you better than that."

Whitney took his hand back and finished the cream and bandage application. Minutes of silence drew Whitney right back to where her father had tried to deter her from.

"Why do you want her to call you Ruby?"

"Didn't I tell you to mind your manners?"

"I know, I know. But we might as well close the chapter."

Ruby tapped his foot loudly and furiously before he even considered answering. "You were listening. You heard my reasoning."

"Is that all?"

"What else can it be?"

Whitney proceeded to wrap his battered hand.

"What she said. Something inside you misses that life and is searching for a way to get it back."

"That makes not one ounce of sense."

"It doesn't?"

Whitney's rich brown eyes saw their way into Ruby's heart. Immediately, he threw up self-protecting barricades.

"One hundred percent. That part of my life is done. I got in, made my name, made my money, made my family, got out, and now we're here. Just like your mother and I planned."

Whitney tightened the wrap some. "The definition of *done* is when something is finished, completed, and has ended. You're not finished with that part of yourself if you still wish to go by a name you claim no longer exists."

Ruby took his hand back and stood. "We have guests waiting."

Whitney stood. The emerald-wrapped dress set off all of her attractive features and hid the rolls she concealed underneath the silk. "Daddy, all I'm saying is that it feels like you're holding on to something. It's like you're here but not really here."

Ruby hadn't moved, which was confirmation enough for Whitney to know she could continue to speak and he'd hear.

"I have eyes, Daddy. I've noticed the first few years we moved here how disconnected you were to the island. You hardly went out, which caused constant arguing between you and Mommy."

"Look at this place. Why the hell do we have to leave? This house is almost the size of the Bahamas!" Ruby snapped.

"True, but you said you got out for your family. However, it seemed difficult for you to fully engulf yourself in the family life."

"What are you saying, Whitney? I don't love my family?"

"Oh, hell no!" Whitney covered her mouth and held her hand out in-between them. "I'm sorry, Daddy. No, that's not what I'm saying at all." She sat down, and Ruby followed suit. He only stood over people whom he wanted to dominate.

"I'm feeling you may have Stockholm Syndrome or something," she said.

"What?"

"As crazy as it sounds, yes. Why else would you want to continue to be called the name given to you by the man who killed your best friend? How is it that you can't fully get that life out of your system? How can the memory of Wesley hurt you more than Ruby? Ruby, Daddy, the man who killed, pumped poison into his community, and lost almost all of his closest friends. Yet, you want to be called Ruby. You obviously have some weird connection to your past that none of us can understand."

"You're talking crazy, Whitney. Come on now. Let's get going."

"Wait, Daddy, wait. Answer me this. Do you remember when you first laughed after moving to the Bahamas?"

Ruby tried to think; however, all he saw was blank. "No. I can't say that I do."

"I do. I remember the first time you laughed since living here was when Uncle Miles came to visit. You transformed into an entirely different person." Whitney hoped her father hadn't taken notice of the moisture that had formed in her eyes. "The whole week that he was here, you could not contain yourself. You went out almost every night, you had more than one drink, and we couldn't get you to shut up. But when he left, when Uncle Miles left, it was like a shadow had cast over our home. It took away all of the rainbows, the sunshine, and the colorful flowers in our back yard that all of our visitors stop by to smell." Whitney forced out a small smile and then continued.

"That night, you and Mommy went at it. I mean, it was so bad I truly believed you were going to get a divorce. She didn't speak one word to you for a month, and you locked yourself in your office and slept in one of the guest rooms. In the argument, you kept telling her you were happy to see your friend, you missed your friend, and I believed you. I was young. It made sense in my young mind that my daddy missed his friend, because I missed mine.

"Then I got older, and I wondered, was it that you missed your friend, or did you miss the life you gave up? Because when Mommy finally spoke to you again, you became some man on a mission to happiness. All day, every day, you made it your business to say, 'I'm happy. I like it here. This is the life.' Then suddenly, you talked Mommy into date nights. Daddy, you tried too hard. Where you trying to convince us that you were happy with this new life, or convince yourself?"

Ruby placed both of his arms fully on the table. "Whitney, right here with you and your mother is where I belong."

Whitney mimicked her father. Her arms settled on the table as well. "But is it where you want to be? I know you love us. I know you want your family. That is something I have never doubted, but if you could, even temporarily, would you bring us back to New York and take back what was yours? Like an entertainer, would you go back on the road one more time and show motherfuckers how it's done?" Using curse words while in conversation with either of her parents was a no-go. However, Whitney needed to tap into the mindset of her father, which she knew he tried to suppress.

A new light came over Ruby's eyes, that spark of light that only flickered on when Miles came to visit or conversations that took place in the past were recalled. Whitney had sat her father down in the hot seat, and it pained her to watch his discomfort.

"Daddy, whatever it is that you feel, I get it. Does what I believe to be the truth bother me? Yes, but that's only because I don't understand. And it's not met for me to understand, but know this, Daddy. I'll always be here for you. I take none of this personally." She rubbed her father's hand.

Ruby snorted and avoided eye contact, although he still listened.

"However, everything I just said, I can't say stands true for Mommy as well."

Ruby met the eyes his genes had passed down to her.

"I know I'm young and got a lot to learn, but speaking from a woman's perspective, when she said she won't go back down that road again with you, she meant it."

Ruby pondered, and Whitney realized she had possibly just seen his heart fall into his shoes.

"You think she meant that?" he asked softly.

"I know she meant that."

Sherry hurled open the door. It crashed against the wall, and Whitney jumped closer to her father.

"Should I tell everyone to come inside my bedroom's bathroom if they want to socialize with the very reason they're all here?" Sherry held out a wine glass that she quickly brought up to her lips.

"That's not necessary, Sherry. We're on our way now."

"How's your hand?" Sherry nodded at the covering.

"I'll live."

"Dammit." Sherry gave her husband and daughter her back and returned to host the party.

Whitney stood there, bewildered. "Was Mommy always so—"

"Dramatic, hardcore, no-nonsense?"

Then finally, they said in unison, "Scary."

"Yup," Ruby replied.

Chapter 12

Brooklyn, NY
1984

"Get the fuck out!"

"Get the fuck out? This is my shit! You're in my crib! You get the fuck out!"

"Oh, so you're not going to go?" Sherry's high ponytail gave off just as much attitude as she did with all its twists and turns.

"Hell no!" Ruby stressed.

"Okay." Sherry's pink high-top aerobic sneakers led her out of the dining room and straight into the bedroom she'd shared with Ruby for three months. She went for Ruby's watch box and plucked the first five out of their slots. Sherry brought them over to the window, where she freed the five watches from her hold and watched them plummet inside the dead bushes that circled their home. Ruby's fast-paced footsteps heading her way amplified Sherry's speed by one hundred and compelled her to grab the entire box and empty into the wind whatever timepieces lingered behind.

Ruby took note of the open drawer that nearly hung off its hinges, followed by half of his girlfriend's body suspended out the window. She pulled herself in and rewarded Ruby with a mischievous grin. Ruby shoved past her and quickly identified all the watches he had purchased throughout the years. He dipped his head inside and sucked his teeth.

"That's the best you got?" Ruby turned his voice into that of a goofy adolescent. "Wow, how will I ever get my watches out the lifeless bushes on our front yard?"

Sherry's expression twisted. Her lips rolled inside her mouth, and her tight fist was all Ruby saw before she slid into the hallway and ransacked his shoe closet.

Awww, fuck. She's going for the sneakers! Ruby raced into the hall. Shoeless, he slid on the waxed floor; however, he caught his balance before he landed on his ass. Ruby stretched his arm out.

Sherry sidestepped his reach and dropped a pair of newly purchased boots on her way up the attic steps. Her back hunched low, she made sure to intensify her hold on the casualty of war. In a haste, she tied each pair of sneakers together by the laces.

"Sherry! Don't fuck with my kicks!"

"Fuck off!" The attic magnified Sherry's voice that temporarily punctured her hearing. She pushed open the diamond-shaped window and held out her first pair of victims. Midair, she swayed the shoes from side to side, building the intensity.

She said out loud, "On the count of three. One, two, three." She tossed the black sneakers out into the Long Island wind. As she imagined they would, they landed on the telephone lines outside their home. The laces twisted together and dangled the footwear above the vehicles that whisked by on the one-way street.

"Fuck yeah!" Adrenaline pumping, she flung the next pair.

Stuck in the attic's entrance, Ruby spewed out his threats and frustrations nonstop. "Sherry! Don't fuck with my shit! I'll throw all your makeup and hair in the dumpster if any of the shit is fucked with!"

"Blah! Blah! Blah!"

Ruby punched the door. He entertained the thought of discarding their handyman's warning about the attic's weight limit while under construction.

"Fuck it," he murmured.

Ruby jogged up the steps. At the edge of the stairs, he shrank by crouching into the pint-size version of himself as best he could. One careful step at a time, he inched inside the tool- and dust-infested space. His head poked out from behind the white-sheet-covered furniture.

"If I go down, you go down. Literally!" Sherry reminded him.

He pushed his arms out and balanced himself after he tilted slightly over to the left. The loose floorboards creaked below him, and his heart raced. He looked to Sherry, who wore a look of accomplishment.

"What are you going to do to my sneakers?" Slowly, he got down on all fours. His lack of fear was no longer as strong.

"The question is, what have I already done?"

The flooring's creaking escalated. Ruby crawled backward, and the board his hand once rested on cracked and plunged onto the dining room table.

"Wesley, you okay?" Sherry attempted to leave the safety of the window seat and haul ass over to her man's side.

"No! Don't move. Let me get out first. The panels won't hold us both!" Ruby backed himself into the doorway, and once he landed on the steps, he ducked his head down.

"Wesley, are you okay? Did you make it out?"

"I'm good! Make your way out slow. Avoid the loose boards."

Sherry did as instructed. The missing panel she overstepped conjured a wave of guilt that settled over her.

Ruby waited for her at the bottom of the stairs, hand
out. She placed her hand into his. He helped her down.
Directly in front of him, he held her by the hips and admired her up front. Bashful, she moved her head around
and tried to avoid his gaze.

"You mean more to me than humanly possible," he
proclaimed.

Her head turned to the side and offered him nothing
but half of her beauty. He re-positioned her stance.

"I'm sorry I'm always gone, but it's for a purpose," he
said.

She chewed down on her lip, her eyes remained stationed anywhere but on him.

"You know that, right?"

Her silence was not only alarming, but nerve rattling.
The screams and yells that society deemed unhealthy
were interpreted by Ruby for their true meaning: love.
Not everyone could calmly express their hurt; therefore,
they wrapped it in aggression and sarcasm. Sherry was
one of those people. She struggled with the battles cast
on her, fought and fought its existence.

"No, I don't." She batted her eyes. Those damn emotions kicked in and pulled the fire alarm and called
on the waterworks. "It's no plausible reason for leaving
home to poison the community you claim to love. You
can throw money wherever and however you please, but
it doesn't clean up your dirt."

"You really feel that way?"

They locked eyes.

"Most definitely."

"I thought you viewed things differently because of
your—"

"Don't bring up my father. This is about you running
the streets like you don't have a woman at home. When
will it stop? What's this hold the streets has on you?"

Sherry stepped out of his grasp. "Stay home for today. Let's spend time today." Her eyes sparkled. They shone with a sprinkle of hope and need.

Ruby's failure to respond drove Sherry to depart from the hallway. Her brightly lit eyes frosted over with dull and solid disappointment. On the bottom floor of their home, she snatched her coat and purse and went for the door.

"Today we give out turkeys. I can't miss this. It means too much," he said.

"And I don't! You're feeding the very people you're killing! What sense does that make?"

"I'm giving back."

"You're giving in to your guilt. You're not doing any of this from the goodness of your heart. You're doing this for the burden on your soul and to make up for what you didn't do—stop your friend's death." Sherry's heart stopped, and her eyes inflated into balloons. "Oh, my gosh," she voiced. "I'm so sorry. I didn't mean that." She stepped closer to Ruby, who only dodged her presence. "I'm sorry. I was mad. I—"

Ruby shoved his way past her and out of the door. He wore no coat. The only source of warmth he could depend on was the turtleneck that clung to his body.

"Wesley! You have no coat! It's freezing out! Please at least let me give you your coat!"

Inside his car, Ruby blasted his radio. Hip hop music drowned out Sherry's apologetic pleas. He backed out of their driveway. Sherry was on the front lawn with tears heavy on her face.

On the side of their home, he was stopped by the red light. Frustrated because he could still see her in his mirrors, he focused on the light. He didn't know why, but his eyes traveled from the green light on up. Once they passed the red circle and the top of the traffic light, they planted themselves of two pairs of sneakers suspended overhead.

Ruby poked his head out the window and looked up. His new sneakers were the neighborhood's entertainment. Folks old and young walked on the sidewalks and pointed up at the shoes.

A young boy no older than twelve told his mother, "Those, Mom! Those are the sneakers that I want."

"You're late," Miles signed.

Ruby closed the trunk to his car, emptied the shopping bag with a winter coat, and put it on. "I know," Ruby hissed. He ensured Miles could read his lips. "How'd it go? How many turkeys were given out?" Ruby dipped his head inside the back of the empty delivery truck. Had he spoken into it, he would have heard his echo.

"All three hundred," Miles's hands answered.

Ruby saw the multiple tables set up on either side of the street.

"The coats are gone, and the raffle winner will have their rent paid up for three months. Pay name is Clarke Cohen. His contact info is right here." Miles held up a scribbled piece of paper.

"Good," Ruby verbalized.

He observed the number of people who lingered around. Some had removed their old coats and warmed themselves with name brand jackets. Others exchanged numbers. The positivity in the air inspired community unity.

"Your future father-in-law's waiting on you." Miles pointed between groups of people.

Alone, the chief jammed his hands inside the pockets of his trench coat, watching Ruby and Miles from afar.

"How long has he been waiting?" Ruby signed.

"Since we started."

"He say anything?"

"Nope. Just stood there, watching and waiting," Miles informed.

"I'll be back." Ruby excused himself through the crowds of people who patted him on the back and repeatedly thanked him for his generosity.

"You ever need anything, Ruby, I got you!"

"This is gonna be a good Thanksgiving because of you! Come on by and get a plate!"

Ruby wished he could accept the appreciation with more graciousness; however, the look on Asher's face erased the good feeling each appreciative voice gave Ruby.

Ruby approached Asher. "Chief."

"Mister popular." Asher chucked a piece of gum inside his mouth. "As much as I appreciate the free turkey,"—Asher's mouth smacked—"I don't like to be kept waiting."

"If you wanted a turkey, all you had to do was tell Sherry. I would have had one sent to you. No need to come down here with us criminals."

"The less communication we have through Sherry, the better. I get the feeling she's not happy with our . . . business relationship."

Ruby did not entertain his observation.

A woman whose arms were filled with her turkey and new jacket stopped in front of them. "Ruby, you're an angel. An angel, I tell you." She nodded at him and continued on her way.

"Now, what is it that you want to speak with me about, chief? Isn't it a bad look to be seen with me? I wouldn't want to upset your brothers in blue." Ruby folded his arms and leaned against a brick wall.

"Maybe, but I don't care much about a lot of things anymore, now that I'll be retiring next month." Asher took his hands out of his pockets.

"Retiring. It's about that time, huh? Where else am I going to find me a pig just as dirty as you to be my eyes and ears of the NYPD?"

Asher refrained from a game of tit-for-tat verbal bashing. "For the sake of my daughter and only for her,"—he threw a death stare Ruby's way—"I've recommended one of my men already in the fold to take my position. He gets the promotion and everything for you remains as is. No rocking the boat."

"Asher, you make me proud."

An older gentleman walking by held his fist out to Ruby and the two gave one another a pound.

"I'm glad I have," Asher said, "because this second part of our meeting won't. You have a snake in your organization, Ruby. He's flapping his gums like a teenager who just got her own room phone."

Ruby pulled his back from the wall. "Bullshit. I run a tight ship. There's no room for disloyalty."

Asher removed his gloves. "Well, it's happening. Someone's poking holes in your ship, and you're sure to go down if you don't start plugging shit up." He examined his wet hands. "Now, these are some damn good gloves. I can be in a blizzard, and my hands will do nothing but sweat." He waved the leather in Ruby's face and shoved them in his pocket.

"Who's the snitch?"

"I don't know yet. Looking into it. Word got through to me from one of my dirty pigs. Said he never seen the kid. I'm left to believe the person supplying the information is only the messenger and not a member of your crew."

Ruby shook his head. "You don't know what you're talking about. Retirement's shining too bright in your eyes."

"Listen here, you piece of shit." Asher positioned himself in front of Ruby and put a finger in his face. "I don't give a fuck what you have to do, but you handle this shit. I'm not going to watch my daughter travel to and from Rikers visiting you because you fucked up and got sloppy. Fix it!" He backed away, straightened his tie that poked out through the opening of his coat, and cleared his throat.

"Thank you for the turkey. Will I be seeing you on Thanksgiving?" he said.

Ruby straightened his posture and smiled at him. "There's no place else I'd rather be."

"Good to hear." Asher tipped his hat to Ruby and walked off. His pace was slow and without a care in the world.

Ruby scanned the street for Miles. He found him posted up next to a telephone booth. Ruby waved him over. Miles dipped in and out of space Brooklyn natives hadn't occupied.

Ruby pointed to his lips. "We have a problem. Asher tells me we have a snake in our grass."

Quickly, Miles's hands said, "Bullshit! He's trying to psych you out. I never did trust him."

"Look into it," Ruby said. "Keep a close eye on everyone. We can't afford to overlook this if it really is something."

Miles nodded. "And if I find out who it is?"

"Take care of him and clean up whatever mess he's made."

Twin girls, no older than ten with missing teeth, approached Ruby. Proudly, they grinned and showed off their jackets by spinning around.

"Thank you, Mr. Ruby!" they both yelled.

Ruby kneeled down with an overly wide smile on his face. "You're welcome!" he shouted as Miles drifted off and the hunt began.

Chapter 13

Paradise Island, Bahamas
2021

Ruby jammed his hands inside his dress pants. "Is this why you're wearing green?"

"Yup. Your wife told me to." Whitney beamed at a couple at the far side of the heavenly green-and-silver decorated living room.

Ruby scanned the room. The ice sculptures, foil balloons, chocolate fountains, and the numerous snack bars that outlined the living room and made way into the garden brought on a headache.

"How did this get done so fast? When did it get done? And who the hell are all these people?" he asked in a state of awe.

Betty walked by and filled Ruby's open hand with a glass of whiskey. He downed it. Ruby shook the hands of those who approached him. Strangers.

"You're disconnected, Daddy." Whitney's dimples jumped out. "You don't even know who's in your midst. If you ask me, Ruby's slipping."

"Chrissy! You made it!" Arms wide open, Whitney took long strides, which led her to her classmate instantly.

Men and women dressed in black and white serving uniforms with a dashes of green swerved in and out of the crowds, balancing trays filled with finger foods or drinks. One server was close to Ruby when several people who gabbed and bragged about their superficial way of life surrounded the tray. Blocked in by strangers and their unwanted pointless dialogues, Ruby removed the Long Island Iced Tea from the server's tray. Never had the drink made Ruby's top five, though with all the activity that raided his mind and home, he needed something strong to ease the anxiety.

"Sir, I'm truly sorry, but that drink is for the mother of the soon-to-be bride." The well-polished, polite young sever pointed to Sherry. She stood not far out of Ruby's sight. Her warped, icy scowl was the first and only thing that stood out.

Ruby pressed his lips on the rim of the slim glass and chugged it down. He banged the glass on the tray and notified the server that he could now make his delivery. The young man hesitated, yet Ruby shooed him along.

A new server strolled by carrying a platter of champagne balanced and well poured. She offered Ruby a glass, and he accepted.

His wife, whose self-control had taken her until her forties to achieve, abandoned it when her husband held up and tipped his drink to her. Sherry scanned her surroundings and, in one rapid movement, threw Ruby the finger and disguised it under the pretense that she was fixing her hair.

Ruby downed the champagne and slid his way through the bodies whose stomachs he had paid to fill. Free from the giggles, plastic smiles, and fake interactions, Ruby managed to guide himself outside to the patio overlooking the garden. A hefty number of guests walked the grounds; however, double that amount filled the inside of his home and absorbed all the air that he badly needed.

"Mr. Evans, is it a little too much for you in there as well?"

Ruby straightened his posture. "Mr. Brown, how are you doing this evening?"

"I'm great. I didn't think tonight would be so . . ."

"Much?" Ruby finished.

"Exactly."

The two men shared a laugh.

"I'll never understand what it is about weddings and babies and birthdays that makes women lose all of their God-given sense. Did you notice the oil painting of Terrance and Whitney next to the replica of the painting in the form of an ice sculpture?" Ruby asked.

Mr. Brown sipped his brown liquor. "Oh, yes. Why do you think I decided I needed a breather?"

Although Ruby laughed, no sound came out.

"Mr. Evans, entertain an old man and tell me what you really think of my grandson." Mr. Brown stepped aside for a small group of people curious to see the garden.

"Mr. Brown."

"Call me Houston. We're about to be family. A lot of the formalities go out of the window."

"Houston. I see myself in Terrance, a part of who I was a long, long, time ago. A young man trying to be someone that he's not."

"Umph!" Houston rushed himself to swallow his drink. "So, you see that also?"

"I'm a man of many talents, Houston. I've seen it for some time now."

"Not many people would like such a characteristic in their future son-in-law."

A couple near the rose bush waved Ruby's way.

"True, but I don't look down on what I don't understand. Terrance is a good man. He's finding his way more and more every day, and if I could help him with that, I will."

The corners of Houston's mouth went downward, and his head bobbed up and down. "That's very mature of you. I can now say I'm one hundred percent comfortable with my grandson entering this family. I've always knew you were humble, but to hear it out your mouth is comforting." Houston finished his drink and looked around for a server to snatch another from.

"Either you're really thirsty or really stressed," Ruby observed.

"Both. That deadbeat son of mine choose a weekend getaway with one of his mistresses over attending his only son's engagement party." The corners of Houston's mouth collapsed. "You know, every day I wonder where the hell I went wrong with that boy."

"Mr. Evans, would you like some champagne?" a server asked.

Ruby lightened the tray by two glasses and handed one to Houston.

"Ever since I can remember, Terrance fought for that man's approval. It didn't matter what it was, Terrance was starved for that fool's acknowledgment, but for reasons unknown to me, that jackass could never reward the boy with a simple *good job*, or *I'm proud of you*. He gave him nothing other than pure judgment and ridicule."

"How was your relationship with your son?" Ruby's lips met the flute.

"The complete opposite. The fool was just like Terrance. Driven to accomplish something, anything, so it wouldn't look like he lived in my shadow. He based his self-worth on his title, and I knew that, so I made sure to always tell him that whatever he accomplishes in life matters. That he matters. To show support. I backed him on all his ideas, no matter how stupid. Now trust me, Wesley. He had some damn stupid ideas I knew were nothing but a waste of my money, but I went ahead with it because—"

Ruby said, "He's your son."

"Correct!" Houston held up his glass, and a little of his champagne splashed out. "I'm sorry, my brother. Where's the maid?" Houston heaved his body to the side, and his jacket hurled open. He scanned the area for one of Ruby's housekeepers.

"No need, old timer. I got it." Ruby removed a napkin from his jacket pocket. Slowly, he bent down and wiped away the wet spot on the floor panels.

Houston consumed the champagne until it was halfway empty. "Wow. A humble man you are."

Ruby stood. "The only way to be."

"Here, here!" Houston raised his glass in a salute to Ruby. He let it down and pointed his finger at Ruby. "You know, he promised Terrance he would be here. Gave him the whole spiel on how there's no other place he'd rather be and that he cleared his weekend all for today." Houston drained his glass. "Lies. All lies, and as usual, Terrance believed everything his daddy told him. Now, don't get me wrong. Since meeting Whitney, he's grown into being his own man and giving less of a fuck about what others think, but it's gonna take some time for him to completely get the desire to make his father proud out of his system."

Ruby sipped on his bubbly as a tray of infused martinis came their way. Houston stole a drink, set his empty flute down, and mistakenly knocked over the three other glasses on the tray. The tray took a hard, wet fall that splashed liquor onto the server. Ruby and Houston stumbled backward. The new drink he seized was no longer more than two drops.

Ruby helped gather the broken glass off the panels. Kneeling next to the server, he asked her, "Please tell my wife to have Betty come out here and assist with Mr. Brown."

"Right away." The server gathered her mess of a tray and took off.

His back against the house, Ruby held his hand out to Houston. "Come on, old timer. Have a seat over here."

Terrance's grandfather kicked back the martini droplets, placed the glass down on a step, and took Ruby's hand. They moved gradually from the back of the house toward the garden's path.

"Take your time," Ruby said.

Houston took a seat. His head dipped back some when he found comfort. "Oh, man. I haven't had one too many since I can't remember when."

Ruby pulled the bottom of his pants up and sat down beside him.

"Pop Pop!" Terrance hurried over to his grandfather with a broad frown and furrowed eyebrows.

"Here comes this asshole," Houston slurred.

Ruby glowered at Houston.

"No, no, not Terrance. That son of a bitch with him. Bastard should have stayed in New York."

Behind Terrance jogged a skeletal young man of colossal height. Speed-walking behind them both was Betty.

"Mr. Evans, what happened? The server said Pop Pop wasn't well." Tension mixed with the chattering of his teeth took over Terrance's presence.

Ruby placed himself in front of Terrance and gripped his shoulders. "Calm down. He's good. The old man just had a little too much to drink, you know?" The corners of Ruby's mouth raised.

Terrance turned around and clasped both his hands behind his head. "He's still pissed over my father not showing. I told him it's okay to let it go."

"It's not okay!" Houston used Betty's arm to help straighten his posture. "He's a loser! An adulterer! He doesn't deserve a son!" he shouted, one arm hurled in all directions.

Ruby walked Terrance farther over to the side, far from Houston's keen hearing. "He's disappointed in his son, and he wants more for his grandson," he said.

"Pop Pop never drinks." Terrance looked past Ruby to his grandfather.

"Years of the same shit has the tendency of pushing people on to untraveled paths. Listen, why don't you two stay here for the night and tomorrow, if need be? Sometimes a change of scenery helps."

"You sure, Mr. Evans? I don't want us to be a burden."

"You're not."

The man Houston referred to as an asshole interjected. "Terrance, I think I should take Pops home. He's losing it over there."

Ruby stepped back and examined the stranger who had rudely interrupted without a mere "excuse me" or "hello." Houston's hollering escalated into excessive use of vulgar language that took a back seat to Ruby's pissed thoughts.

Terrance started to answer the man, "No need. Pop Pop and I are going to—"

"Terrance." Ruby faced his rude guest with his back slightly hunched and hands folded behind his back. "Your friend lack manners, so maybe you can introduce me to who's under my roof?" The tension held in Ruby's mouth resulted in his eyes bulging out just a little.

"My apologies, my man. This all you?" Terrance's guest whirled his finger in the air.

"Mr. Evans, I'm so sorry." Terrance shot his comrade a hard stare. "This is my cousin Felix. Please excuse him. He's not familiar with proper formalities."

"Yeah, excuse me," Felix echoed while he returned Terrance's bitter look. "It's not something I'm proud to admit, but my cousin over here is right. I haven't had much opportunity to practice proper etiquette. You're home, though, is dope." Felix held both hands out in front of him. "I'm sorry. I mean your home is lovely." One side of his mouth picked up.

"Where you from?" Ruby interrogated. His arms journeyed from his back and crossed against his chest.

"I'm from Chicago."

"What are you all over there talking about? Terrance! Don't let that rotten apple over there get inside your head!" Houston shouted.

Guests whispered to one another after they walked past Houston.

"Fuck up one or two times and you're labeled the back sheep of the family. Doesn't matter if you came up on your own without the help of Daddy or Grandpa, ya dig?" Felix chuckled.

"No. I don't *dig*," Ruby emphasized.

Terrance stepped forward, putting his body between his cousin and future father-in-law. "Listen, Felix, you taking Pop Pop home isn't necessary. Mr. Evans offered us to stay the night. You know, have Pop Pop sleep it off."

"Don't I get an invite, Mr. Evans?"

Ruby scowled.

"Come on, lighten up. I'm just playing. You know, a little jokey-joke." Felix double-tapped Ruby's shoulder.

The reddening in Ruby's cheeks was the main hint given to Terrance that he should get Felix away. The continuing tapping of his finger on his arm was his second clue. Terrance moved in closer to his cousin and wrapped his arm around his shoulders. "Felix, help me get Pop Pop into the house, and I'll hit you in the morning."

Terrance led Felix over to their grandfather. He turned behind him and mouthed to Ruby, "I'm sorry."

His grandsons on either side, Houston walked back inside Ruby's home with Betty leading the way. The four of them made it into the home as Shelly and Whitney came out and scurried over to Ruby.

"What the hell happened? We tried getting here sooner when you told me to send Betty out, but dammit, give motherfuckers a few drinks and hors d'oeuvres and they talk your ear off," Sherry complained.

"Whitney, Terrance's cousin. What do you know about him?"

Whitney held on to her mom's arm and removed her heels. "Oh, yes, that's better. I don't know much, except that he's basically the outcast of the family. In and out of jail and uncouth. His mom died and left everything to him."

"Why is he here?"

"Terrance mentioned something about him being here on business. Said he was keeping an eye on an investment he had over here. Or was it that he's looking into a business venture he'd like to get into out here? I'm sorry, I really don't remember, Daddy. I'm a little toasted."

Whitney and her mother laughed.

"Those infused martinis were no joke," Sherry admitted.

"I told Terrance that he and Houston could stay the night and tomorrow if they choose. Houston's having a difficult time with accepting his son's a douche."

"You did, Daddy? That's so nice of you."

"Would have been nice if you ran it by me," Sherry jabbed.

"You didn't run by me throwing a party that could be mistaken as Whitney's wedding with motherfuckers I don't even know trolling up and down my shit. Also, I didn't think I'd have to ask permission for my daughter's fiancé's inebriated grandfather to stay the night in my own home, so he won't go back to his house and break a hip." Ruby detected the rise in his voice and calmed down by taking several deep breaths.

Sherry's neck cocked in Ruby's direction. "I told your ass all about the guest list. Maybe if you were paying attention and not living in the past, it all wouldn't be such a surprise. And did you say your house? You still on that shit?"

"Okay, Mommy. Come back on inside with me. You know good and well I don't like leaving folks around all of y'all good stuff. I don't care how rich this group is. Sticky fingers is sticky fingers." Whitney snatched her mother by the wrist and yanked her toward the house.

Sherry's heels banged against the ground as her hair bounced. She tried to turn around and look back at her husband in hopes of giving him the finger or perhaps mouth a good "fuck you," but Whitney picked up the pace when the thought hit Sherry's mind. Her newly acquired speed led her to do nothing other than focus on not tripping in her shoes.

Three hours later

It was pushing 2 a.m. when Ruby made it to the guest room that night. Before he stripped, he sat on the bed and played back in his mind everything that had transpired over those last few hours. Thinking of all the chaos made Ruby want to yell out and wake his household. Parties were not Ruby's thing. They never had been, not even back in the day when it was appropriate for him to show his team some appreciation by supplying a little downtime. The planning, the hosting, it all landed on Sherry. All Ruby did was give her the ends to have it all emerge. So naturally, Ruby saw this night as being nothing different. That was, until the last partygoer departed, and Sherry waltzed up the stairs barefoot, her shoes abandoned somewhere downstairs.

"Sherry, where you going? The caterers and band still have to pack up," Ruby called out to his wife.

Step by step, Sherry made it closer to her destination. "Then let them pack up."

"Are they already paid? What's theirs and what's ours?"

Sherry leaned into the railing. "I don't know. This is your house. Figure it out."

True to form Sherry, gave him her customary middle finger. She held it up until she made it to the top of the stairs and vanished.

There, Ruby stood stuck on stupid while the help asked many questions to which he'd known none of the answers. There were questions about what china, drinkware, and silverware she'd like to keep. Supposedly, there was a dining set company that had sponsored the party for exposure to all of Sherry's uppity and well-off associates. As a thank you, she had her pick of china that wouldn't be available for sale to the public until next year.

After every check was cut and numbers collected, Ruby concluded Sherry had paid close to nothing for that party. She had received deals up the ass just by making agreements to advertise their businesses on her personal and business social media sites. She used her status to get the best without having to pay for it. Ruby was impressed. Confused by all of today's modern ways of posting on the internet for exposure and the goal of gaining followers, he was fascinated nonetheless.

When no stranger further occupied his home, he went to his bedroom to show his wife appreciation. Yet, things were never that easy when it came to making up with Sherry. Their bedroom door was locked, and a Post-it rested alongside the doorknob that read:

You have many options in YOUR house to sleep, so pick a room.

On the floor sat his pajamas. Ruby settled for the second-largest guest room their home offered. It had a view of the ocean opposite the garden, and it smelled of the sea. His thoughts seemed to get lost in there a majority of the time, and life's problems disappeared. Ruby undressed slower than necessary. The need to rush was not a priority. He just wanted to be, although he wasn't entirely sure what that meant in his case.

He tightened the string on his pajama pants then slid on his white wife-beater. For years, Sherry had tried to insert two-set pajama pieces into Ruby's nightlife routine, but he couldn't tolerate the comfort change. It wasn't him. Like life in the Bahamas, it felt stuffy, rigid, and without flavor.

He opened the balcony doors and stepped out. The water spoke harshly and with such high aggression that early morning. There was no sense of welcome or tranquility in the waves that hit.

"What are you trying to tell me?" he asked.

If there was one thing Ruby could stomach outside of the safety and happiness the island brought his family, it was the ocean. He and the sea had an understanding. The water spoke, and Ruby would listen. Its flow intensified when Ruby's phone chimed, interrupting their conversation. The longer the phone went off, the angrier the tide sounded.

On the writing desk, far from the freedom the two doors offered, Ruby's cellular phone vibrated and blasted its electronic screams. On the front of the screen, the option to accept or decline Miles's video call was written in white words.

"Miles! To what do I owe the pleasure of this call, you shithead?"

Miles scratched the stubble and shaving bumps heavy on his chin. "Fuck you!" he signed. "Did you tell my goddaughter I apologize for not being able to make it?"

"Yeah, I told her. She understands. She only wishes she could meet this woman who has you smitten enough to vacation with her. Your old ass still getting pussy, and twenty years younger at that. Ain't that about a bitch."

Miles's saggy face perked up a bit. "We all can't find the love of our lives early on and live happily ever after. Some of us have to keep on searching."

Reading Miles's hands reminded Ruby of how far their friendship had come. So many days, they had bonded over the disgust they shared for the same man and the anger and darkness JoJo had brought into their lives. The darkness had transformed them into alter egos that kept them in their grasp. Their past lives had given Miles the ability to read lips perfectly and Ruby to sign.

"Ruby, there's something you need to know." The bags that hung low beneath Miles's eyes grew heavier. "Things aren't good in Brooklyn."

"Okay, have Bungee step in and do what needs to be done. Clean up the mess of his protégé. Those new in power sometimes have difficulties adjusting. Brooklyn has to get used to the new head in command. It just takes a little finessing."

"It's not that simple. This is no typical fuck up."

Miles looked up and quickly signed to someone off camera. "Give me a little time. I'm on an important call." He nodded. "Close the door on your way out."

Lightning lit up the skies and shook the stars. Ruby heard the door shut on Miles's end, and then his friend continued uploading his bag of bad news.

"Bungee and Con are dead."

Ruby felt his insides rattle, but on the outside, his form was stock-still.

"Tony and Linden fell off the map. I can't find them or their families. All the Kings, outside of us, are gone," Miles concluded.

Ruby took a seat. All at once, as if it was agreed upon, the ocean waves crashed into one another, the lightning cracked in the sky, and fist-sized raindrops flooded the island grounds.

"Hold on." Ruby minimized his chat with Miles and opened the Brooklyn Kingpins tree put he had put together on an app called Outside Tree. He traced the street name of Bungee's successor.

"Miles. What about Straw?" he called out. "Is he good? What does he know about this shit, and what is he doing to rectify the situation?"

Miles dropped his head. By the time Ruby maximized the screen, he had picked himself up. Miles told him, "Straw's responsible for all of this. I've got word that he feels it's time for a new kingdom to be born. Out with the old, in with the new."

The balcony doors rushed open. The force brought on by the wind caused the glass windows embedded in the doors to blow out.

"Shit!" Ruby guarded his face with his arm.

"Ruby." Miles's face momentarily froze, then came back to life. "Everything we built has dissolved." The screen slowed and turned into small pixels. Before the lights went out and all forms of communication shut down, the chat ended with Miles telling Ruby, "Your legacy is gone."

Chapter 14

One Week Earlier

Outside, under tree branches with sprouting flowers, Felix sat alone. Comfortable with his outdoor furniture selection, he remained still. Head dipped backward and eyes closed, he ordered his body to act as dead weight in order not to lose the direct rays of sunshine that hit his face and made him feel as if closed off inside a tanning bed. The vitamin D that stirred and bubbled within his skin created a moment of zen that sent him off into a relaxed state of mind. Although surrounded by plastic-wrapped tables and chairs stacked against the corners of the outdoor glass dining area, his mind led him to believe he was a hostage in a spa determined to grant him inner peace. Involuntarily, Felix's body drifted down and didn't stop until he came to and pushed himself up.

In Felix's battle to regain serenity, the arrival of his mentor had gone unnoticed. Inside Felix's unfinished bubble, his pale, clammy-skinned adviser, who was in crucial need of a return to his home island of the Dominican Republic so the sunbeams could replenish his flesh, scanned his future place of business.

"When do you open? You've built this place fast." Bungee slid a finger across the only table that was set up and wiped the light dust particles off on his pant leg.

Felix wiggled around a few more times before he settled for what seemed to be the closest he'd achieve to the comfort he once had. "In two months. Just in time for fall. I'm calling it Friskies. I want all of Brooklyn here sucking down my chicken and gravy." He licked his lips. "I call this here the bubble. I dedicate this to my grown and sexy patrons." He turned his friend's attention to the glass ceiling. "Picture the leaves and flower buds tumbling down and the evening rain washing it all away just as dinner is served." His narrow, slender face gave off a smile that resembled Spider-Man's Green Goblin.

Bungee leaned against the large, solid table. "Felix, what are you doing with Brooklyn?"

The corners of Felix's stretched mouth fell. "What am I doing with Brooklyn?" he repeated. His face was a puzzle in need of piecing together. "What am I doing with Brooklyn? Oh, what am I doing with Brooklyn! I'm doing a little revamping, is all." He crossed one leg over the other with folded hands on top of his knee.

The lines in Bungee's forehead made an appearance. "Does your revamping include undoing years of proven success for every dealer that comes into play?" He stabbed his finger into the table. "Because if that's what you call revamping, I'm not liking your renovating skills, and I'm not liking you going on killing sprees. You're making shit hot. We don't do hot."

From where Felix sat, he could see the hard white flakes from the gel that smoothed Bungee's hair.

"Bungee, why so hostile? Have you forgotten right before you left your well-kept, oiled machine of a business that I'd mentioned making a few changes?"

Bungee turned fully in Felix's direction, the table no longer a crutch. "A few changes. Not a transformation. There are home invasions and pregnant, strung-out women nodding off in the middle of Brooklyn's streets." Bungee bent down and held on to either side of the table. "And why the fuck are the pigs telling me they haven't been paid? Are you trying to get us hemmed up?"

Felix used the tip of his nail to scratch the top of his eyebrow. "I think it's time for a change. Sort of an out-with-the-old, in-with-the-new way of thinking. Now, don't get me wrong. Your old school, prehistoric way of doing things got us far and done us well, but this is a new day and age. We have a new generation of men more willing to go about this business not so . . ."—Felix tapped his finger against his jawline—"restricted. There's a need for freedom, and with that freedom, I believe we can achieve much more, much faster."

"By breaking ties with the NYPD and killing off your neighborhood, you're doing nothing but making a scene and breaking alliances. I taught you better. Respect Brooklyn and her people, and she'll respect you! You don't kill your men. They keep this shit going!" Bungee's voice deepened. "Having more friends instead of enemies ensures dirt won't stick. Had you wanted to do things other than how I taught you, you should have never—" Bungee stopped talking. "You son of a bitch." Rays of sunlight lit up multiple areas of the restaurant. Bungee shoved the table to the side. The open space granted him access to hoist Felix up by the shirt.

"You played me. You planned this shit, didn't you? You never wanted to be a part of a legacy. You wanted to make your own." He shook him. "Your punk ass cheated your way to the top. You faggot!"

"You catch on fast." Felix chuckled. "You always were swift."

Bungee's hammers-for-hands constricted and pulled him closer. "You think this shit is funny? I should body you right now and put down the dog I trained."

Felix poked his lips out and pecked Bungee on his mouth. Bungee's eyebrows plummeted. He shoved Felix into his seat and used his hand to repeatedly clean his mouth. He spit, wiped his mouth, and spit some more.

Felix reached under his metal chair. "It's 2021, Bungee. You know better than to use the F word." Felix exposed the first piece he'd ever fired. It had been a gift from Bungee. He aimed it at the man he had learned from, killed for, cried for, and almost died for. "Get with the times." Felix blew two bullets into Bungee's chest and one in his dome for his offensive language. Bungee's limp body dropped sideways onto the floor.

Felix bent down and closed Bungee's eyes. He stroked the man's tough hair.

"Perry!"

Not long after Felix called for his minion, Perry appeared from inside the halfway finished eatery, hands and feet gloved and sheets of plastic in his arms. He didn't look at Felix or the body while he rattled off instructions. "There's a change of clothes inside. Leave what you're wearing in there and don't return here until morning."

Perry never looked a man in the eye when he spoke. For so long, that had irked Felix; however, when he learned that in Perry's culture it was a sign of respect, he grew accustomed to it.

"Will do. Perry, can I be transparent with you?"

Perry looked ahead while Felix untucked his shirt.

"I'm going to miss Bungee. He was a passionate mentor, but dammit, don't it feel good to be rid of that mother-fucker!" Felix did a horrid attempt at what he claimed was tap dancing. "The whole flamboyant, pretty-boy, proper-speaking crap can fuck a motherfucker up, ya dig? Make him lose his street cred." He unbuttoned his skinny jeans.

Perry didn't respond. He stood in place like a member of the Queen's Guard.

"I like me some dick, but acting like a bottom bitch ain't my thing. I need to see my shit going in and out that butt-hole. But you know what they say? Sometimes you gotta do what you gotta do, and I had to put on a show, ya feel me? No matter how much they say they not, suckas are homophobic and think we're weak." Felix wrestled his head out the T-shirt. "So, if I wanted in the game faster without being seen as a threat to that bitch-ass position, I had to play the ass-kissing part. Had to be a yes man, a right hand." Clothes in hand, Felix walked up to Perry. His long nose was almost touching Perry's.

"I like you, Perry. I know your people ain't down for my butty-sticking ways, but you respect it and never say shit. Keep it up." He patted his shoulder. "When you're finished with this mess, let Con know I'd like to meet with him tomorrow."

With a confident stride, Felix walked into the front of his establishment stark naked.

Chapter 15

Paradise Island, Bahamas
2021

Not more than five minutes after the electricity went out, the backup generator kicked in. Rather than reconnect with Miles and clean the mess made by Mother Nature's aggressive tone, Ruby checked on his loved ones, except for Sherry, followed by his housekeepers. His sight validated that all were well and without knowledge of the disturbance. Covered by a baseball hat and hooded sweater he hadn't worn in years, he passed his bedroom door and slid a folded piece of paper with the words *I'm sorry* under the door.

In a car that he had barely driven, Ruby was sure that if he inhaled deep enough, he'd smell that new car smell everyone raved about. He took in the pounding and crushing sounds his tires encountered on the road and didn't wince over the light raindrops the open window spit at his face. The storm's downgrade from savage to merciful helped Ruby's thoughts fall into place.

The distant ride out to the farm reminded Ruby of its purchase and renovation. Flashes of the land's rebirth, along with the consistent hopes for it to never be inhabited, settled in front of Ruby's vision. His hands took over and guided the steering wheel to his destination. The action allowed Ruby's mind to take flight and relive the past.

The black fence separated and protected miles of rich green land. Although once shabby and broken, it was what had pushed Ruby to buy. Its strength, regardless of its age and weathering, allowed it to survive so much. Its longevity and will to stand firm was what reassured Ruby. He drove along the fence that led him back in time to when Ruby officially became a part of the music world and a brother in blue.

Brooklyn, NY
1987

"Yo! Yo! Can I have everyone's attention?" The man with a medium build stood on the sticky table with empty beer bottles, overturned drinking glasses, and cigarette butts. The microphone he held had the letter *G* painted on it. After he made numerous attempts to calm the amped crowd, finally, the rowdy voices simmered down and gave their attention to the man the streets knew as Scratch.

"I just want to say something real quick. We all know why we're here, and that's because my road dog, my ace, my best friend since kindergarten, Shane Gray, a.k.a. Glock's first album went *double platinum!*"

The loyal hip-hop listeners broke out in a sea of applause. Whistling and feet stomping added to the craze when Scratch started to dance on the table, beer bottle over his head. The golden liquid splashed out and landed on faces beneath him. Once the table began to rock, Scratch took on the stance of a surfer. He let up on his movements and returned to his speech. He held his head high and raised his bottle to the top floor of the rented loft. Eyes squinting, he fought against the cigarette smoke and flashing club lights to find his friend, who looked down at the party from the second floor.

"You did it, homie. All those days and nights recording in basements, bathrooms, and selling tapes out of our trunks paid off, my man! You the king! Congratulations!"

Every head on the lower level raised their glasses to Glock. Off-key, each fan and longtime friend screamed until their throats hurt, "Congratulations, Glock!"

Glock held a microphone, which was identical to the one Scratch handled, up to his lips. "Scratch, get your drunk ass down before you bust your ass."

The crowd fell out in laughter.

"I'm not paying for your medical bills, motherfucker. We all know you don't have no insurance."

The already entertained group roared louder.

Scratch spoke into the mic. "Fuck you, motherfucker. You are my insurance, medical, life, all that shit!"

Glock's one dimple blossomed. "Nah, serious, though. Thank you to everyone that's here, because every one of you has a part in my success. Either you let me sleep on your couch when my pops and I were beefing, put somebody on to my tapes who otherwise would have never gave me a chance, or did something as simple as be a part of the audience while I battled homies on street corners and in parks. Whatever you did, how little it may have seemed at the time, it wasn't. You helped get me out there and gave me the confidence I needed to keep going, even after Crossroads annihilated me in our first battle."

Boos let loose in the crowd.

"But y'all still stood by me and didn't dip on a motherfucker. That's love right there. Thank you. So, if y'all gonna toast me, it's only right I toast y'all. To Brooklyn, baby!"

"To Brooklyn!" the loft yelled out.

Glock's first single blasted out of the speakers and reminded partygoers what had made him reach the top at the speed of light. Waitresses, wearing outfits that recalled Glock's leading ladies from his videos, circulated in the room. One server, dressed as Glock's first ever leading lady, walked the steps to the second floor in high-top sneakers, tight shorts that hit her knees, with suspenders over a tight, short-sleeve shirt. She emptied her tray of drinks on the small tables beside Ruby and Glock.

When she caught an up-close glimpse of Ruby, she took her time standing straight after leaning down to deliver the drinks. Her cleavage almost touched her chin and threatened to topple out of her shirt—and into Ruby's hands if he let them.

"Can I get you anything?" Her long tongue traced over her lips. She dipped her head to the side so her jumbo curls rolled down her shoulder.

Without giving her a look, Ruby waved her off. Taken aback by his behavior, she sucked her teeth and went for the exit.

"Damn, you cold-blooded." Glock sipped from his glass.

"My woman will catch two counts of murder if I fuck around on her. The headache's not worth it."

Glock took in more liquor. He looked around at the few approved people who shared his space in his section. They were occupied in conversation and drinks. Glock spit out his thoughts. "I want to personally thank you, man. If it wasn't for you, I wouldn't be here. You financially backed me and made this all happen. I appreciate that. You're gonna get your money back, all of it."

"I been meaning to talk to you about that."

Glock leaned forward. "Shoot."

"You don't have to pay back everything. Only sixty percent." Ruby bent over and rubbed a smudge off his sneaker.

Glock noticed the footwear that not even he could get his hands on. "Sixty percent?" he asked.

"Sixty percent," Ruby reiterated.

"Why? No disrespect, but don't nothing come for free, so what you want from me?"

Ruby followed Glock's stare as he looked over his appearance. Although he knew what decorated him, he still looked over his gold nugget chain and gold-and-diamond pinky ring.

Ruby reached for the champagne the cleavage-revealing waitress had left behind. "Your friendship," he said just before the crystal met his lips.

"My friendship?" Glock concentrated on the opposite side of the room. Three men who always stuck to Ruby's side whenever Glock met with Ruby were watching him watch them. "Ruby, by the looks of it, you don't need no more friends."

"I can always use friends. Not every friendship is the same, because not every friend is the same. I am broadening my horizons when it comes to friends and taking on new kinds." Ruby finished the bubbly. He stationed his elbow on the armrest closest to Glock. "You live for this. The glitz, the glam, the music. This is your world, and in every world comes different connections. So, this is where you come in, friend." Ruby waited. "You pay me only sixty percent of what I put into you, and if and when I never need you, you're there."

Glock sat back. "So, I'll be indebted to you."

Ruby bounced his head up and down a little. "In technical terms, yeah, but I don't like to see it like that. I like to view it as us being friends. I was there for you, and when the time comes, you be there for me. And when I say you, that includes everything that comes with you. Your business crew and your street crew. You can't forget where you came from. Friends like you don't come around often. Cat from the hood who chased his dreams, that's not seen every day."

"Sixty percent?" Glock asked again.

"Sixty percent."

Glock put his arm up and snapped his fingers. One of his bodyguards posted in the corner got the bartender's attention. Right away, the bartender brought over another rum on the rocks. Glock inhaled it the instant the glass met his palm. He put down the glass, turned to Ruby, and held out his hand.

While they shook on it, Glock let him know, "What's mine is yours."

Ruby stopped shaking and covered Glock's hand with his other. "This is the beginning of a beautiful friendship."

Once their holds were broken, one of the corner boys Ruby had brought along to the party and had ordered to remain on the lower level, crashed into the room.

"Hey, Ruby, can I speak to you over here right quick?"

Ruby followed his worker a few feet away from where he sat with Glock and explained what he knew. Ruby darted out of the VIP room. He pushed through the building doors when saw the 911 across the screen of his beeper. Ruby didn't wait for the men he came with to catch up. He got in his car and ran lights on the way to Sherry's.

Sherry lived on the eighth floor of an apartment building. The eighth floor was the most sought-after floor because it was the quietest floor, and that was because a cop lived there. When kids needed somewhere to smoke or feel each other up, no one went into the eighth-floor staircase. It was where no bad could be done. That was, until that evening. The hallway was filled with police officers, some dressed in uniform, and others in clothing they looked to have slapped on after being called out of bed.

"He's dead. He's fuckin' dead. I can't believe this shit."
Officer Gallo paced the hallway, both hands clasped
behind his head. He wore faded jeans and a sweatshirt.
Narcotics always dressed down.

Ruby pushed his way past the men in blue that on a
regular day he would try to ignore.

"At least he got the son of a bitch," Ruby heard a high-
pitched male say. "They took one of us, we took one of
them."

Ruby made it to the door where a uniformed officer
blocked his path.

"You can't come in here, sir."

"My girl, my girlfriend Sherry, she's in there!"

"I'm sorry. You can't come in here. It's a crime scene."

Ruby shoved the cop and looked over his shoulder. He
spotted Sherry crying into the arms of Miles.

"Sherry! Sherry!"

Makeup running down her face, Sherry searched for
who had called her name. She saw Ruby being pushed
back by the officer who denied him entrance.

"Wesley!" Sherry ripped herself out of Miles's hold. "Let
him in! Get your fuckin' hands off him and let him in!"

The cop got out of Ruby's way. He fixed his shirt and
straightened his tie.

Sherry smashed herself into Ruby's arms. "He's dead.
He killed my father!" Sherry's sobs quieted the room
while casting a heavier blanket of sadness over the apartment.

The sounds of photographs being taken caught Ruby's
attention. A few feet away from where he stood consoling
Sherry, in the kitchen, her father lay dead next to a young
Hispanic teen.

"I was getting ready to come to the party." Sherry spoke
fast, too fast. It took Ruby all he had to stay focused on
what she was saying. "You told me you were sending

Miles to come get me, so I walked to the front of the house to get something. He came in. He just fuckin' came in and started shooting! He shot Daddy, and Daddy returned fire."

Sherry started to shake. Ruby tightened his grip on her, but she loosened it and continued speaking.

"He, he, he held his gun at me! He wasn't dead, but Miles . . . Miles came in and shot him. He could have killed me, Wesley!"

Ruby eyeballed Miles, who told him with his hands, "The snitch."

Ruby looked closer at the body. He'd never seen him before a day in his life.

One of the officers went over to Sherry. "Did you say that kid over there saved you?" He pointed to Miles.

Sherry shook her head persistently.

"Did she call you Wesley?" He gave his attention to Ruby, who said nothing. "Are you Wesley Evans?"

Sherry jumped out of Ruby's arms. "He had nothing to do with this, so you back the fuck up!" Her finger was in his face as Ruby pulled her back.

"Mr. Evans, can I speak to you over here, please? It will only take a second."

"No, no. Why do you want to speak with him?" Sherry demanded to know.

"It's okay. Go back over there with Miles. I'll only be a minute."

"No. I'm not going anywhere."

Ruby put his forehead against hers. "Please, you've gone through enough."

She dragged herself back over to Miles. Ruby and the officer stepped inside the living room. There, they held close to a corner next to the window.

"Listen here, Ruby. I know all about the shit you and Asher had going on. He schooled me on everything and had me do my share. Now, I'm sure he told you that come his retirement, I'll be taking his place."

"He might have mentioned it."

"Lucky for you, I got the job. We just didn't announce it yet. My moving on up is a big damn deal. The mayor is a good friend of mine, so if he's a good friend, and you're a good friend, you know what that means."

"We all friends," Ruby said sadly.

"Exactly. Now, your boy over there, the deaf one. We can paint him as a hero, and I can have his file magically disappear all by you adding ten grand on top of what you were paying Asher to keep you and your boys out of cuffs." The young, tight-suit-and-ponytail-wearing guy picked the lint off the arm of his jacket.

"Or?"

"Or I can paint this shit how it really is, a drug bust gone wrong. Let the world know Asher was dirty and shit got out of hand when a deal went bad."

"I don't know who the fuck that dead kid is, and if I don't know who he is, then that means he wasn't working for me."

"I don't care if he worked for the President of the United States. It's not about the truth, but how we can make it look. Now, what do you wanna do? You want a friend, or you want an enemy? And word around town is you don't have a lot of foes, so I doubt you want to start now."

"Fine, but with the increase comes the mayor's friend-ship and my whole crew's files expunged," Ruby said.

"That, and when the time comes for me to run for mayor, I can count on you to contribute." He showed gums so large they took away from his teeth.

"Deal."

Ponytail wrapped his arm around Ruby, turned him to the officers scattered about, and told him, "Welcome to the family."

All the men and women watched as Richie embraced Ruby. Each of them nodded, and just like that, Ruby became more untouchable.

Sherry sat facing the wall. Her tears were her only real company. Ruby signaled for Miles to step aside some, away from Sherry.

Ruby stood directly in front of Miles and touched his own lips. "What happened?" he verbalized. Although Ruby doubted if anyone in that apartment would speak on the details Miles was about to give, he still played it safe by blocking sight of Miles.

"The kid was trying to make a name for himself. He bamboozled Asher, had him think he was rolling with us and had shit to tell. He's been watching you and Asher for some time now. Knew there was a connection, so he took his shot."

"Who gave you this info?"

"Motherfucker fell in my lap. He didn't know who I was. Walked up on me and a few guys around the way. I had some time to burn since I offered to pick up Sherry, so I chilled outside. He knew the guys I was with, started bragging about how he had this cop under his thumb and was about to come up off your name. Showed his piece and everything. Tried to act tough and say he was heading to the cop's house now and was sure things would go his way. Lip reading is a beautiful thing, homie."

Ruby gave Miles a pound. "Good looking out. You saved Sherry. You my brother for life."

Miles's smile rose then fell. He pointed behind Ruby. When Ruby turned around, he saw Asher's body being carried out.

"Where are you taking him?" Sherry shouted. "Wesley, where are they taking him?" Sherry charged the men who transported her father's body away, pulled and yanked on their coroners' jackets. "Where are you taking him? Where are you taking him?"

It took Ruby, Miles, and two narcotics officers to restrain Sherry.

"Where are they taking him? Where are they taking him? Daddy! Daddy!"

Paradise Island, Bahamas
2021

Ruby pulled up on the dirt road behind the stable. What would have been the home to horses, had there been horses, held firm and appealed to the eye. Ruby took into consideration his old age. He didn't recall the distance from the barn to farmhouse being such a stretch back in the day when he had found the land. He closed in the tedious space made messy by mud and puddles with short, slow steps.

At the back door, which he had argued to have sealed off but was overruled by the owner, he slid the key inside the first lock and redid the action with the other two keys. It was darker than any home he'd ever been in. Ruby found his way into the kitchen lit by candles.

"Your lights go out too, or was it just on the farm?" Tony flicked the cigarette lighter on and off.

Ruby removed his hoodie and sat across from his longtime friend. "Nope, I got hit." He double-tapped the barrel of the firearm.

"Miles told you I got out of dodge."

"Yeah. He told me."

Tony covered the lighter, tossed it on the table, then touched the long braid that hung off his chin. "You tell him where I was? That I'm alive?"

"That's not how this works. The less people to know about spontaneous moves, the better. I'll tell him when things ease up."

Tony got up from the table and limped over to the liquor cabinet. "Want a drink?"

"Nah, I had my share last night. We threw Whitney an engagement party."

"Whitney's getting married? Damn, we're old."

"Tell me about it."

Tony moved the flashlight to the middle of the table and set his drink down in its previous spot. "Back in the day, when my time came to leave the game alone and you told me that my retirement plan entailed an emergency flight home . . ." Tony sat back and pointed his finger to Ruby. "Man, I thought you were straight bananas, bored even, and needed something to spend your money on." Their laughter roared, the kind of natural, honest belly hollers you only have amongst those you feel you're most secure.

"I knew you did. Took me two months to get you out here to see the place and another two months for you to accept all the paperwork on it. Damn, you're a stubborn motherfucker."

"I know." Tony placed the glass up to his lips. The burning sensation that torched his throat delayed him momentarily. "But I'm glad I was eligible for the plan. I wasn't ready. When I found out crap went south, I was in a vulnerable position. Out of town with family."

"How did we get here, Tony? What do you know?"

"What do you know?" Tony shot back.

"Still have to be in some form of control, I see."

"Old habits die hard," Tony admitted.

Ruby snorted. "I know we're at war with one of our own. Felix goes by the tag Straw. He's picking off past kings. What am I missing? What do you know?"

They heard footsteps overhead. Tony looked up. "I'm good, Halle! He's here!"

"Hi, Ruby!" called down a tiny, soft voice.

"Halle! You still holding?" Ruby asked, halfway joking, halfway serious.

"Don't you know it!" The sound of a gun cocking echoed throughout the house.

"Tony keep me abreast!"

"Copy!" Tony rested his hands in his lap. "Halle had a family reunion over in Texas during the beginning of the month. During our stay, I got word of Bungee's death. Thought nothing of it. We can't live forever. Two days later, I heard about Con. This OG suffers from no 'Old Timers.' I remember the signs of war, so me and my wife left the reunion early and caught a flight out here."

Tony plucked the single cigarette held behind his ear, set it inside his mouth, and lit it up. He blew out two smoke rings before he continued with his truth telling. "We've been here for the past five days, waiting for you to show. Following all the steps to the emergency retirement flee plan."

"I found out not even a full twenty-four hours ago about any of this. Besides the obvious, what do you know about this cat Straw?" Ruby asked.

Tony released the nicotine out his nose. "He was a charity case. Boy's a homosexual. Before Bungee took him under his wing, no one would fuck with an openly gay thug. It didn't matter what he brought to the table."

Ruby retrieved the liquor bottle off the kitchen counter. He poured himself a shot and dulled his nerves. "But Bungee brought him into the family because he has a soft spot for homosexuals."

Tony used his hand to put out his cigarette. The palm of his left hand darkened with circles. "In the words of Halle, don't you know it. And that's why none of us said boo. No one was trying to tell Brooklyn's king, whose gay brother was the victim of a hate crime, no gays allowed."

Ruby leered at the barn. It appeared so tiny from the window through which he looked at it. "Bungee accepted him with open arms. Welcomed him, taught him, and set him up for life. Why kill him? He got what he wanted." Ruby voiced his thoughts out loud.

"Did all this sun burn your common sense to a crisp? We've seen this before. He wants everyone with enough muscle who can intervene gone. He doesn't want to be a part of the family. He wants to *be* the family. He's chopping us off one by one so he'll be the last man standing, the head honcho. What a way to flex, huh?"

"Lately, Sherry's been on my back. Accusing me of missing the life and trying to find a way back in." Ruby took another shot.

"And?"

"And what?"

"Are you?" Tony turned his fingers into the shape of little guns. He pointed at Ruby and made explosion noises.

Ruby sidestepped the question. "How am I supposed to tell her I'll have to go out to New York to handle this?"

"You don't. You have Miles handle it." Tony settled his feet on the chair Ruby abandoned.

"If Miles could have, he would have, and I would've known nothing other than when it was time to attend funerals."

"Then I'll do something. Enough of the duck, duck, goose shit!" Tony sat his hand on top of his weapon.

"No. That's what he probably expects. You're the first one out of us all expected to make a sudden move. You're impulsive. That's always been your weak point. So you do nothing. You be the target he's made you, while I collect everything there is on this little prick. If he's as smart as he acts, he's changed everything—the stash houses, meeting spots, runners, anything and everything associated with us."

"Now, I followed directions and came here at the first sign of danger, but, Ruby, listen now. I don't know how much longer I can stay in your witness protection. Arthritis or not, I'm still about that life," Tony reminded his longtime friend.

"I know that's right!" Halle hollered from upstairs.

"You. Do. Nothing." Ruby emphasized each word slow and clearly.

For a while, Ruby stayed quiet. He wanted those three words to sink and marinate inside Tony's hard skull.

Then, he asked, "How does this bastard look? Where is he from? Does he have any family and friends? I want to know it all, even the name of the fucker's dog."

"He's what his name says. Tall and skinny. Other than that, I got nothing. But I will say, I think all of this is the little fucker throwing a tantrum. It's being said the little shithead has no connect. Bungee died before he could formally be introduced to Hynes's replacement. He has no in."

"Who's his replacement?"

"Bibiano, his oldest son. He does business different from Hynes. He needs more than his father's green light. He has to meet his sellers in person, and they have to be vouched by someone he knew of in the business for years."

Tony went for his lighter. He sparked the fire on and off a few times when a thought came to mind. "But you know who would know the rest of your answers and more? Linden." The fire shot out. "Did you offer him a getaway too?"

"You know I can't say."

"Let's say you did. It would be in your best interest to speak with him. He remained close to Bungee. They had more than a mentor-protégé relationship. They were best friends. If anyone knows anything worth knowing, it's him. But I have to warn you about something." Tony gave Ruby an unsettling stare.

"Talk."

"Linden got brain damage from a car accident. Made his memory go to shit. So good luck getting anything out of him." Tony paused. "That is if you can reach him."

Chapter 16

Kauai, Hawaii
2021

"I know what you're doing." Sherry took a sip of her champagne paired with a strawberry inside.

"What am I doing?"

"You're trying to make up for that 'call me Ruby' crap. Trying to get on my good side with a family vacation to Hawaii. You're trying to suck up."

The snort that invaded the jet turned both Sherry and Ruby's head. "My goodness that girl can snore. She needs to see an ENT."

Whitney slept with her mouth open and her head drooped to the side.

Ruby returned to his book. "Maybe I am. Why must you bring it up like that? Why can't we just enjoy our time together?"

"Because this doesn't make anything go away. I'd be a fool to turn down a trip, but that request you made, we still have to talk about."

Ruby turned the page. "There's nothing to talk about."

Sherry shifted herself so she faced her husband entirely. "Do I look like boo-boo the fool to you? Do you really think all of these years of us being together I can't tell when you're not telling me the whole story? Don't insult my intelligence, *Ruby*," she cut her eyes at him. "I'm not the one."

She made herself comfortable and covered her eyes with a satin sleep mask that read *Sweet Dreams*. "During our stay in Hawaii, I'll let things go, but the moment we step foot off that island, you have some explaining to do. Don't think I forgot about Cape Town." Sherry lifted the blanket over her. "Whenever there's a screw-up, a getaway is never far behind."

Cape Town, South Africa
1992

"You promised."

Ruby opened his eyes. The aromatherapy diffuser kicked out lemongrass and tea tree oils that soared up Ruby's nasal passage. He watched as the diffuser transitioned from color to color and listened to the sounds of waves rock and slap against the shore.

"What are you talking about?" he asked.

"Last year, you promised that by this time this year, you'd be done with the business. And you're not."

Perhaps it was Ruby's mind playing tricks on him, because the diffuser turned the color gray, not a typical color sought out to achieve relaxation.

"I will. Just—"

"Give me some time," she finished for him. "I have. I've given you years. The first four, I never questioned your departure. During our engagement, my mouth kept shut, but *you* mentioned making an exit before we married. We married, and you've then postponed it with promises, and now you're trying to postpone yet again. This time, with distractions of trips during the holiday." Sherry's tone when she spoke her last sentence came off soaked in frustration.

The diffuser abandoned its body of gray and moved on to red.

"It will happen."

Both of Ruby's and Sherry's masseuses delicately raised their heads and with simple, side-to-side movements, cracked their necks. They then positioned their heads to face the opposite sides of one another.

"Is it really worth it? Worth all the heartache, secrets, guy?" Sherry asked.

"We're not talking about this. Not now."

"You need to uphold your promise."

"Did your mother give your father this much grief while on the force?" he asked.

"That's different."

Ruby's head turned to his wife. "Dirt is dirt, Sherry." He waited for her to turn to him, but she hadn't. The furthest she got was she to lift her head, temporarily hold it high, and lay it right back down.

"Women marry men who remind them of their fathers," he said.

Ruby was ready. He waited on his wife's immediate comeback that would pluck a number of his nerves and drag out the argument.

Yet, she said nothing. The masseuse asked Ruby to lay fully on his side. He caught a glimpse of the diffuser returning to the color gray when Sherry responded.

"They also learn from their mothers' mistakes."

Sherry's masseuse instructed her to lay on her back.

"Get out, Wesley, and get out soon, or I'll make the move for you, and I'll leave."

Ruby's body stiffened. The masseuse increased pressure where she massaged.

"You won't. I won't let you."

The hands set to crack, ease, and rub away tension throughout Ruby's body ceased.

"Is there a problem?" he questioned the masseuse.

"Oh, no. Not at all. I'm out of oil. Let me get some more. And please, turn on your back."

Ruby did as he was told. The masseuse walked past Ruby. When she no longer blocked his sight of his wife, he noticed Sherry's dried tear streaks thick on her right cheek.

Finally, for the first time since they had stepped inside the spa's couples massage room, she gave her husband the respect to look at him. "You don't have a choice. My mama ain't raise no fool, and my father schooled me."

Had Ruby transformed into his spirit animal at that moment, he would have shown enlarged, ravaging teeth while he roared in Sherry's face. The outcry would chill her skin and rustle her hair.

"Sorry about that." The masseuse worked her way up from Ruby's legs. The entire time, Ruby and Sherry held strong in their leering battle.

The masseuse positioned Ruby's head in the direction of the diffuser. Within seconds and without warning, its colors quickly jumped back and forth from gray to red. Ruby had enough.

"What's with the diffuser? Aren't this thing supposed to be relaxing and positive?"

The masseuse glanced at the machine. "This model is supposed to be able to pick up on strong emotions. Looks like someone's very emotional right now."

Ruby was in his head. He hoped to see a smile on his wife's face, but all he was met with was the back of her head.

"You outdid yourself, old man! Is this what I have to look forward to when I'm married and Terrance messes up?" Whitney flopped down on the sectional and picked at the olive and cheese platter.

"This is what you get when a man handles business."
Ruby couldn't help but dig into his statement's double
meaning.

Sherry stepped in from the dining area situated on the
terrace. The back of her floral sandals slapped against
the floor, and her thigh-high dress flowed in the wind.

"It's nice," she declared. "Very nice, especially for
something booked on such short notice." Sherry opened
the room" double doors and continued on her tour.

"Someone's still pissed." Whitney nibbled in a white
piece of cheese. "But I'm glad to see you're trying to make
peace, Daddy. Hang in there." She squinted, then headed
over to the bar to see what spread was laid out.

"It's about to be lit! Look at this! There's clams, lobster
tails, shrimp, and oooh . . ." Whitney folded her hands
and shut her eyes. "There's calamari, Daddy. I love
calamari."

"And it's all yours. Dig in, sweet pea."

In the process of fixing herself a plate, Whitney danced
in place. She swirled her shapely hips, and when she
made it over to the crab legs and bite-sized salmon,
she started to twerk.

A heavy knock on the massive mahogany doors resulted in a balding, elderly white man draped in a black-
and-gray uniform complete with white gloves to hustle
out of the kitchen. He made a beeline for the front door.

Whitney plopped herself on a bar stool and popped a
shrimp inside her mouth. Before she finished chewing,
she questioned her father. "Daddy, who's that man?"
She swallowed. "He appeared out of nowhere like some
superhero."

"He's our butler."

"What's his name? Jeffrey?" She licked her fingertips.

Ruby blinked, slow and steady. "No more nineties
throwback shows for you."

The butler welcomed a young, wide-faced girl with a button nose into the suite. Ruby met her at the door with an extended hand.

"Olina, nice to meet you in person."

Olina took his hand and with great enthusiasm, expressed her happiness to be of service.

Ruby called Sherry and Whitney over and introduced the two to the young lady in front of them. "This young lady is Olina. She is going to show the two of you down to the spa. I've booked surprised appointments for you that I want you to take full advantage of." Ruby slid his hand into his wife's.

"That's nice of you."

Olina stepped in. "We have one of the best spas in the world. Presidents, along with kings and queens travel to experience our services. I'll be with you the entire time, waiting on you hand and foot as you receive the pampering you deserve." Her smile could have belonged to a cartoon character.

"Yesss! Thank you, Daddy! I'm long overdue for some pampering." Whitney stepped next to Olina, where she picked her brain on the celebrity clientele she bragged the hotel catered to.

"Sherry?" Ruby called out. "You like your surprise? Couldn't have you visit this fancy hotel known for its spa services and not have you indulge." The flash of Ruby's teeth and gums took Sherry back in time to when his smile had first mesmerized her.

She pushed out a smile. "You're right about that. I've read about it in a magazine a couple of weeks ago." She smiled a little more for good measure. "But what about you? I thought this was a family vacation. What will you be doing while we're away?" Sherry told herself to keep her cheeks high and mouth wide.

Ruby made his way over to her and held her by the waist. "You know what they say. When the cat's away, the mice will play." He placed his lips on hers. "I'm just kidding. I'm going to take a nap. You know, jet lag."

Sherry rested her forehead against his. It was her safe haven. "Okay. Will you be here when we get back?"

"Refreshed and ready to take on Hawaii."

The automatic frosted-glass doors opened. Two couples and a group of elderly women who clung onto maps of the island made their way out of the hotel ahead of Ruby, who catered to the back of the mob. Tourists jumped inside tour buses and vans, their conversations carried by the wind as they rode past.

"Mr. Evans, it's a pleasure to meet you. I'm Tampa. I'll be your driver for the day."

Ruby held his phone up to the middle-aged man's face and compared the photo to real life.

Tampa exposed all of his front teeth. "It's me, the one and only." He grinned.

Content with the outcome, Ruby put away his phone and dipped inside the back door Tampa held open. Inside the air-conditioned vehicle, Ruby handed Tampa a piece of paper torn out of a notepad.

"This is where we're headed. You wait for me while I'm in there. You don't move for anything."

"You're the boss."

Tampa's driving could have put the city that never sleeps to bed. He managed to maintain the perfect speed all while avoiding the bumps and rocks that disturbed the road. Ruby did some sightseeing from behind the tinted window. After this meeting, he promised himself he'd do what he misled his family into believing this trip was for—having family time.

Things looked different from the last time Ruby was
on the island. Nonetheless, it still gave off the feeling
of strength and patience, the two things needed to survive life after Brooklyn. Paired with Tampa's driving,
Hawaii's nature, agriculture, and native people sucked
Ruby into a slumber.

Chapter 17

Kauai, Hawaii
2021

"Mr. Evans, we've reached your destination."

Ruby's eyes shot open. He blinked a few times before he became aware of his surroundings. He slapped both of his cheeks.

"I'm up." He straightened his back and looked at the window. "Pull over to the side of the house."

Breaking twigs and dead leaves underneath its tires, the truck pounded its way to the side of the mountain. Tampa parked. "I can drive to the front. This land is unkept. You'll walk through weeds and grass full of insects." Unable to ignore the weeds that touched their windows, Tampa's tanned face frowned.

"Afraid of a little nature, Tampa?" Ruby pushed the door open, sure to use enough strength to overthrow the greenery.

"Yes." He hugged the steering wheel. "I've seen what this island can do."

"I'm sure you'll survive. Stay here." Ruby slammed the door shut.

Weeds and thorns grown on a selection of majestic flowers snatched hold of Ruby's shorts and Hawaiian button-down shirt. On his journey to the small wooden home, his outfit was snagged by Mother Nature a time

or two. On the doorstep, Ruby wiped his sandals off on
the faded mat that once read WELCOME. Out the pocket of
his flowery shirt, he pulled the key that gained him entry
into the semi-shabby home.

Under the roof once weakened by rain, Ruby listened to his own footsteps groan and screech above the
hand-woven rug. Up the short stairs that led to the only
bedroom in the house, Ruby watched in confusion and
slight entertainment as Linden sped around the room
and filled a duffle bag with paperwork, photos, and
trinkets that he knew Linden valued because they had
belonged to his parents.

Ruby grinned on his way inside the room. "Where's the
fire?" he teased.

Uneasy and out of breath, Linden picked his head
up out of the bag. "Ruby, thank goodness you're here.
What's our next move? What do we do? Wait, wait, I
forgot." He ran over to Ruby and planted his hands on
his shoulders. Each of his hands shook. "We have to go to
Hawaii to that place you got me, remember?"

Ruby searched his friend for the man he grew up
with in his twenties. Other than weight gain, stretched
skin, and thinned hair, Linden was physically who he
remembered, but mentally, no one was home.

Ruby held Linden's face in his hands. "We're already in
Hawaii, Linden. We don't have to go anywhere." Ruby's
head moved from left to right, and Linden made his head
do so too.

Linden stepped back and looked around. "We are in
Hawaii?"

"Yes," Ruby reassured him.

Linden closed his eyes and repeated over and over,
"We're in Hawaii. I'm here to meet with Ruby. I'm in
Hawaii, and I'm here to meet with Ruby." His eyes ope-
ned. "I'm sorry. I forgot. I got here a few days ago. I'm

sorry, Ruby. Sometimes I become confused. My head's not what it used to be." He touched the top of his balding head.

Ruby knew he should get everything out of his old comrade before his mind checked out yet again, but he found it hard. To rush and push for details would force Ruby to admit that Linden was no longer himself. It would erase him from what he once had been—the most organized, time sensitive, responsible creature there was.

The tie-wearing guy who refused to cover himself with baggy gear was coined the nerd of the group, not solely for his style, but for his intellect, which outran Ruby's book-obsessed mind. He had been the ultimate good-guy-gone-bad because he chose life in the streets over the free rides offered from Princeton, Brown, and Columbia. How could that guy have become so lost?

Linden sat on the wicker chair beside the window. Ruby parked himself in the center of the room. He could feel the guilt and sorrow claw at his eyes. The fact that he'd known nothing about his friend's accident and acted not even as a support system brought Ruby down. How could a group of friends who conquered a city that foreigners flock to no longer speak? Miles was the only person from his past that Ruby kept in contact with. The others, he had long forgotten about, pushed to the back of his mind once he touched down in the Bahamas.

But memories could never die, and now he saw why. He didn't crave the past because he wanted back in. He craved the past because it needed him back in.

"Linden, we have a big problem."

"Straw? Right?" Linden's eyes pleaded for Ruby to confirm he was right.

"Yes. Straw. What do you know about him?"

"Everything," Linden revealed. "At least, what I could find." Linden went to the closet. Off the top shelf, he brought down a box with a manila envelope inside. "He's a manipulator. He becomes whoever he has to be, whenever he has to be it, to get what he wants. He plays on people's emotions. That's how he got in so close with Bungee. He gets in where he fits in. When Bungee stepped down and it became official Straw was next in line, I felt uncomfortable, so I did some investigating of my own. Got ahold of his birth certificate even."

"What do you mean? Didn't Bungee look into him before he even brought him into the fold?"

"Yes, he did." Linden dug inside the envelope. "But in my opinion, he was too clean, too perfect. Too much like Bungee's kid brother Hector." Linden laid out pages of an article collected out of a New York newspaper on the floor. "That article in three pages summarized Hector's life and death down to a T, one of the few times reporters got something right based on a person of color. Hector's death was the reason more gay pride marches broke out and new laws were passed. He made noise, so much noise that Bungee had to go on hiatus and I had to fill in for a while. Politicians and reporters dug too much into the family's life. Multiple interviews were held, charities were named after Hector to bring awareness to hate crimes. Bungee couldn't risk being exposed."

"Wait, wait, wait." Ruby sat on the bed. "You stepped in for Bungee?"

"Yes. What else was there for us to do? It was the best for the business and Bungee's family."

Ruby's head rocked from left to right. "How come I knew nothing about this?"

"After Miles retired, you disappeared and became Brooklyn's ghost. We heard nothing from you. You stopped checking in, so we assumed since you were done, you were done. I even questioned when I made it out here if you'd show."

Ruby avoided eye contact. "How long did this hiatus go on for?"

"Six months."

"Damn."

"Things were hot, and Bungee was going through it. Had the rest of the world not caught wind of the injustice, he still would have needed time. He was in no space to make the type of decisions and moves needed to push our shit. And he damn sure couldn't hold meetings with New York's law enforcement, politicians, and our connect. Nine out of ten times, things would have gone sour."

Ruby swiped the article off the floor. He tried to read it, but only words such as *brother*, *murdered*, *homosexual*, *college-bound*, and *straight-A student* stood out.

"If you're feeling guilty, don't," Linden said. He read Ruby like he used to, which wasn't hard. But Linden also did what many didn't. He spoke on his observations. "He got the money you sent. Did with it what you asked, paid the funeral costs and put the rest in Bungee's daughter's college fund."

"Yeah, money fixes everything. It just washes away the guilt." Ruby folded the pages in half and handed them back to Linden.

Linden cleared his throat. "Anyway, everything written in that piece down to the non-profit organizations that Hector was a part of, Straw was a member of."

"So, it could be a coincidence."

"It saddens me you say that, Ruby, considering you're the one that taught us all nothing's a coincidence." Linden pulled out three additional sheets of paper. "So, I did some more digging. Had my contacts pull up Straw's documentation of membership. Look at the dates of entry. It's one month before Straw made contact with Bungee. I know the date because I was with Bungee the day he met him. It was my birthday. We had a few drinks

and smokes at a cigar lounge. He told Bungee he admired
Hector and knew of him, met him while being a part of
the organization. That's bull. Hector died two months
before Straw joined any of these groups."

Linden grabbed a highlighter off the windowsill. He
opened the newspaper article and on page two, he high-
lighted something. "And here it states Hector's favorite
basketball team was the Knicks." He showed Ruby the
highlight. "Now, here's a photo of Bungee and Straw at
a Knicks game. They had someone in the crowd take a
picture of their backs wearing matching Derrick Rose
jerseys."

Ruby took the picture. "Bungee couldn't stand the
Knicks. He was a 76ers fan."

"I know. Straw was a Knicks fan."

Linden looked over the worn newspaper articles and
Ruby wondered. Was Linden really ill? Was he still in
there and just needed some time to come out and stay
out?

"Here it goes, something else. On page one, they mention Hector's birthday on March 18, 1997. Straw said
he shared the same birthday as Hector. The kid's twenty-four like Hector was, but he wasn't born on the
eighteenth." Linden pointed to where the ink read March
18, 1997, then pulled out a copy of Straw's birth certificate. He held it up. His finger underlined the date. "April
5, 1997," he read aloud.

"Tell me Bungee just didn't take kid's word for this shit."

"He didn't. That's my next line of proof." Linden held a
photocopy of a New York State ID. "He showed Bungee
his ID." He held the ID and birth certificate out for Ruby
to take. "Take a look at the names. What does the ID say?"

"Pierce Harper."

"And the birth certificate."

"Felix Brown." Ruby looked at the line where it mentioned Straw's place of birth: Chicago. Ruby slowly lowered the papers down on his lap. "Linden, do you have a photo of Straw?"

Linden snapped his fingers. "Of course! That leads me to my next discovery. He couldn't claim to have known Hector if they hadn't at least known one or two of the same people. In the article, there's a photo of Kelsey Wood, Hector's son. The date on that paper was January 20, 2019. Here's a picture of both Straw and Kelsey at a candle lighting ceremony for Hector. This was posted in a teen magazine two weeks after the only article with a visual and written mention of Kelsey was put out for the world to see. And in Straw's case, to use. He's a manipulator, Ruby. He becomes who he needs to be to get where he needs to be."

That's exactly what Tony said.

Ruby eyeballed the photo.

Son of a bitch. Ruby felt his heart double in beats. His body temperature plummeted, then heated up and caused his body to break out in drops of sweat. The hand that held the proof of Straw's identity vibrated.

"Rube, you okay?" Linden dragged his seat closer to Ruby.

"Why didn't you share all of this with Bungee?"

"Because I got into my accident." Linden rubbed his left arm, then the corner of both eyes. "I forgot about it. And when I finally would remember, I'd forget again." Linden's leg started to bounce up and down. "I was given medicine from my doctor. Something new, a drug the government is trying. I agreed for them to test it out on me. So far, so good. There're times I can go days at a time without forgetting. I keep track of those days on my calendar. The longest I've gone was one week. Recently, things have gotten a little better. Sometimes, instead of me completely blacking out, I'll have short bouts of memory loss, but I'll come right back and remember. Like what you just witnessed."

The papers slid out of Ruby's grasp. His body weakened.

"I write notes to myself, post them around the house, so when I do come back, I can pick up where I left off. After two months of me taking the pills, I remembered what I had to show Bungee." He held the envelope high in one hand. "I made arrangements for Bungee to meet me at my home. Made sure I had my proof where Bungee could find it in case I blacked out, and a letter explaining my findings. I had it all mapped out. Took advantage of what was left of my mind to use." Linden started to sob. The anguish stuck in his throat and pushed out tears. "I waited for him to arrive. My mind stayed with me. It let me keep focused long enough to learn he had died."

Linden folded into a ball of tears. "The man I ran with as a kid, stood as his best man at his wedding, made me the godfather to his daughter, he died. He, he—" Linden paused, took a deep breath, and continued to talk. "He took me in after my accident. Had me stay with him for a while. When I noticed the meds were doing me some good, we decided I'd try living alone again, you know. Try and give me back a sense of independence." Tears drenched his face that he didn't bother to clean. "For some reason, I can never forget the day I learned about Bungee's death or his funeral. That is the one thing I wish my accident would take away from me."

The room fell mute. There was nothing said for minutes on end. During that time of nothing, Ruby thought *fuck it* and allowed the hurt from his spirit to fall out of his eyes in silence, absent of judgment and the belief men should not cry. These two men, whose brains were remarkable and fear nonexistent, cried like on the day they left their mothers' birth canal. When the pain had let up and the need to push on returned, Ruby reinstated the discussion.

"What happened next?"

"When I heard about Con not long after Bungee, something felt wrong, told me to get out. One of the notes on my bathroom mirror told me if something feels off, go here, this address written down. And here I am. I took the directions you left behind for me and read it every day in hopes it'll stay in there. At least, until I got here."

"Everything you're telling me now, is it because of your notes?"

"The pills and my notes. I study my life every day. You can't depend on medicine. Some are man-made, and anything man-made can be taken apart."

"I know that kid, Linden. He's the cousin of my daughter's fiancé. He was in my home a few days ago."

Linden leaped out of his chair. The envelope he had held on to for dear life fell to his feet. "Why are we still here? We have to go now!" Linden moved as swiftly as he had been moving when Ruby walked in on him.

Ruby held out his hands. "My family is okay. They're here in Hawaii with me."

Linden plucked a tissue out of its box and dabbed his face down. "You piece of shit. Damn near gave me a heart attack." A few more dabs of his face and Linden stopped moving altogether. "Ruby, is your daughter's fiancé here with you?"

"No. Just my immediate family."

"That's good, that's good." Linden bit down on his lip.

"So, the fiancé is back home. Where he lives, is it in the same area you live?"

"Fuck. Linden, are you zoning out?" Ruby snapped his fingers in front of Linden's face. Linden shoved his hand out of his face.

"Answer me," Linden said.

"Yes. My daughter's fiancé is back in the Bahamas where I live."

"Then, if Straw wanted access to your home, he can get it." Linden swallowed. "Ruby, don't tell me you have a home office where you still use boards to help you visualize your next move when a problem arises?"

Ruby's skin lost its melanin. He took his phone out and dialed his estate.

"Evans residence. Who may I ask am I speaking with?"

"Betty, I have something important I need to ask."

"Sure, Mr. Evans. What is it that you need to know?"

Ruby placed her on loudspeaker. "Has anyone been by the house?"

"Since you and your family have been away? Yes. That young man Felix. Terrance's cousin."

Ruby's hold tightened on the phone. His brown hand turned bright red. "What did he come by for? What is it that he needed?"

"Mr. Evans, what's going on?"

Holding back the feeling of stupidity and fury, Ruby demanded that she answer.

"He said his grandfather left behind something the night he stayed over."

Ruby swallowed the rock in his throat. "Who escorted him around the house?"

"Well, well, I did, of course. Yes. I showed him to the guestroom Mr. Brown occupied." She paused for a moment. "I then left him unattended to handle a situation that required immediate attention."

Betty called her boss's name. After she stated his name twice, he gave out orders.

"I want you to look around the entire house. Only you. And anything you see that's out of order, I want you to report back to me."

"Should I visit the lower level? Your office?"

"Have that be the first place you look." He hung up and practiced controlling his breathing. He envisioned Betty carrying her round body around the house and carefully observing each and everything that made his home a home.

Ruby watched the clock. It took exactly thirty-three minutes for Betty to return his call.

Ruby didn't need to say hello. Once he put the phone to his ear, Betty stated her findings right away. The more words said, the more time wasted.

"Nothing out of place in your office, but he's been down here. The bastard left a deep scuff mark on the floor."

"What about my board? Does anything look tampered with?"

"Linden's home address. But I looked around and found it under the file cabinet. I think it's been there for some time. The ink is faded."

Riiiiiiight. I never did pick it up.

"He was also in your bedroom. The bedsheets were ruffled, and photos of your parents and friend that passed are missing. But he left a note on top of the frames. It says, *Tag, you're it!*"

Son of a bitch thinks this is a game.

"Betty, listen to me. You and everyone on staff get out of there now. Go home and don't come near my home until you hear from me."

"Yes, sir."

Ruby ended the call. "He was in the house."

"Then he knows where I am," Linden clarified.

"Yes and no."

"What is that supposed to mean?" Linden's already thin face sank in deeper.

"He knows you're in Hawaii, but not exactly where, so let's take advantage of this setback and get you out of here."

Chapter 18

Early that morning

"Good evening. Ms. Betty, isn't it?"

Betty gave her mother-of-a-smile of comfort. "Yes, it is."

"I'm sorry to disturb you this evening. You probably don't remember me, but I'm Felix, Felix Brown, cousin of Whitney's fiancé Terrance." He held out his hand.

"Oh, yes, yes, yes. How can I forget such a tall gentleman such as yourself? What can I do for you?"

"This is quite embarrassing, but the night of the engagement party, when my grandfather became heavily inebriated, he stayed the night here in one of the Evans' guest rooms. Upon his return home he has, I really have no idea how, just discovered he's missing his wallet."

Betty's oval face twisted. "Did he? I've been in that room many times following the celebration and seen no wallet. Are you sure he lost it there? We were outside for some time in the garden."

"I'm positive, Ms. Betty." Felix flashed his set of equally big teeth. "Terrance himself told me he placed all of Pop Pop's valuables in the nightstand next to the bed."

Ms. Betty snapped her fingers. "Now it all makes sense. That room is hardly ever occupied. I forget time and time again to check the drawers."

Felix's joker of a smile enhanced. "I would be in debt to you if you'd please retrieve my grandfather's belongings. I would offer myself to do the deed, but I'm sure you wouldn't want a stranger inside your home." Felix's smile receded.

"Stranger? You are far from a stranger, Mr. Felix."

"I'm sure others would beg to differ. I've come to learn that people immediately think the worst. There's no trust or understanding in this world anymore. Only pure judgment. I'm sorry I have held you up long enough. I'll wait right here in the safety and awareness of your security cameras while you get my grandfather's possessions." Felix stepped fully in the view of the small camera above the door.

Betty's right hand rested over her heart. With her left, she opened the door more, so she no longer blocked its entrance. "Come on in and get your grandfather's wallet. I trust you." Betty stepped to the side.

"Ms. Betty." Felix took her hands into his. "If I were a few years older, I would not rest until I made an honest woman out of you." He patted the top of her hand and stole a kiss.

Betty's cheeks turned different shades of red. The giggles she let out were one of a schoolgirl whose crush had told her hello.

"Aren't you a breath of fresh air? Follow me. I'll show you to the room he was in. This place can get you lost if you're not familiar with it."

Two middle-aged men dressed in the same uniform as Betty, only differing in that they wore pants and bow ties, acknowledged their guest and asked if he'd like a beverage.

"Thank you, but no thank you."

"Gentlemen, this is Mr. Felix. He's here to collect an item left behind at the party. I'll be showing him to guest room number two if needed."

Her staff nodded and went on about their business.

"Why do I get the feeling you're someone important here?"

"I don't know about important, but I'm the head housekeeper. I oversee a staff of three. And when we make it to the guest room, you'll understand why several hands are needed. Let's get going."

Felix looked over his head at the luxurious light fixtures and artwork he had never seen the big deal in owning. The place looked different without the glitz and glam of party décor, snobby guests, and catering staff swarming the joint. Felix lagged behind Betty. He slid his fingers against the main living room's furnishings, vases, and even wallpaper along his way to the guestroom.

He followed her through the main dining area and past a downstairs library before they hit stairs he didn't recall seeing the night of the party.

"Ms. Betty, why don't I remember seeing these steps the other night?" The unknown irked Felix.

"Because there are different routes to getting to where you need to go in this house. Mr. Evans' idea. Said he wants his home to be a maze. I don't know why. Anyway, that's why I mentioned getting lost if you're not familiar."

"How long have you worked for the Evans, Ms. Betty?"

"Going on fifteen years. How Mr. Evans likes to tell it, they had their share of head housekeepers, but when I came in, it was love at first sight." Her aged face perked up. "I've had a long day. How about I show off some and we take the elevator? These old legs of mine aren't what they used to be." Betty called for the elevator with a soft hit of the button. On command, its thin, long doors opened.

"You're from America? Yes?" he asked.

Betty hit the second-floor button, yet it was the faded button with the letter *B* engraved on it with a small sign beside it that read OUT OF ORDER, that Felix noticed.

"Yes, sure. That's why Mr. Evan believes our working together was meant to be. I was born here in the Bahamas but grew up in New York."

"What part?"

"Brooklyn." Betty stepped off the elevator and walked down the long hallway. Every door was closed and painted in different earth tones. "I moved back to help with my mother's failing health. A friend of mine gardens for the Evans and told me he was looking for help. I interviewed, and it seems right. When I mentioned I was a Brooklyn girl, I had the job!" Betty clapped her hands together. "You know what they say. It's nothing like a Brooklyn girl!" They turned a short corner.

"I may have to steal you from Mr. Evans. You're sure winning me over."

Betty stopped at a door splashed in deep green. "You can try because if there's one thing I've learned about Mr. Evans, it's that you never steal from him."

Betty pushed the door open. Both faces were hit with cool air from the air conditioner. The room intercom went off, and out came a voice Felix identified as belonging to the butler, who offered him something to drink.

"Betty, you're needed. The door is jammed, and the alarm won't let up."

Her eyes rolled. "Lord have mercy," she mumbled. She held down the button and spoke. "I'm on my way." Her hands folded together, she said, "Mr. Felix, I'm truly sorry, but I really must—"

Felix stopped her from finishing by waving his hands in the air. "A leader's job is never done. I'm sure I'll be in and out. On second thought,"—he gave the room a once over—"I may have to give Terrance a ring and confirm whether it was the end table he said he placed the wallet in, or in one of these hundreds of drawers this room has."

The intercom went off. "Do what you must, dear. When you're ready to be escorted out, hit the button with the letter *G* on it, and I'll be back up." Her legs whisked her away.

"They surely are working you too hard, Ms. Betty. What a shame."

After she was gone, Felix counted to ten and then left the room. At the end of the hall, he made his way into each of the rooms one by one. Inside one of the rooms, the balcony doors had been boarded off.

"How ghetto. Black people can never have nothing."

Felix kicked a pair of Oxfords that were in his way to the side. He opened the closet and was greeted by a nice amount of clothing on hangers. He took the sleeve of a shirt and brought it up to his nose. Deeply and vigorously, he inhaled. He noted the scent left behind and moved on to repeat the process on a pair of jeans and pajama pants.

"They all smell like Ruby. Am I detecting marital issues?" He looked at his watch wind down. He bolted out of the room and dipped in and out of two more rooms that held no value to him. One evidently had belonged to Whitney since childhood, and the other, Felix guessed, housed Betty. It was in the last room at the end of the hall where Felix found hope.

"A master bedroom fit for a king. Dammit, Ruby, you sure know how to do shit." He waltzed over to the pillows and took a whiff. "Honeysuckle mixed with a pinch of jasmine. Mrs. Evans, you sure are sweet." He leaned over to the neighboring pillows. "And there goes that cologne again. Bold and dominating. My type of man." Felix's reptile-like tongue slithered out from between his lips and licked the pillow that supplied Ruby comfort and support.

Lost in a moment of blissful lust, Felix found himself on his stomach spread eagle, his face drowned inside Ruby's pillow. Coming up for air, he caught sight of a marble-decorated picture frame that protected an image of a young Ruby and an older woman. Adjacent to that photograph was one of an older man dressed in a war uniform, and next to that, Ruby posed kneeling down to the ground in front of a graffiti wall alongside a heavy-set brother.

Felix sat up, crossed his legs Indian style, and laid each frame out in front of him.

"What do you three have in common?" he said out loud. He did a quick survey of the room. Besides the faces of his wife and Whitney that the walls held, these photos on the nightstand were the only three that sat close to Ruby's side. And then it clicked. The tip of Felix's finger landed on the face of the older woman. Then they slid on over to the older gentleman, and then to the heavy-set brother.

"Mommy, daddy . . ." He paused on the heavy guy. "Bungee never mentioned you having a brother." He held the photo close to his face. He hoped the close proximity would reel in a soul connection. Felix brought the picture closer until it hit his nose. "Who are you?"

"I want to tell you not to get close to any of your soldiers. But that shit's damn near impossible when you're around a motherfucker you gotta trust with your life and your money."

"Why would you not be cool with the homies?"

Bungee tapped the ashes from his cigar into the ashtray. "Because there's soldiers that die. And if it happens to be one you fucks with hard, the loss fucks you up. Back in the day, Ruby lost one of his main men. Boss

*never seemed to be the same again. In fact, I think that's
what distanced him from us all."*

"What was the guy's name?"

"Mayo."

Felix stood up and pushed himself into the air. He held
the photo of Ruby and his deceased friend against his
chest while he jumped up and down on the king-sized
mattress. He dropped down on the bed, legs opened and
frames in between.

"Now what should I do?"

*"If there's one thing I've learned about Mr. Evans, it's
that you never steal from him."*

Felix snatched a book off a nightstand.

"Oh, sweet old Betty. You really are something special."

Felix relieved each of the frames of their long-held
photographs. He looked around for paper but settled for
the novel he had moved aside. He ripped the title page
out of the beginning of the book and scribbled something
down from the red-ink pen he carried in his pocket. Felix
had completed the drawing of his smiley face when his
watch gave off his four-minute warning.

"Fuck! I need more time." Felix hopped out of the bed.
He rushed back to the room Betty had left him in and
pressed the button *G*.

"Miss. Betty, I just feel horrible. We're waiting on a
call back from Terrance. The wallet's nowhere for me to
find." He held down the button. A loud, screeching noise
blasted through.

"Mr. Felix!" Betty yelled. "Hang tight! I'll be up there as
soon as I can. Five minutes! Please give me five minutes!"

"That's perfect," Felix told her.

"What the hell did you guys touch?" That was the last
thing Felix heard.

Felix sneaked back into the master bedroom and
continued the invasion of privacy inside the electronic

walk-in closet. Like a child, he hit each of the buttons. Drawers opened and closed, the tie hanger moved up and down, and all of the shirts and pants swayed from side to side. The last button he hit pushed all the clothing to either side of the closet and revealed an elevator.

"The fuck kind of 007 shit is this?" Felix's watch beeped, informing him one minute had passed. "Guess I'm going on an adventure." He ducked inside the small elevator and pushed the only knob stamped with the letter *B*. The elevator faintly rattled. Before it touched down, Felix leaned over and slid the gun from the ankle holster.

After two steps were taken, lights flickered on. The space carried a large metal desk, file cabinets, a computer, and a fax machine—a true live-in business office. The wall behind the desk hosted a board that was half dry-erase, half chalkboard. Felix approached it.

"What are you doing?"

The world map sat high on the board above five smaller maps. Five destinations on the world map were circled in red. Two out of the five had an X over them. Hawaii, the Bahamas, Canada, Australia, and Japan—each place circled carried its own map below. Felix leaned over, his hands on his knees, and observed the small headshots on the corner of each small map and its circled areas. The large Xs covering the faces of Bungee and Con was the clue needed for Felix to piece together the puzzle. The three faces that remained untouched verified that Felix had hit the motherlode. Each photo had addresses attached, all except Linden's.

"You made this too easy, Ruby. Way too easy."

Chapter 19

Kauai, Hawaii
2021

"Fuck!"

"Still nothing?"

"No! Neither one of them are picking up their damn phones!"

Ruby called Sherry again. This time, he prayed to himself that she'd pick up.

Hi, this is Sherry Evans. I'm unavailable—

Ruby hung up. "Did you get through to Tony?"

Linden shook his head. "Nope."

"Did you try texting?"

"I tried everything. No answer."

"Fuck!"

Ruby called Whitney.

You've reached Whitney, and unfortunately, I'm—

"Fuck!" Ruby punched the back of the driver's seat several times. The car swerved, and Tampa quickly regained control. Ruby slammed his back against his seat and covered his face with his hands.

"Focus, Ruby. Now is not the time to fall apart. Put things into perspective. You're in Hawaii. Even if he found this out faster than we think, we still have time to get your family out of Dodge. It takes ten hours to reach this island from the Bahamas."

Ruby nodded. "That's right, that's right." His finger tapped wildly against the side of his temple. "Tampa, put the pedal to the metal, my man!"

"Try Tony again," he said to Linden.

Linden held his phone in one hand, then set it back on his lap. "Where did you say Sherry and Whitney were?"

"At a spa."

"You're not going to get through to them. Those places supply lockers for attendees to place their belongings in."

Ruby closed his eyes and counted to five. "Sherry dragged me to those places dozens of times. How the fuck can I forget?"

Ruby caught Tampa staring through the rearview mirror. "Tampa, what's the problem?"

"I can call the spa. I got the number right here. All you have to do is press CALL." He waved his phone around for Ruby to see, then held it out to him.

"Fuck yeah!" Ruby snatched the phone and punched the CALL button. After the first ring, Ruby reminded Linden to keep trying for Tony.

"Waterstone Spa, this is Jessica. How can I assist you today?"

"I'm looking to get in contact with my wife, Mrs. Evans. She's having a deep tissue massage, seaweed mud wrap, and what's it called?" Ruby snapped his fingers. "The buffing manicure and pedicure services."

Both Linden and Tampa gave Ruby a blank stare. Ruby held his middle finger up to them both.

"Oh, yes. Sherry. And she's accompanied by her daughter Whitney. Such a lovely mother-daughter combo."

"Yes, that's them. Can you have my wife come to the phone immediately? It's an emergency."

"I'll do you one better and transfer your call to their room. They're in the middle of their massage. Please hold."

The phone beeped twice before it was answered by a woman's joyful, perky voice.

"Mrs. Evans, please."

Sherry and Whitney's laughter echoed into the receiver from the background. Sherry spoke into the phone with such glee it ripped Ruby from the inside out.

"Wesley—Oh, I'm sorry, I mean Mr. Ruby." Sherry giggled, and their daughter joined in. Sherry snapped her fingers, "Hey, Dollface, pour me another. Shit's good."

"Sherry, I need you to get Whitney and yourself out of there now and go straight to the room. By the time you two get your stuff, I'll be there."

Ruby could hear the loud smacks of Whitney's lips parting from a glass. "What are you talking about?"

"Dammit, Sherry, focus! Get our daughter and get the fuck out of there! This is serious!"

"Ma, what's Dad saying? Why are you looking like that?"

Sherry's voice drifted from the phone. "I don't know. He's being dramatic about something. Here, you speak to him. He's killing my vibe."

"You have got to be shittin' me!" Ruby shouted.

"Daddy?"

"Whitney, get yourself and your drunk mother the fuck to my room now. We're leaving as soon as I get there."

"Why? What's wrong?"

Ruby could picture his daughter's forehead lined with stress and her bottom lip trembling.

"Just do it!" Ruby ended the call. His leg bounced, and he intensely rubbed his bald head from back to front. His glare yet again met Tampa's in the mirror. "Hurry the fuck up and get us there already!" he roared. He chucked the phone into the front of the car, where it smacked into the windshield and formed a spider web crack.

"Linden, have you reached Tony?" Ruby's eyeballs appeared to have bulged out veins popping.

"No. Had I, you would have heard me talking."

Ruby set his attention out the window.

"Wesley!"

"Don't call me that!" Ruby broke. "Don't refer to me as that weak piece of shit! I'm Ruby. Do you hear me? Do you understand me, you brain-damaged son of a bitch?" What spit did not hug the corners of Ruby's mouth shot out in front of him. The veins in his neck met the intensity of his fury.

"What's wrong with being Wesley? He's who you are today," Linden calmly replied.

"Exactly! All of this shit wouldn't be happening had he been able to take care of shit from the beginning." Ruby pounded his fist against his chest. "Wesley's the weaker me, the little boy who pissed his pants when his best friend was murdered in front of him. The little fucker did nothing! Said nothing!"

"What are you talking about, man? You told me that story. You got JoJo and Goldie back."

"Years later, after I was forced to transform into Ruby, the only part of me capable of getting shit done! Had Wesley been able to, we wouldn't be in this situation. My family wouldn't be in danger, Bungee would be alive, and you would still have your mind intact. Wesley's the reason Ruby was born. I can never respect the weak."

Linden's dome moved from side to side. "You have it fucked up. Ruby's the cause of all this, not Wesley. Had you been yourself from the beginning, you would have never had this life. As for myself and the guys you don't know how we would have turned out. Just like this alter ego of yours you choose to blame everything on, we made our own decisions. You just had a hand in our ill doings." Linden crossed one leg over the other.

The air of silence made it possible for Tampa to speak. "We're three minutes away."

Linden acknowledged him with a nod of the head.

"I can't be Wesley," Ruby let out. The car jerked and rattled their bodies. "Every error ever made was because I allowed Wesley to make a decision." Ruby wiped his mouth with his hand. "The night Mayo died, my gut told me not to let Miles go without him, but I didn't listen. My punk ass was nervous about going out on a real date with Sherry, on the low. I wanted Mayo and his lady to come along. Mayo had a big personality. He would have lightened the mood. I got too close to Miles and Mayo, became friends instead of straight business. Allowed them to make decisions I should have made."

"Like?"

"Like not taking out Mayo's stepfather. Mayo thought it was enough that he roughed him up and scared him a bit when he laid hands on his moms, but I knew more should have been done. Me going ghost when I retired was me trying to be a family man and letting go of this life, giving Wesley a chance to live. Falling in love with Sherry got her father killed. Those feelings and trust are weaknesses no kingpin should ever possess. This life should be a lonely one, but I didn't listen."

The automobile pulled up in front of the hotel. Ruby's body was halfway out when he started to shout out orders. "Tampa! Keep the engine running!"

The automatic doors opened.

"Linden, keep trying to reach Tony. And if you do, tell him to head out to Brooklyn asap. We'll meet him there in a few days."

Linden walked as swiftly as he could to keep up with Ruby so he wouldn't shout in a lobby filled with vacationers. "Brooklyn? Why are you going back to Brooklyn? Straw's in the Bahamas."

"Because after I put that sack of shit in the ground, I'm going back home to regain order."

"Wait, wait! Now, wait a damn minute!"

Three elevators opened all at once and kicked out a full house of people. Ruby and Linden made their way through the stampede of guests and into an empty elevator.

"You're going back to work again?" Yellow-tinted teeth and overgrown nose hairs made themselves undeniably visible when Linden invaded Ruby's personal space. "You're old as dirt. What the fuck are you going to do?"

"Repair my home." Ruby hit the button engraved with the letters *PH*.

"Your home? Your home is in the Bahamas."

Ruby clasped his hands in front of him. The truth he had let out moments ago in the vehicle rejuvenated him and gave him the clarity and acceptance he needed. "That's Wesley's home. I told you I can't be him. I was a fool for trying."

"*We*. You said *we*. I'm no good in my condition."

"That's why you're coming. I'm going to put you up. Get you around-the-clock care. Make up for lost time."

Ruby led the way off the elevator. While he fiddled around in his pocket for the room key, Linden asked one last question.

"What about your family, Ruby? Sherry's not going to go for this. What are you going to do about them?"

He found the key; however, he didn't show it right away. Ruby's stance became stiff.

"I don't know."

"Because if you mean what you say about not being able to live as Wesley, that includes your family. You'll be walking away from your family."

Ruby somewhat tilted his head. "I know."

Chapter 20

Kauai, Hawaii
2021

Inside, Ruby expected for the suite to be lively and filled with his wife and daughter scattered about, running from room to room, packing what they had come with and purchased from the spa's gift shop. He had prepared his hardened vocals to scold and demand they end their searches and get out of the room now. Sadly, there was no one in the room to reprimand. The butler that Whitney had named Jeffrey met Ruby at the door.

"Have you seen my wife and daughter?"

"No, sir. Not since you've sent them off to the spa. Is everything okay? Is there anything I can get you?"

Linden sarcastically replied, "Yeah, his family."

"I can do so for you, sir, if you insist. The spa is not far from here," Jeffrey assured.

"I would highly appreciate that. Thank you." Ruby applauded. He went inside his wallet and handed over a one-hundred-dollar bill.

Jeffrey tucked Benjamin Franklin securely inside the pocket of his vest. His shiny, hard-bottom shoes tickled the tiles on his way to the door. Before he could reach for one of the two doorknobs, the door opened and Whitney charged inside, one hand pulling at her hair. Her left foot was a complete manicure, while her right was covered in the red nail polish she flew in with.

Ruby screamed at his daughter while she walked past him and over to the bar. "Why the hell are you two just getting up here? We have to go now!" He stomped his way over to Whitney and snatched the glass of vodka from her hand. "You playing games with me, little girl?" Ruby seethed.

Whitney's mouth clenched together tighter than an asshole and rotated upward. "Your wife is the reason why we're just getting up here. If you haven't noticed, Father, I'm walking around with a half spa worth of beauty done on me, while miss diva over there is fully pampered."

After Ruby scrutinized his daughter's appearance, he studied his wife's as she sat down and clicked on the television.

"You see!" Whitney pointed out. She grabbed her drink from her father's hand and downed the shot. "Said she wasn't going nowhere until they finished with her nails and toes."

"Pour yourself another drink, Whitney," Ruby awarded his daughter by saying.

"Don't mind if I do," she huffed.

"You think this shit is some joke, Sherry? Pack your shit. There's someone dangerous on my ass and everyone associated with me. I need you and Whitney out of here now!"

Sherry crossed her legs and used the remote to turn up the volume. Ruby cut the television off manually.

"This is no time for your tantrums. Get up. We're leaving."

"You're out of the game, Wesley. Why would someone be on your ass? Besides, you're in the bedroom sleeping. You know, jet lag," Sherry said calmly. She set the remote down beside her and politely placed her hands into her lap.

Ruby looked to Linden, then to their butler.

"Mr. Belvedere, how about you take a break?"

Alone with only the people Ruby had known, he gave the fast version of his dilemma.

"I am, but some new cat over in Brooklyn is tearing the city apart and killing off every kingpin that came after me. I have to put this dog down," he explained. Then he remembered.

"Whitney." He went straight for her. "Give me your phone now."

"My phone? Why?"

"Give it to me, dammit!"

Whitney stuck her hand inside the pocket of her Bermuda shorts and pulled out the smartphone. She slapped it in his hand. She released it like it was hot coals. Ruby took it, and against the gigantic pillar fit for the palace of Greek royalty, he smashed it over and over again into the decoration.

From there, he tossed it to Linden. "Get rid of it now."

Linden went off to the balcony.

"Dad! What are you doing? How am I supposed to get in touch with Terrance?"

"Did you speak with Terrance since we got here?" Ruby hoped for answers other than the one he figured was coming.

"Well, yes. I let him know we got here safely."

"Does he know where we're staying? The name of the hotel?"

"Daddy, of course. He's my fiancé. Why wouldn't I tell him that?"

"Get your shit now!"

"Daddy! I'll do as you say. Just tell me what this has to do with Terrance, please!"

Ruby was used to his demanding ways without an explanation that needed to be given. However, seeing how his wife could not have shown less interest in the situation and being that his daughter was at least trying to work with him, he deemed it fair he communicated with her.

What he was about to say caused the inside of his throat to itch and his eye to twitch. He'd had many conversations with many people concerning the crimes he committed, but to have to actually warn your offspring about what you'd have to do was a hard pill to swallow.

"Terrance's cousin. I now know why his family's not fond of him. He's a real bad man. A bad man I'm going to have to—" Ruby turned to his wife.

"Go on. Tell her what Ruby does."

Linden reappeared off the balcony. He stepped in quickly.

"Daddy, please just tell me."

"I'm going to have to take care of him." He tried to soften the conversation by giving a half-smile that kept falling. Although he knew the attempt was useless, he had no other way of handling the awkwardness.

"I thought you were done with that life." Whitney's voice lowered. She backed up a little. Her stance appeared as if it crossed her mind that he'd harm her as well.

"I am." Ruby hit his chest with his hands. "This is just something that I have to do. This is something out of the norm that only I can handle."

"And what about Miles?" Sherry questioned.

"This is bigger than Miles," Ruby shot at Sherry.

She snickered.

"Is Felix a part of your old life?" Whitney asked.

"Very much, and he's hurting a lot of people. I'm sure he found out Terrance's connection to me, and that's why he came to the party, which now means he now knows where we live. So you and your mother have to go somewhere no one knows about."

"Daddy, you're not going to hurt Terrance, are you? I don't think he knows about any of this. I don't think he'd set us up like this. Daddy, please not Terrance. If anything, I'll call off the wedding. I'll leave and never contact him again. Just please, please don't hurt him." Whitney had pushed her way into her father's arms and drove her nails into his skin. With her head burrowed in his shoulder, tears on his shirt, Ruby struggled to pull her off so he could look her in the eyes and tell her his truth. She clung to him, stuck to him, like a child fearful of being left on the first day of school.

"Whitney, Whitney. I need you to listen to me. Are you listening to me?"

Her cries were loud. The fear had drowned out everything else.

Again, Ruby faced his wife. "Sherry, help me!"

"No. Not when it comes to this." Sherry walked to the other side of the room where the second bar sat.

Ruby ripped Whitney off him. Her face was a painful mess. "Listen to me, Whitney. I'm not going to hurt Terrance. He has nothing to do with this, and if he does, it's only been his cousin using him. I know this. Terrance is not built for this life. He's just a means to an end in his cousin's eyes. Nothing is going to happen to him. Do you understand me?"

Whitney took a second before she answered. She examined the room. She looked at her mother, back turned, drink in hand—which had been considered her usual as of late—and Linden, who looked out of place and uncomfortable. His was the same face she remembered periodically seeing as a kid, just older. "Yes. I, I understand."

"Calm down. Terrance has nothing to do with this, but I need you to promise me something."

Whitney nodded without giving eye contact.

"You tell me him nothing about this. Ever."

Sherry banged the glass down on the bar. "This is what you want. To drag your daughter into your shit and start her marriage off with a lie. Fuck you, Wesley! You will *not* taint her life too!"

"That's not what I'm doing!"

"It's exactly what you're doing, but you're too selfish and hell-bent on getting back to your old fucked up life to see it. Why? Why is that life so important to you, Wesley? Why can't you just let it go?"

Ruby's phone rang. He looked down at the phone from his pocket and saw Miles trying to connect. He hit DECLINE.

Sherry took a hit of tequila straight from the bottle. She walked over to where everyone else in the room stood with the drink in her hands. "What is it that you want, Wesley? What is it that you really want?"

"We have to go," Ruby mentioned once more.

"No. I'm not going anywhere. This has gone on for too long. The disconnect. The fakeness. After your request the other night, things are starting to make sense, but I want to hear it out your mouth. I want you to tell me yourself." Sherry approached her husband and pushed a newly manicured finger into his chest. "What's in here?"

Ruby confiscated the liquor from her and stepped closer into her face. "This shit stops now. I'm tired of your drunken ways," he seethed between his teeth, out his soul.

Sherry forced herself on her tippy toes so that her act of intimidation was just as strong as her husband's. "And I'm tired of you living in the past."

Had a video been recorded from behind the lenses on the sets of televisions around the world, this ultimate marriage stand-off would have been shown on the Discovery Channel. The animalistic strength and battle for respect outweighed any human wars.

Linden pulled his friend away by the shoulders, creating a healthy personal space for both of them.

"Ma, let's just pack up and leave. You and Daddy can sort this all out when we get home," Whitney told her mother.

"I'm not going anywhere until my husband speaks to me." The sheer desperation coated with agony shot out of Sherry and into the hearts of everyone in the room like Cupid's arrows.

Linden placed one hand on Whitney's elbow and the other on her wrist. "Whitney, let's go get your things. Lead me to your room."

Although Linden didn't know where he was going, Whitney's inability to move led her anywhere but there.

"What's going on, Wesley?"

It had been years since Ruby could remember having seen Sherry's face overrun by tears. Her hardened death stares and creative cursing combinations were the go-to moves Ruby had become accustomed to. So, to see pure and soul-tugging grief made Wesley fight to come out and stay out.

"I think Whitney had it right. We have to go. When everything's taken care of, I'll send for you and Whitney to come home, and there, we can talk about this." Ruby went for her hands.

Sherry slapped him away. "You're not understanding me. I'm not going anywhere until we talk about this right here and right now. No more running." The tears kept flowing.

Ruby balled his lips inside his mouth and pushed them back out. "What do you want to know, Sherry?"

"What is it that you want? Do you want back in for good?"

Ruby looked to every closed door ahead of him. He hoped someone would come barging inside and interrupt the conversation that needed to be had.

"Answer me. No one's coming to save you."

It was things such as that—the capability that Sherry had to read his thoughts without much if any clue at all—that joined them and made them one. The bond was sealed with such strength that to hide anything became nearly impossible.

"Yes, I do. I wish I never left."

"We had an understanding. You did what you did for some time, and you'd leave so we could live in peace and be a family."

"I know, but that's not what I want. I can't live like this. I can't live as Wesley. He's not who I want to be, who I'm used to being." Ruby tried again to touch his wife, and again she rejected him. "You want me to be someone I'm not," he finally told her.

"What are you talking about?" Her voice cracked into hundreds of large shards. "You sound crazy. This, this talking in third person has got to stop!" Sherry's hands balled into fists that flew in the air.

"It is crazy." Ruby stepped back and tried to swallow away the dryness his throat had formed. "Crazy that I've become different people to live. And now that it's time to pick a life, I can't, because whichever door I walk through, I'll be walking out on something important."

"And what will you be walking out of if you choose your family, Wesley? What do you deem important to let go?"

"Me."

Sherry took a seat at the bar. "Wesley," she said in-between big bouts of breaths, "Ruby is a persona, an alter ego, a street necessity. He is not who you are. Wesley is who you are."

Ruby shortened the distance that separated him from Sherry. "And who are you to tell me who I am? Because here I am telling you who I am, and you're telling me otherwise."

Sherry jumped out of her seat, turned around, and tossed one of the seafood platters off the bar across the room. Calamari flanked the floor-length curtains. "You can't be someone you've made up! If I act like Catwoman, does that make me Catwoman? No! Let it go, this—this obsession that you have with being someone else. Just let it go and live, please!" The pleading and desperate need was something Ruby had never witnessed from Sherry on this level.

"Life as Ruby is easy. It comes with a significantly low level of pain and stress when I cut Wesley out. I'm not built for a life of happiness. To be happy, you must know how it is to hurt, and when I live as Ruby, he takes away all feelings. It's liberating. Whereas living as Wesley comes with too many liabilities."

Sherry's head pushed back. She held her hands out in front of her. "Are you calling Whitney and me a liability?"

Ruby rushed in front of Sherry. This time, despite her pulling away, he grabbed ahold of her. "I didn't mean it that way. It came out wrong."

"You're pathetic! A man in his sixties, and he's picking the streets! What sense does it make? You're a lost soul, Wesley. A fuckin' lost soul!" She tried to rip her wrists out of his hands and failed every time. "Get the fuck off of me!"

"We can still be together. Just let me be me! Let me do what I do best!"

"I accepted you! All of you! I gave up peaceful nights worrying about you. I lost my father because of you!"

Ruby opened his mouth to cut in.

"No!" Sherry warded him off. "The only reason my father worked with you was so he could keep you close. He begged me to leave you alone, but I wouldn't, so to maintain my safety, he jeopardized everything to keep you protected. And you're going to go back to the world that took away the most important person to me?" Unaware of where the muscle came from, Sherry tore herself away from Ruby. Her chest pumped hard and swift.

"Daddy was never a dirty cop, just a good father to dumb-ass daughter." The bun once high above Sherry's head now tumbled down her neck.

Ruby's video message went off.

"Who's that?"

"Miles."

"Miles can handle this. You just don't want him to. You just want an out from here, so you'd get back in out there." Sherry's lip turned up and nose flared. "I'll go wherever you want me and Whitney to go for our safety. I will cooperate on that end, but Wesley."

Ruby could see her hands shake.

"If you leave and do this street shit and I go wherever you send me, I'm not coming back home. I'm not living life backwards. It's either you come with us, or you live without me. Whitney's a grown woman and still needs her father. Trust me, I know. So, if she wants to continue having a relationship with you, that's her business."

"Why can't I have both? Why can't I be who I am and have my family? Why can't you bend for that?"

"Because I've already broken my back bending for you!" she shouted. "I never wanted a drug dealer. I wanted Wesley, the bookworm, the thinker, the good guy." A sob leaked out of Sherry before she could catch it. "Without Wesley, there is no Ruby." Before she faced him, she dried her face. "Your parents must be turning in their graves right now because you've just killed their son."

She snatched her clutch off a stand that held a vase filled with purple and yellow flowers. "Tell Whitney I'll be in the car. I'll get everything I need wherever my new home is. I'll consider it a fresh start." Sherry headed for the exit, but before she found it in herself to open those doors, she told her husband, "To think a small, small piece of me actually hoped—no, believed—you were trying to make things right by coming on this family trip. But now I see it was all just smoke and mirrors."

Not lingering around to hear his rebuttable, Sherry rammed open the doors and then shut them furiously.

Planted in place, Ruby was left feeling what he loathed most, having lost another loved one. "Damn you, Wesley. Damn you."

Chapter 21

Paradise Island, Bahamas
2021

The food that his body had half-digested into slimy chunks of numerous colors blew out from Tony's mouth and ruined the cloth that covered his face. Perry removed himself from Tony's chest and lowered himself down to Tony's strapped, confined head.

"Where is he?" Perry's accent made anyone who crossed his path question his origin. He was no American. His drawl was too potent and dense; however, his clarity and accurate pronunciation were what boggled American minds. "Now that you're conscious, tell me, where is the man you call Linden?"

What additional water Tony could extract out of him, he did. The drenched face-covering formed into a second layer of skin and made suffocation approach sooner. The mental exhaustion and physical abuse stole the volume in his voice.

"Waterboarding. I've read up on that torture tactic, just never had the guts to use it," he whispered, drained and lightheaded.

"I don't need to research. I've lived these ploys. Now again, where is your friend?"

"I don't know."

Perry picked up the pitcher of water off the floor and slowly poured it over Tony's face. Had his body not been fastened down from the ankles up, his figure would have toppled onto the floor. All control departed Tony's body, along with his mental abilities.

I'm going to pass out, was all Tony could fathom. However, thankfully, before unconsciousness swept over him again, the poured water ceased.

"Are you ready to talk?"

Tony coughed. The natural reaction added to the fire that scorched through his insides.

"I don't know. Find him how you found me." His eyes drifted to the back of his head. The few words Tony let out decreased his energy immensely, yet he held on to the small voice in his mind that coached his survival and cheered on his strength.

"He's not dumb like you. He is discreet. My connections cannot trace him. He is no pig like you, who insists on constant food delivery. My time is thin. Tell me now where your friend is."

"Why is it so important for you to kill us? Because your boss is too much of a bitch to follow tradition?" Tony used his words to delay the torture of drowning. What air he wasn't denied, he used to his advantage.

"Where is he?" The swishing sounds of water dancing inside the walls of the pitcher flooded Tony's ears and screamed louder the closer it got. "I ask once more. Where is he?"

"Why is it so important?"

"All of you dying is important."

Creaking from the farmhouse front door, followed by light footsteps, insulted Tony's ears.

"I work alone. We do what you ask. Please leave right now," Perry said.

Tony sensed a bit of discomfort and heard the shake in Perry's voice.

The robotic, electronic voice akin to Apple's Siri that replied to Perry compelled Tony to put his mind at ease and concentrate on the stranger in the room.

"Is he dead?"

"No, not yet. I want to know where his friend is, this Linden."

Seconds passed by. The quietness supplied Tony with the chance to hear tapping and punching from fingertips onto a slick surface.

"You know where he is. You have everything you need. Do not stray from what you know. Kill him."

"No address was found. Only locations. I am a man of precision, and with that comes the need for great detail and accurate timing."

Again tapping. This time, the aggression and speed matched Tony's heartbeat.

Tony's ears rang double and snatched his attention above his head. Although his sight had been temporarily out of order, Tony heard small, slow, steady footsteps.

Halle.

To know his wife was near and no longer ridding herself of cabin fever gnawed at Tony's insides and magnified his anxiety. There were years spent training Halle for if-and-when situations such as what they currently sat in. Now that it was time for the student to be tested, all Tony wished was for her to run.

"I will get you what you need. Do your job. The faster it's done, the faster I introduce him to his new connect," the robot reminded.

Underneath the cloth, Tony beamed then seethed.

The rumors were right. Bastard killed Bungee before he could link him with Bibiano. Now he needs a new in.

"Where's his wife?"

Perry didn't respond automatically. The room fell quiet. Had Tony been asked, he'd say he was sure he heard the scar-faced man's heart go off track in his chest.

"Wife? I was told nothing about a wife."

It was nothing but a dream, a man's dream to keep his woman safe, especially a man who had married a strong-minded, strong-willed woman whose determination to protect overrode reality. So, Tony laughed at the errors of Perry's ways and the price he'd paid because of it. At the end of Tony's entertainment, bullets flew down from the top stair's railing. Slugs after slug migrated from the left side of the living room to the right. Shells that dropped amongst the floor added a melody to the act of death that raged from a woman on a mission. Windows and picture frames were blown out. Feathers burst like a strawberry Gusher that met its demise from decorative couch pillows that old women from foreign countries had hand sewn.

Halle's fit of revenge stumbled upon Perry, and with a programmed mind to kill on sight, she shot at him, and this time, kept her gun aimed in one direction. Perry's chest absorbed five bullets that shoved him back and knocked him into Tony. Both bodies, one which had taken its last breath, plummeted down on the oak wood and stayed put until the firestorm of bullets shut its mouth and took a breath.

Free from the cloth that covered his face and added to his torture, Tony looked around, and when all movement concluded, he called out, "Halle! Halle!"

Halle leaned her shotgun down at her side and leaned over the railing. Her first line of sight was of her husband, turned on his side, stuck to a board. "Tony! You okay? I didn't get you, did I?"

Tony let out a sigh of relief. "Hell no! If you would have got me, we wouldn't be speaking right now. I'm tied down here. Come undo me!"

"I'm coming, baby."

The last piece of glass decoration that hadn't been shattered was a clear glass apple, caught inside the coffee table's built-in cup holder. It had been pushed off from the table and broken in two.

The man with no voice had made it out of the shadows of the home entertainment center and stood in the middle of the war zone. Gun pulled, he settled it on Halle. She leaned over for her gun. The abrupt reaction caused her to duck the bullet he sent her way.

Halle ascended from behind the railings. As steadfast and confident as her enemy in his line of fire, she, too, pulled the trigger. However, only one gun freed a slug that tore into the air like a cannonball during battle. No longer awarded for her high-speed movements, Halle was hit in the neck. She managed to reach for her wound. Weakly, she applied pressure to the fountain of blood that flowed out.

Halle's and Tony's eyes met when a second bullet struck through her forehead. Her body buckled and fell forward into the railing that held her upper body in place and allowed her head and arms to dangle like rag dolls.

"Halle! Get up! Get up!" Tony's body bucked. The energy lost during the act of torture had returned with the strength of ten men. His powerful movements pushed him on his back and in view of his wife's murderer. "You're dead! Do you hear me? You're dead! Everything you have ever known is dead!" The strap that held his chest in place popped. "You were always the weakest one!"

Voiceless and heartless, the man of no words whose glasses had drops of blood on the lenses, stood over Tony. With his right hand, he waved goodbye, and with his left, he let go of the bullet that slowly stole Tony's life. Fidgeting and bleeding, Tony was left where he lay, his arms stretched outward. The dirt, rocks, and twigs caught beneath the tires on the road used to leave the farm popped, smashed, and echoed through the night. It was those sounds and the noise of the tires that hammered down with every movement that Tony focused on before he died.

It was the talk of the night that carried Tony's finger to write out four letters on the wooden floor using his wife's blood. When it came down to writing out the fifth letter, his finger hung in the air, tempted, determined, and heart set on finishing the name. Then it dropped beside the incomplete name he'd dared to say.

Mile.

Chapter 22

Kauai, Hawaii
2021

The hotel lobby was filled with extravagant plants, no less than six feet tall, with humungous leaves used to fan royalty on hot summer days. They took space on the corners of the floor, primarily adjacent to the entrance. It was a man-made forest of beauty for the inside, and the hiding place for Ruby to watch his family's departure. The driver hired to take his family to the airport loaded the last of their belongings. It took a lot, but Whitney managed to pack her things *and* her mother's without the help of no one other than Linden. Ruby thought about his last moments with his daughter up in their room. He felt a sharp pain surge through his stomach. He felt like a horrible father.

Ruby watched from the bedroom door as his daughter rushed to get everything together. The imagery took him back to when she was a child and her main objective was to clean her room within a set time she had given herself. Not much had changed. Whitney was still that little girl, this time in a grown woman's body, who tried to appease both her parents any way she thought possible.

Whitney had set two of her bags in front of the doorway. "How long do you think everything will take? When will you come to where we're going?"

Ruby couldn't look her in the eye when he responded. "I don't know. Felix is in the Bahamas, but his mess was made in Brooklyn. Both places must be cleaned up."

Whitney stopped packing. "If you don't come with us right now, is it over between you and Mommy?"

"She says that, but it's not."

Whitney slammed her makeup bag inside her luggage. "You're delusional."

"What?"

"You're delusional if you think she'll take you back. I warned you. She will leave you." Whitney zipped up the bag. "Will I see you at my wedding?"

Ruby walked in the room, took the hair products she held out of her grasp, and sat her down on the bed. "I'm not leaving you. I'm your father. I will never abandon you. What's going on now is just a temporary bump in the road, a growing pain. This is no goodbye."

Whitney's eyes started to fill with tears.

"I admire how you believe that, Daddy."

"It's the truth."

Whitney stood. "Be careful, Daddy, please. I'll grant you your wish. Terrance will know nothing about any of this."

Whitney's agreeing to start her marriage with a secret for the sake of her father killed a piece of his heart.

"I should have never asked that of you. That, that's not me."

Whitney touched the gray on her father's face. "Yes, it is. It's Ruby." She playfully tapped his face a couple of times and returned to putting away all traces of their presence.

***

Ruby closed his eyes. He prayed the simple action would remove the memory of his bad parenting from his mind forever. When his eyes opened, he pushed a green leaf with a yellow hue from blocking his view of his family. He watched the car move a few feet. When it suddenly stopped, Sherry got out.

Go to her. That part of your life is over. Let it die. Allow yourself to be happy, Wesley.

They will be there when we get back. Order must be restored. In time, they will understand. You've come too far, Ruby. Don't stop now.

People walked by the plants Ruby had jammed himself in. For ten minutes, Sherry stood and waited.

You're making the biggest mistake of your life. And for what, the streets? You blame me for your pain, but we both know who's to blame. Look at her. She's waiting on you, Wesley. She wants you to choose your family.

What would it have all been for if we allow it to go to shit now? We're not dead yet. Why not fix what he helped make?

Whitney got out from the other side of the automobile. She embraced her mother, who at first appeared to push her away. She put up this front for a good ten seconds before finally sinking into her child. Whitney held her mother by the back of her head, and although Ruby could not physically hear their cries, he felt it.

I hope it's worth it, Wesley kept telling him. *I hope it's worth it.*

There was no more stalling in hopes of Ruby's arrival once Sherry got inside the car for the second time and took off. Even when the car turned out of view, Ruby remained staring at the road.

"Ruby."

He hadn't heard his name called the last three times by Linden, who stood outside the groups of plants granting him his privacy.

"Ruby."

Still without a response, Linden went for Ruby's ringing phone secured in his pocket. Ruby grabbed his hand and squeezed.

"What are you doing?" The void look and dead glare dressed on Ruby's face was a thing of the past resurfaced.

Still, Linden treated the situation just as one would when in contact with a wild animal. "Your phone is ringing," he informed his friend. "Don't you hear it?" Linden spoke softly and carefully selected each word.

Ruby loosened his hold and placed the tension grouped in his hand on his cell. He accepted the video call that blurred in need of desperate attention. Miles's face appeared live on the screen. Without any greeting, Miles's hands dove right into conversation.

"About damn time. I've been trying to reach you!"

"Well, you got me," Ruby sarcastically replied.

"Ruby, listen to me. If you know where Linden is, you need to tell me."

"Why would I know where Linden is?" Ruby shot back. The visual of his family leaving stained his memory and left him in a mood he wouldn't allow himself to shake.

"You offered me your version of a retirement parachute plan. I forgot about it until now. I know you, Ruby. You wouldn't look out for one king and not another. Where is Linden?"

Three toddlers sprinted around the lobby ahead of their parents. Each had a firm hold on the plastic buckets that carried their toy shovels and other toddler beach essentials. They hollered and darted in and out from behind walls as the hotel personnel speed walked to their next assigned station. Their mother called for them. Her voice deepened yet seasoned with a hint of sweetness when she was gawked at by fellow parents and the elderly.

Ruby examined his surroundings. "I'll call you back I'm not in a secluded place." Ruby took off for the elevator. Linden was on his tail, just as he had been since they reunited. Linden rubbed his knee while they waited for transportation to the top of the building.

A herd of people fell out from the elevator's doors. Ruby bum-rushed himself past the vacationers who took their sweet time walking, admiring the lobby's custom design. Ruby slammed his hand against the key panel. A loud, irritating beeping nose pierced Ruby's ear. Linden clicked the alarm off from his watch and dug out of his slacks a Ziploc bag full of white, red, and yellow pills. He popped one of each color.

The discomfort Ruby struggled with internally multiplied when he witnessed the necessities needed to help get his friend back on track. "Those help you with your memory?"

"Yeah. I take a few others for other shit I got going on, but these are the most important. Got to stay sharp if I'm going to be around you."

Back at the suite, Ruby locked his phone on its station and returned Miles's video call. After two rings, Miles's face appeared on the screen.

"What is this about you needing to know where Linden is, Miles? You know that whatever I know, due to the circumstances, I can't share anything." Ruby reverted to signing. The significance of the situation required he and Miles lose nothing in translation.

"Circumstances have changed. This is not your call. Hynes wants to meet with all the living kings. We have to fly out of Cuba this instant."

Ruby fought against the questionable glare his facial features gravitated to display.

"He got wind of what's going on," Ruby asked for clarification, "and wants to meet with all remaining kings."

"Yes. You, me, and Linden. It's imperative you tell me where he is. You know Hynes doesn't like attention on anyone he's in bed with, so he wants to meet with us all and hear in person how we plan to rectify the situation."

Ruby and Linden shared a brief stare.

Miles repositioned himself in the seat of his car. "Tell me where he is so that I can pick him up and we can get things handled."

"If I did know where Linden is, why would you have to go get him? He's a grown man, Miles. What's with all the hand holding?"

Linden paced back and forth. He bit off each of his newly grown nails one after the other.

Miles looked away from the camera. "Linden got into an accident some time ago and suffers from some severe memory loss. He's going to need help traveling. I can go get him, and we'll meet up with you in Hawaii and go from there. We have to all be on the same page about what we're going to do about Straw."

"Why am I just hearing about this, about Linden's accident?" Ruby placed extra aggression in his hand movements. Had he not put fury into the palms of his hands and fingers, he was sure he'd ram them through the phone.

"Why are you just learning about everything? You cleaned your hands of everything and everyone the day you retired. Don't shoot the messenger."

Ruby wiped away the imaginary spit on the corners of his mouth and leaned back in his chair. "He wants to meet with just the three of us, huh?"

Miles threw his hands in the air in an overly dramatic gesture. "Yes! Are we both now deaf?" Miles's finger roughly tapped against his ear.

"Nah, man. I heard you loud and clear."

"Good." Miles rolled down the driver's seat window, which gave Ruby a clean, clear picture of the black fence that outlined the rich land behind him.

"I'll be in touch," Ruby rattled off.

"Wait!" Miles's hoarse, struggling voice let out.

Ruby ended the call. There he sat, engrossed in the screen that showed nothing but a black and white background packed with apps.

"You know, I'm not supposed to drink while on these meds, but fuck it." Linden took a swig from a decanter. "What's our next move?"

Before he could say, Ruby took a couple of more minutes to mourn his longest-standing friendship. "We go get Tony's body."

Chapter 23

Flying to the Bahamas
2021

Ruby's attention sat stuck on the white and light blue clouds. Thoroughly, he watched the puffy cotton balls slide from place to place out the oval aircraft window. During such a questionable and regrettable time, the puffballs that hovered over the world succeeded in supplying Ruby with a moment of peace. This peace he locked himself in for two hours without offering a word to Linden. He backed himself further into the leather seat. Its ability to take on the shape of his body and pull him gave him the security only a mother's womb could.

A stewardess in a clean-cut tailored suit draped over her oddly shaped thin frame graciously and with ease rested a chicken salad and cognac on the table in front of Linden. Silverware and condiments neatly surrounded his meal. He poured clear dressing on the salad and mixed it amongst the leaves.

"Maybe we're wrong. Maybe Tony's fine and we're reaching." Lettuce and cherry tomatoes filled Linden's mouth. The small tomato squirted sweet juices when he bit down.

"We're not." Ruby's clouds began to take on recognizable shapes. "There's only one reason Miles wouldn't mention Tony having to meet with Hynes. And that's because he's dead."

Linden shrugged. After he pushed aside onion slices and penetrated chicken with his fork, he talked with a mouth full of meat. "I know. Just tried a little hopeful positivity. We can use a whole lot of that these days." He swallowed the grilled chicken, dipped a piece of lettuce and tomato into a puddle of dressing, then felt it was time to state his peace. "But I'm sure there's a legitimate reason why Miles is not telling you about Tony. You've been gone a long time, Ruby. Retired or not, Miles kept his hands in the game one way or another. He's probably doing just that. Handling business. Things changed, brother."

The biggest puffball took on the form of a lion's face, and the smallest one, a howling wolf.

"Well, I'm back now, and his stint as a lone wolf is done with. I don't give a damn how long I was gone or how much shit changed. This shit is mine."

Linden stuck his tongue out and rocked his head from left to right. "Damn, this shit is good." He raised his glass. "Got that kick to it." Linden stomped his foot down until the liquor's burning sensation eased up. Coughing some, he asked, "You sure you recognized that black fence?"

Ruby snapped his head in Linden's direction. "Positive. I can't call it, L. I can't, I can't say what it is,"—Ruby tripped over his words—"but something's going on." Ruby's face tightened and his jaw locked. It almost took the jaws of life to loosen his jaw muscles so he could speak. "My gut's telling me this shit is bigger than we think."

Linden licked his top lip and allowed his napkin to clean the rest. "What are you trying to say, Ruby?"

Ruby pointed his jagged finger, the result of a broken finger never cared for as a child, at his friend. "Miles is up to something. You're right about one thing. Things did change, and that thing is Miles."

Linden rang for the stewardess. Out of the front of the jet, she appeared from behind the curtains.

"Another glass, darling."

"You need to slow down. You need to focus," Ruby demanded.

"I will. But the look in your eye is telling me I'm going to need it for whatever pill you want me to swallow."

The hostess reemerged, glass in hand. However, before she got the chance to set it down, Linden snatched it from her and emptied it in one gulp. Unintentionally, the words *Oh, my!* stumbled out of her mouth.

To regain her professionalism, she plastered on a phony smile and asked, "Is there anything else I can get for you, Mr. Falconer?"

"No," Ruby intercepted. "Mr. Falconer had enough. Thank you, Natalie."

Without bothering to clear Linden's surroundings of his empty glass, she retreated to the cockpit.

"My gut's telling me there's something," Ruby whispered in a husky tone. "He hasn't spoken to me this clear and adamant since the night Mayo died."

"So, that's where this is all coming from?"

Ruby's face shifted into various positions.

"You're paranoid. Scared some heavy shit is going to go down, just as it did with Mayo, and you'll be at fault. This game will do that to you. Have you seen shit that isn't there? Why do you think I'm the shortest reigning king?" Linden brought his empty glass up to his lips.

Ruby leaped out of his seat and slapped the glass out his grasp. Fist full of Linden's collared V-neck, he snatched him out of his seat and got into his face.

"Don't mock me." Ruby's already gruff, brazen voice became flushed with fury. The cockpit's curtain was blown open, and with no more than two long strides of her lengthy legs, Natalie stood at Linden's side, a Taurus PT111 pushed into his dome.

"If I said I have a gut feeling something's wrong, then something's wrong." Ruby lifted him higher. "Why is Miles in the Bahamas instead of overseas? Everyone followed directions. Why not him?"

"Like I said, he's not trying to hide. Maybe he's trying to take care of things."

"Had that been true, he wouldn't have told me shit. Wouldn't have let me into the fold since I'm so-called retired. He wants me in on this." He didn't bother to offer the fact that Hynes had retired and there was no meeting. That alone infuriated Ruby. He wrapped his fatty hands around his friend's neck. The action was automatic and with ease. When he looked up at Linden's face, he didn't see a comrade, but years of trial and error. Years of hurt. He squeezed.

"What do you know?"

Linden gasped for air and bucked his body "Nothing." The one-word response was followed by low gurgling sounds.

"You're lying." Ruby put what strength he had into his hands. The pressure he put on them made his palms change color from white to rosy red.

Linden pulled at his hands, grabbed at his face. Blood drawn from above Ruby's eyes alerted Ruby of his actions and kicked to the curb the mentality of everyone being out to get him. Ruby dropped him. Like a piece of spaghetti, Linden slithered down on Natalie's shoes and held his neck. The imprint of a hand started to take form, and discolored cheeks and lips began to lighten. Violently, he coughed. The rush of air pumped life back into his lungs.

Out of breath and tight in the chest, Ruby stumbled back into his chair. Lightheadedness pulled his card and tamed the beast.

The weapon still locked on Linden, Natalie asked. "You okay? Need me to get you something?"

"Lower your gun," he ordered.

She did just that, concealed her weapon within the holster strapped to her thigh and stood momentarily before making her exit.

Still caught in the middle of a coughing fit, Linden spit globs on the carpeted floor.

"Nothing's what it seems!" Ruby yelled. He jammed his finger into the side of his head, poke by poke, until his finger bent and cracked his own knuckle. "I know it! I just know it!" The unknown was what scared Ruby most next to living as Wesley for twenty-four hours, seven days a week.

"Why?" Linden asked, dry and breathless. "What the hell can Miles have against you?"

"I don't know." Ruby took a second to think some more. "I don't know, but I'm not going against my gut. Not this time."

Brooklyn, NY
1983

"Isn't she . . . isn't she . . . isn't she . . ." Leon stumbled backward against a building's brick wall. When he stood himself up straight, he fell back again. "Isn't she . . ." Leon stopped his singing and thought out loud. "Damn, what's the rest of the words?"

"Lovely. It's *isn't she lovely*," an elderly man whose balance depended on his cane limped on by and filled in the lyrical blanks for Leon.

"There we go! Thank you, my brotha!"

The old man trudged along and now hummed the song along the way.

Leon slid down the wall and took a seat on the cracked concrete. This time, he sang the tune in its entirety. From the inside pocket of a dingy, ragged checkered blazer, he held out a small baggy packed with coke. In front of his face, he kissed it and went on with his one-man show.

"From liquor to the snow. Boy, how the mighty has fallen." Leon dipped the pinky nail he had purposely grown out into the white and held it under his nose. After he inhaled, he finished his tune. He drifted back to his childhood, when his parents played all the oldies but goodies.

The good old days. When everything made sense.

A neighborhood kid who used to pay Leon to purchase liquor for him, now grown, walked by with his arm around his lady.

"How you doin', Leon? Keep your head up, man."

Leon's bony fingers moved slowly, one by one, and his lips stayed sealed. He watched the youngster in his baggy clothes and heavy jewelry walk by.

"Stay up," he mumbled. "I ain't never been down, motherfucker."

He reached under his Kangol, broke the seal on the tiny vodka, and offed it.

"Burn, baby, burn," he said to himself about the small flame that ignited in his chest. "Just like the first time." Mouth stretched open, long stretches of laughter spilled out from Leon. When he found himself unable to breathe, he slammed his mouth shut, and a flash of pain zapped through him. Leon moved his jaw around. His taste buds absorbed the taste of salt, and with a push of the tongue, he spit out a tooth.

Leon examined the rotten and bloody fang in amazement. He rotated the tooth between two fingers. "Well, I'll be."

After boredom fell upon him, he tossed the enamel in a bush and stood up. Lightheaded and with a sudden urge to giggle, Leon teeter-tottered and smashed against the brick wall once more.

"Dammit!" He grabbed his lower back and stretched out his underweight figure. After he made several failed attempts to get up, headlights brightened where he lay and beamed in his face. Leon blocked the light with his arm. The gap in his mouth where a tooth used to be was visible for all to see.

Mayo got out of the car. "Uncle L, you okay? What you doing laying out here?"

"Mayo, my man, I think I fucked my back up." Hand against the wall, Leon pushed himself up as much as possible. Eyes shut and teeth clenched, he fought against the pain.

"I'ma help you up and take you home, a'ight?"

"I'd appreciate that, sucka." Leon tried to laugh, but it activated his backache.

Mayo waved Miles over. Together, they helped Leon to the back seat of the Jeep.

Miles's hands told Mayo, "Damn. High again."

Mayo started the ignition, then signed back, "Like a kite."

The trio drove down a few blocks. Leon groaned and moaned. Not long after, Leon's dramatics began when they pulled up in front of Papi's.

Mayo unfastened his seat belt. "I'll be right back. I need to get a pack of Newports and a Chick-O-Stick real quick."

Mayo hadn't gotten the chance to fully get out of the car before Leon had his pinky back in the cookie jar. Miles watched him from the rearview mirror killing himself some more.

"It helps with the pain," Leon tried to justify. He took a couple more hits, then involuntarily leaned his head back, eyes low and mouth open. Drool found its way out one corner of his trap.

"You've been good to my nephew. A good right hand."

Miles heard nothing he said, so his attention remained set out the window.

"Oh, fuck. I forgot he can't hear." Leon positioned his hands in front of his face and moved them around. Throughout the years, Miles had helped Ruby care for his uncle, which alone had forced Leon to learn to sign. He was good at it, a fast learner, but when high, that quality slowed down. In search of the proper finger formations, he moved his hands around. He fought off the pain, leaned forward, and tapped Miles on the shoulder. He dropped back in his seat when Miles turned around.

Leon signed, "You're a good right hand."

Miles gave a fleeting smile.

"A'ight, good. This sign language shit ain't so hard when high," Leon mumbled to himself. He continued to speak. "That's why I owe you an apology."

The left side of Miles's face rose. He went to speak.

"No need to respond. I'll make it quick." Leon dropped one of his hands. Outside his pants, he scratched his sac. "Your dear old auntie. Yeah, I might have lied some years back about what I know."

Miles shifted himself more in Leon's direction. "What about her?" his hands asked.

"What the cops said about a junkie doing her. Yeah, that was true."

Miles felt his limbs grow numb and his breathing turn shallow. Leon tipped his hat, and like a junkie magician, made a small bottle of liquor appear out of nowhere. He went to unscrew the top just as Miles dove to the back seat and pulled Leon in.

"Talllk!" his voice box scratched out.

Eyes dilated and his chapped lips curved down, Leon verbally told him, "I was the junkie. It was an accident. She was at the wrong place at the wrong time. First time I dipped in that white. Had a bad trip." Leon started to drift off. He instantly came to and literally spit out the words, "I'm sorry." His eyes closed.

Miles shook him and slapped his face. "Talllk!" he strained to say.

It wasn't until Miles looked deeply at Leon that he saw how much of a shell of his former self he'd become. He'd grown to care for Leon despite his downfalls, and used his emotions to blind him to Leon's fast decline. But now that he focused on who was in front of him, he took note of his wrinkled skin and whisker-covered face, signs of old age his aunt never got to take on. Salty tears started to rise in his eyes.

A frightened, dumbfounded stare covered Leon's face when he screamed out, "Jojo! Jojo covered it up! Couldn't have Ruby's uncle going down. He had to keep the little man happy."

Slowly, real slow, Leon's weathered frown turned upside down. The vehicle chirped, and Mayo opened the door.

"Yo, Papi a trip," he said loudly, "He said he's thinking about opening an ice cream shop. Fuck he's gonna open an ice cream shop for?" He flung the bag of treats inside and flopped down in his seat.

Miles pushed Leon into his seat and sat back down himself. His face twitched, and his lips trembled. The outside view was nothing but a blur.

"After we drop Leon off, I'll drop you at your crib." Mayo pulled off. He rattled his spare hand around in the paper bag, pulled out his Chick-O-Stick, and bit the plastic off with his teeth.

Whistling snores flew from the back of that car to the front.

"Damn, he's out. That shit will fuck you up. Not to mention have you do some crazy shit," Mayo voiced for the sake of conversation.

Still living in a world of shock, Miles moved his lips. Mayo didn't see, but they said, "Yeah, it does."

The two walked Leon up the steps to his fourth-floor apartment. The elevator was out, again, so the men relied on their strength and willpower to lug Leon's dead weight to his home. Out on the staircase, Mayo stopped to catch his breath and complained, "Damn, that elevator never works. Why don't Leon let Ruby get him out of here?"

Miles nudged Leon ahead, his way of telling Mayo to keep it moving. Leon's front door was cracked open.

"Damn shame. Left his door open again."

They dragged Leon inside his place. They kicked aside clothing, liquor bottles, and Chinese food containers out of their way and created a path that led from the front door to the bedroom. They dropped an unconscious Leon on the twin-sized bed. Mayo put an ear to Leon's mouth.

Miles signed, "What are you doing?"

Miles stood up, covered Leon with a sheet, then signed, "Making sure he's still breathing."

Mayo removed the old man's tattered shoes while Miles zeroed in on Leon's slow, light breathing. Mayo gave Leon one last once over, then headed for the door. Miles caught up with him and had his hands say, "I'll stay behind. Make sure he's good."

Mayo looked past Miles and to the bed. "Nah. He'll be a'ight."

"I'ma stay. To make sure."

Mayo scratched behind his ear. "Nah, man, let's just go. Besides, Ruby doesn't want either one of us rolling solo. Shit's a little hot right now with Curry and his boys, remember?"

Fuck, Miles thought.

"You'll be alone when you drop me off. No difference," Miles pointed out.

"Me and Coke gotta make a run. I saw him in Papi's and told him to meet me in front of your building around ten." Mayo squinted to see the time on the alarm clock a pair of dirty drawers sat on top of. "Come on. Let's go. I ain't trying to be late. He'll be good." Mayo cut off the light, grabbed Miles by the shoulder, and led him out of the room. To keep from showing his shaking hands, Miles kept them stuffed in his pockets.

One hour later

A loud click sounded in the front of the apartment and granted Miles access into the junkyard he'd visited countless times before. He followed the trail left behind by him and Mayo not long ago. The tip of his finger slid across the blade of the pocketknife he carried. He stood in the doorway of Leon's room. An empty bed. Leon lay sprawled out on the floor, his back to the door and the side of his face dunked inside a puddle of his own vomit. Miles stepped inside and closed the door behind him.

He kneeled down and rolled Leon onto his back, and he pushed the blade against his Adam's apple. On the verge of applying all the pressure needed to slit open Leon's flesh, Miles saw movement out of the corner of his eye. The bedroom door was slowly opening. He slid the knife underneath Leon's body before he stood and turned toward the door.

Mayo flicked on the ceiling light. When Miles came into sight, Mayo stepped back a little. He placed his hand on his chest before signing, "Fuck you doing here? You scared the shit out of me."

Out of frustration, Miles hurriedly signed, "I lost my keys. Got to my place and didn't have them. Thought I might have dropped them here. Found them on the floor

next to Leon." He pulled his keys out of his pocket and
wiggled them in the air.

Mayo's thumb pointed behind him. "How you get in
here then?"

Always quick on his feet, Miles covered his dirty tracks.
"Ruby gave me a key for whenever he needed me to check
on Uncle L. I keep them separated from my own keys.
How'd you get in here? Why are you here?" he asked. He
took control over the conversation.

"Ruby gave me a set too." Mayo pushed his lips in and
out.

Miles tilted his head while he signed, "Why are you
here?"

"A'ight, a'ight, don't say anything to Ruby, but I hide
some of our stash here. Instead of going all the way to
the stash house all the time, I pop in here. Leon's place is
closer to where we make our usual runs."

"You hide junk at a junkie's crib?" Miles's face had
dumbest written from top to bottom.

"Leon knows nothing about it. It's in a loose floorboard
under the dresser. Shit, if it wasn't for you being so
concerned,"—Mayo turned his tone into a high-pitched
girly squeal—"I could have got everything without you
knowing and been in the Bronx by now. Then maybe
Coke wouldn't have had to stop and take a shit on the way
back here."

I was the junkie. It was an accident. She was at the
wrong place at the wrong time.

Miles's teeth began to clench and his legs shook.

"Help me clean him up." Miles bent down. He slid the
knife from under Leon and tucked it in his sneaker.

They put Leon back on the bed and used Leon's filthy
laundry to clean up the vomit. On their way out, the smell
of puke stuck to them.

Miles let Mayo know, "I'll check in on him in the morning. Make sure he's still breathing."

Mayo carried the drug-filled bookbag by the handle. "And don't tell Ruby. You know how he gets when Leon's on his binges."

"I won't tell him shit," Miles's hands admitted.

There was no sleeping aid, greasy food, or boring movie that could put Miles to sleep that night. In the darkened room, his only supply of light came from the streetlights and occasional passing car headlights that peeked through the blinds. When he wasn't imagining the multiple ways he'd kill Leon, he was trying to talk himself into going back to the apartment before the sun rose.

But that would be too risky now that he knew Mayo could pop up at any second. So, he forced himself to lie there until daybreak. He'd make another visit, do what should have been done years ago, and when being questioned, he would explain that Leon had been dead when he got there. It would then come out what had transpired the night before, and Mayo would be his alibi and back up his reason for making an appearance. Besides, that was why he had been given a key, to help keep an eye on his friend's junkie uncle.

The sky turned from night to day. The blackout room Miles lay in, watching the time in a sweat-soaked shirt, was raided with sunlight. Dressed in the same clothes from the day before and sneakers still on his feet, he got out from his bed and rubbed his heavy, burning eyes. The only framed photo in the apartment hung next to the bedroom door. Before he left, he gazed at the photo and thought, *This is for you, Aunt Haddy.*

Miles took the stairs down to the lobby. He had no desire to wait for an elevator, let alone see anyone. He was
making his way to the building's back door when he saw
a disheveled Mayo, holding the back of his pants up with
one hand, banging on the glass to be let in. Miles went to
open the door, but a little girl beat him to it. Mayo rushed
up to Miles. Hands on his knees, he struggled to take in
air.

Finally able to speak, he said out loud first, then with
his hands for confirmation that his friend understood
him, "We gotta meet Ruby at Leon's. He's dead. Ruby
found him this morning. He died."

Chapter 24

Every five seconds, the windshield wipers moved steadily from right to left, then left to right. Streaks were left behind from the previous job, and the caused a slight buffering sound everyone eventually got used to. The further the car rode along the black fence and beat against the muddy road, the deeper the vehicle appeared to sink into the earth.

Ruby turned on the radio and listened to the weatherman predict heavy rain and flood warnings. "Stay off the roads and stay indoors. Roads will be blocked off and businesses shut down early to limit outside activity. If you're outdoors now, you have approximately one hour to reach a safe haven."

Ruby listened as the weather station broke down in great detail the likelihood of a fatal outcome if people didn't follow directions and remain indoors, preferably on high ground. Far off in the distance, the farmhouse came into view. For a few moments, the aggressive raindrops splattered against the windshield and converted into running lines that blurred the home and played tricks on the eyes. The storm, paired with the darkness that fell on the island, made the otherwise simple home into a haunted estate.

While the tires slapped against the brown puddle, its water beat against the windows. Ruby cut off the weather forecast shortly before his phone vibrated inside the cup holder. Without hesitation, he opened the text from the only people who had the spare phone's number.

We're here safely. And yes, I got rid of Mommy's phone before we made it to the airport. I love you, Daddy.

He read the text over and over and took peace in his family's safety. He wrote back.

Keep that phone with you at all times. I'll check in when I can.

He pressed SEND, then sent a new message behind it.

I love you both.

Ruby debated whether he should open a window and stick his head out so that when he reentered the automobile, he'd hide his tears under Mother Nature's suffering. He pushed down whatever emotion Whitney had evoked.

Natalie pulled up alongside their destination. The three exited as is. Raincoats and umbrellas had proven useless against the downpour. Head down, Ruby followed close behind a gun-carrying Natalie and in front of a zipped-lipped Linden. The fully opened door left no thought to the imagination as to what lay inside.

Pulling his feet from being swallowed by the mood, Ruby looked over his shoulder at Linden, whose teeth chattered and thin body shivered.

"Still means nothing!" Linden hollered over the rain and wind. "Could mean anything."

Ruby turned back around, continuing to trail behind Natalie. They walked up the steps and, regardless of the eye-blinding thunderstorm, watched their surroundings.

"Wait here." Out of uniform and dressed as a civilian, Natalie went inside first, her weapon trained in front of her. She never got used to it. For all the years she'd protected the dirt of the earth, she never got past the smell of death. The first sniff was always the worst. The stale blood and bowels that passed after life was lost hit her so strongly that she could taste it in the back of her throat.

She didn't need to walk farther. The center of the living room verified there was no life inside the hideaway of the man she had once worked for. She swept her bang to the back of her head.

"Enter at your own risk," she warned, gun still in hand at her side. Natalie waited for the old men to step inside. She tried to avoid staring at the bodies.

"Shiiiiit," Linden dragged on. He wiped away the water off his face the best he could.

Linden walked around the living space and observed everything that had been pierced and destroyed by bullets. The blood that stuck to the walls, floors, and even the ceiling could fool anyone at first glance into believing it was an actual paint job. There was so much blood everywhere.

"Who's this?" Linden stood over Perry's body and looked him over. "Wait. I know him." Linden's memory began to fog. He took a closer look at the damaged, crimson red face and forced himself to remember.

"Never seen him before," Natalie offered.

"I have. I know I have." With the sleeve of his wet shirt, Linden wiped away the blood that covered the man's face.

Ruby's attention first fell on the second floor. For a second, he took in Halle's body hanging over the bars, her deep browns opened to the world. He walked underneath her corpse, which led him straight to Tony. His knees threatened to buckle. Like his wife, the windows to Tony's soul stayed open. Ruby said a prayer before he used his two fingers to shut them and grant him peace.

"I remember! He's Straw's flunky, his hitman. He's a foreigner. Was a solider over in his country somewhere," Linden explained. "How the hell did they manage to take him out?" he thought out loud.

Natalie pointed up. "Halle. Must've caught the mother-fucker off guard."

Linden followed Natalie's direction. "No, Halle." His feet dragged him closer under the body. He bumped into Ruby, who was on his knees. "Oh, no! Oh, no!" Linden blubbered. He started to slap his hands into his face. "I didn't want to believe it. I didn't." He made his hands into a fist and punched at his skull. After five times of repeating the action, he got it out of his system and joined Ruby down on the floor.

"We gotta do something. This cannot go unpunished. We gotta do something," Linden rambled. He pushed Ruby to the side and put his ear to his long-time friend's chest.

Natalie held back the growing emotion in her chest. "I'm calling the cleaning men. They have to take care of this." She bit down on her lip. "I'll make sure they know his family gets the bodies." Natalie gave the two their space, pulled out the phone stashed in a Ziploc bag from her pocket, and made the call.

"He's gone, Linden." Ruby tried to move but lost his balance. His hand touched the floor and kept him up. Wetness and a feeling of thickness taped itself to his hand. He looked down at the blood that stained him and read the word not far from the small pool of gore he had tripped into.

"Do you believe me now?"

"Huh?" Linden looked to see what his friend was talking about. He read the word for everyone to hear. "Mile."

The two shared a stare. "That bastard killed Tony, but why? It makes no sense," Linden confessed.

Ruby felt himself gravitate to Tony. Not long after he set his sight back on him, his eyes shot open, and Ruby heard Tony's voice in his head.

The little shithead has no connect. Bungee died before he could formally be introduced to Hynes's replacement. He has no in.

Ruby punched the floor. He punched it over and over again until he heard and felt bones crack. "That traitor!"

Linden stood by Tony's side. He didn't move an inch throughout Ruby's antics.

Ruby got up. "He's working with Straw."

Linden's gaze turned confused. "What?"

"Miles is working with Straw," Ruby huffed. "It started with Straw wanting to do things his way. So he went on a power trip. Killed Bungee and Con just to prove he can, but he didn't know Hynes had retired and the new connect requires he's vouched for."

Linden stood to his feet, and Natalie walked over.

"Miles is going to vouch for him. That's why he's not in hiding. He needs Miles, but they want us dead first."

"No," Linden intercepted. "If Straw has him in, he would never waste time chasing after us before securing the connect. So he's not the one dragging his feet."

"Fuck!" Ruby yelled. He yelled with everything he had in him. He pulled strength from his toes to the hairs of his head and jammed it into his chest, where he released it out in his screams. This went on until his throat grew sore, dry, and numb. Even then, he fought to yell.

Natalie made her way closer to Linden. "What am I missing?" She kept her sight trained on Ruby.

"In exchange for a meeting with a connect, his best friend wants us dead," Linden said.

Natalie's uptight shoulders dropped. "What? Why?"

"I don't know. But there's two things I do know, and that's that the dead don't lie, and that Ruby will find out what he needs to."

The worst of the storm had passed, and everything the residents of the Bahamas had been warned about was nothing more than a false alarm. Standing outside of the vehicle parked in front of his home, Ruby felt relief and the removal of fear that had weighed down the environment's sense of peace. Whenever the possibility of death came around and mankind had to take action, energy shifted and was easily felt through the six degrees of separation.

"Natalie, get him to the airport and never leave his side, especially when you two land in Vermont. When he takes a piss, I want you right there watching like he's taking a drug test. I'll contact you with directions when you land. Be safe." Ruby banged on the top of the car for her to move.

"Hey!" Linden hopped out of the car. "I'm no kid, Ruby. You don't just ship me off to summer camp when you please! Have some respect, motherfucker!"

Ruby balled up his lips. "This is for your own safety, L. No disrespect intended. This needs to be done."

Linden raised his arms up. "I need to come with you and have your back. I'm all you got!"

Natalie eavesdropped and watched the show through the car's outside mirror. When Ruby caught her staring, she turned away.

Ruby toyed around with the proper words to use with Linden. "Your position in this all hasn't changed. Retired or not, your brain is what kept us all alive. When you were in power, that was the first and only time blood wasn't shed, and that's because you outsmarted everyone. You stayed ahead of all the competition like a game of chess. Now, although you have and will, you're no killer. That is one area of expertise you don't succeed in. And right now is imperative because your strength is under maintenance. You need to fall in line right now. It's nothing personal."

Linden's alarm went off.

"Take your medicine. I'll be in touch." Ruby took his friend's hand, and they shook on it.

"Be careful," Linden told him. Although his face hardened, his voice still managed to express concern. "If you need me, let me know."

Ruby nodded and walked up to his house. When he heard the engine start and the car pull off, Ruby watched the vehicle gain distance. No one would hear him, but he said anyway, "I can't because you said it yourself. You're all I got left."

"Where are we going?" Linden swallowed his pills and pushed them down with the warm water he kept in the rental.

"Vermont."

"What is your name again?" Linden pulled himself up using the back of the driver's seat to get a better look at Natalie.

"We've been together all day. You know my na—" Natalie stopped herself from speaking. "Shit, Ruby warned me about this."

"About what?"

"My name's Natalie. We had a mutual friend I used to work for. Tony."

"You know Tony? Have you heard from him lately?"

Their vehicle slowed down and fell in line with a number of cars waiting to cross over to dry land. Ahead was a flood that took over the road and forced cars on either side of the street to take turns and drive slowly across the water one by one.

"Damn, look at this." Linden looked on momentarily then sat back.

Natalie inched the car forward, their turn at entering the street pool leisurely approached. Linden pressed for the window to fall and welcomed the cool, fresh air that hit his face. Cars across from theirs eased by. Drivers sat chest to steering wheel for added control of the automobile.

"I hope we don't miss our flight," Natalie thought out loud. The line of cars came to a halt.

Linden sipped the last of the bottled water. He cleared away what droplets seeped out of his mouth and made eye contact with the back seat passenger in the truck across from them. Straw straightened his posture, then looked more intently into Linden's face. After Linden blinked one hard, swift time, he watched Straw smile and wave at him. Then he saw the hand that hadn't acted as the welcome committee pointing a long-barrel gun at him.

Linden screamed, "Gun!" He ducked down and lay across the floor. Bullets, one after the other, ripped into the car and didn't let up until all four windows were blown out and tires deflated. The silence the car experienced after the vehicle sank down to the ground was short lived and followed up by additional slugs coming their way.

"Aw! Fuck!" Linden grabbed at his shoulder and rocked his body from side to side. Blood leaked out of him, which he plugged with his finger. "Natalie! I'm hit!"

Tires were heard swerving and crashing into the water. From behind, Linden and Natalie were bashed into and moved a few inches before the van that had wrecked their bumper went around the stranded truck and took off.

The end of the bullet storm left Straw yelling out to his driver, "Go! Go! Go!"

Cries and slow, shifting movement outside blared inside Linden's ears.

"Natalie, you okay?" Linden grunted. He turned on his back, a firm hold still on his arm. He tried to push himself up and yelped. When he pulled his upper body up, he was faced with a leg full of blood that kept on discharging.

An unfamiliar face poked inside the back window. "You okay? Do you need medical assistance?" the stranger asked.

"Yes," Linden huffed. "I've been shot in my shoulder and leg."

"Hang tight. We called for an ambulance."

It was silly to think at the time, but Linden was relieved the stranger sounded American. He did no good with accents outside of his own. The guy looked to the front of the car, and his face dropped. He turned away and covered his hand over his mouth.

Sirens wailed from what sounded like miles away, but they quickly ate at the distance and parked nearby.

"Help is here, sir. They're coming now." If the stranger didn't focus on Linden, he focused on the approaching paramedics.

Linden's removal from the bullet-riddled car happened so fast that he experienced it all in blurry bouts. Laid out on a gurney, Linden was on his way inside the ambulance when shouting and constant curse words swarmed his way. Ruby had shoved his way through the crowd of onlookers and made it to Linden's blood-soiled body.

"Who did this? Was it Straw?"

The tallest paramedics held his arm out in an attempt to maintain the separation between Ruby and Linden. "Sir, you can follow us to the hospital, but we have to get going." The man's accent was heavy, yet clear.

Ruby shoved his arm away and shoved himself closer to Linden and repeated, "Was it Straw?"

"Ruby? What are you doing here?"

Ruby stumbled backward.

"Sir, we have to get him to the hospital. If he doesn't recall who you are, he could have sustained head injuries that need medical attention now."

"No, he suffers from memory loss. He had an accident some years back," Ruby spilled out.

"All the more reason for us to move immediately."

Ruby granted the space needed for the men and women to do their job. All were inside the back of the ambulance when Ruby called out, "Hey! There was a woman with him. Did she make it?"

The paramedic who went to close the back door shook his head and stuck his thumb where Ruby should look. A few feet from where Linden had received medical attention, a white sheet was being placed over Natalie's body.

Ruby approached the body. His presence ended the medics' conversation.

"Can I see the body?" Ruby asked. "I'm a friend."

The sheet was pulled down to her neck. "I don't know if this helps," the rather old, thin-haired Caucasian man went on to say. "Maybe it can bring some sort of comfort during this difficult time. She put up a fight. Fought hard to stay with us, even kept repeating the word . . ."

His partner chimed in, "Straw."

"Yes, kept saying the word *Straw*. If you ask me, sir, that helped keep her alive just a little longer. I'm sorry for your loss."

Although Ruby knew who the culprit was, the strength and fight it had taken for her to confirm his assumption while she transitioned awarded her his everlasting respect.

"You have no idea the comfort hearing that supplies." Ruby took the initiative of covering her again. He stepped aside and allowed the men to do their jobs.

Chapter 25

Paradise Island, Bahamas
2021

"If I have to step in and do your job, it defeats the purpose of using you. You're therefore deemed useless." Whatever Miles typed, the electronic voice spoke over the video chat.

Straw put the small Scotch glass up to his lips. Before he consumed it, he said, "You put in a little work, so what? You choose to check in on Perry." He tasted the liquor and sank deeper into the seat.

"I'm glad I did. He would have been the only one dead had I not, and everything would have taken longer to execute. I've waited years to get myself in the position to destroy everything that makes Ruby, Ruby. I will not wait any longer."

Straw shrugged. "Three out of four's not bad. Any*who*, moving on, how do you suggest we reel in the big fish? You're not the only one on a time contraint," Straw pointed a black painted nail at the tablet screen. "I need to make money, and if I'm going to do that, I need a connect." The small glass slammed down on the mini table attached to the back seat. "So, talk."

Without a thought, Miles's fingers typed at an exceptionally alarming rate. "Speak to me that way again, and I'll cut your tongue out and use it to lick your asshole you like played with so much. I'm nothing like these wannabe thugs you associate with. I'm the real thing. Don't push me." Miles's elbows leaned on the desk he sat at.

Straw looked from left to right. "Okay now. Point taken. My apologies." He held his hands out and crossed his legs.

"Ruby's stalling. He knows something's going on. He's not taken or returning my calls. So, we have to flush him out, make him come to us."

Straw tapped his chin with his finger. "Tell me more."

"We dangle what he loves out in front of him and make him come out and save it."

Straw sat up and clapped his hands. "Oh, goody! A hostage situation. Let me put in a call to my cousin. I'll have his fiancé and her mother in my possession faster than you can spank me." Straw searched for his phone.

"No!" the robotic voice called out. "Not them. Brooklyn, that's his real baby.

It's time we put the nail in the coffin and end where it all started. Burn as much of it as you can down to the ground. Start where he grew up. It's time the homeless rate in the Big Apple rises."

Straw's mouth dropped. "Arson," he whispered. "I have never!" Without taking his focus off Miles, he unzipped his pants and reunited his hand and his manhood. A blank stare filled his face while his hand moved up and down as his bottom lip dropped.

"Fuck are you doing?"

Straw's body bucked, and a high-pitched moan tumbled out of his mouth. Miles ended the call. His timing was perfect because had he stuck around for only seconds more, the visual of discharged semen hitting the video chat would have scarred Miles for life.

Straw collapsed in his seat. His body shifted to the left when the vehicle made a sharp turn and came to an abrupt stop. His driver rushed out of the car and vomited on the side of the road.

"Oh, boy," Straw said to himself. "Heterosexuals are so sensitive."

Three hours later

After Ruby saw both Linden and Natalie off, his body and mind shut down. He was in the car when he started the engine and nothing happened. He couldn't move, and his next plan of attack was foggy and amateurish. After five minutes of ordering his body to pull off and having not one limb move, he took the hint and gave into the need to disconnect from reality and shut off before he lost all sense of himself. No matter how much the drug life was glorified, it took its toll. With everybody that dropped and every disloyalty uncovered, it ripped a piece of your soul out and left you panting for life.

Ruby took the opportunity to do and think of nothing, but not before he thought out loud, "I'm going to kill them. I'm going to kill them both." To hear his thoughts aloud manifested a sense of calmness to fulfill him. That is when he was able to breathe in and out without disturbance.

Ruby shook off the stiffness that came over his body, cleaned the corner of his eyes with his finger, and snapped back into the real world. His hands on the steering wheel and foot on the brake, Ruby was prepared to take off. He put on his signal just as his phone screamed from a text message.

Holding off from driving, Ruby opened the message from an unknown number. He clicked the link attached and was led to a New York news channel website. A live video showed burning buildings.

"The fuck?"

Ruby tried to look closer when the camera zoomed in and revealed that the area in question was where he had grown up. Blocks and blocks of buildings and houses were ablaze. Fire trucks swarmed the neighborhood, and residents stood dressed in their nightclothes, crying and in a frenzy. He heard a man repeat, "Everything's gone. Everything I have is gone." Women in headscarves and slippers paced up and down the street, hands on either side of their heads, with tears drowning their cheeks.

The newscaster came into view. Her makeup was clean and simple, and her hair pulled back into a tight ponytail.

"This is Yolanda Cast reporting live with News at Midnight in Brooklyn, New York. What you are now unfortunately witnessing is approximately five apartment buildings and a number of brownstones on Broadway and Hancock threatening to burn to the ground, while firefighters work profusely to get the flames under control.

"According to two residents who were taking their nightly jog, they saw several masked men drenching the homes with gasoline and setting them ablaze. After firemen pulled up to the scene, two more calls were put in, reporting homes on fire in Coney Island and Downtown Brooklyn. Sadly, the fires in these two additional areas include neighborhood stores.

"Tonight, hundreds of families will go without a home to sleep in and will be forced to stay in hotels paid for by the government."

Ruby searched the websites of other New York news stations and watched over and over again as the chaos continued to unfold. People were seen holding handfuls of items, others were barefoot, and some screaming, begging firefighters to rescue their pets.

Ruby felt an additional piece of his soul disconnect from him, and his heart tightened. He punched out of the videos, and a new text hit. He opened it. The rage it brought on deleted the hurt.

Come out, come out, wherever you are. Come on home. We'll be waiting for you.

Chapter 26

It took a total of forty minutes for Ruby to collect himself and wrap his head around thoughts that led up to the demise of Straw and Miles. He had to block out all the violent scenes he created to clearly set up his next move of not only bringing his enemies to him, but demolishing what they set out to obtain outside of killing him.

Ruby scrolled down the contacts under the letter *F* and tapped on the video camera next to the contact titled FRIEND. It took three rings for a face Ruby hadn't seen in more than ten years to emerge.

"Ruby? Get the fuck outta here. How are you doing?"

"Albert, or are you still going by Glock?"

Glock pulled down the fitted cap he wore to conceal his thinning hair. "I go by whatever. It's nothing for me as long as it's not hurting my pockets."

Ruby pushed out a small laugh and dove in to the reason for his call. "Friend, it's about that time."

The excitement on Glock's face fell. "I didn't see that coming. Only you would have the memory of an elephant. What do you need from me, brother?"

"I need back into the game. And when I say that, I mean I want everything I once controlled."

"You want me to talk to Bibiano, get you in? Be your shortcut?"

"Not just that. I want to control what comes in and out. Everyone and everything have to go through me to get to Bibiano."

Glock repositioned himself in the seat at his desk. "What's this about, big bro?"

"The less you know, the better."

"I hear you, but you do know Bibiano is going to want something out of this. Nothing is free with him."

Behind Glock, Ruby watched the office door open and a tall, dark-haired woman, whose legs could have been mistaken for broom handles, entered. Glock followed Ruby's stare and opened his arms for his wife to drop on his lip. She sprinkled his face with kisses. She noticed that Glock's computer screen held a man who was watching them.

"Who is this?" She brought the screen closer to her, and she squealed. "Ruby!" She bounced on Glock. "Mi esposo, is this Ruby?"

"In the flesh."

"Marquesa, beautiful as ever!"

"How are you? Where have you been? I should order a hit out on you. You missed our wedding." Marquesa loaded Glock with more kisses. His face trapped in her hands, she laid a five-second kiss on his lips. After she pulled away, a string of spit connected the two. "I forgive you. Your fifty thousand dollars brightened my disappointment."

"I'm sure it did."

"So, what are we talking about?" Marquesa covered her exposed knee with the fabric of her long, floral dress.

"Baby," Glock said softly. "We're talking business over here"

"I can talk business. Try me. Ruby, what are we talking about?" Although she appeared through a screen, her presence demanded, if not threatened, to be respected.

Ruby looked over at his friend, who rested his elbow on the back of his chair and threw his other arm up in surrender.

"Well, Marquesa, we were talking about your brother, Bibiano."

Marquesa rolled her eyes and tossed her arms in the air. "What did that little toad do now? Was he late with a shipment? Wait, no, no. He's reneging on an agreed upon price! That small, small man. No worries, friend. I'll take care of this." Marquesa was off of her husband's lap when Glock pulled her back down.

"Marq, relax. Ruby's retired, remember."

She put on her thinking face. "Oh, yes, yes, yes. Then why are you talking about the imbecile?"

"I want back in. And I want everything that enters the five boroughs and its surrounding areas to go through me and me alone."

Marquesa pushed thin strands of hair out of her face. "So, you want to be the only man connected to Bibiano. Umm, smart. But what is in it for my brother? He may be the family idiot, but he is still my brother, and I must make sure he is protected."

"Peace of mind. The fewer people connected to Bibiano and the Roque family, the better. I can guarantee he'd remain out of sight and out of mind. I made New York what it is. It's because of me your father made more money in my hometown than with any other dealer in the United States. I'm sure Bibiano would like the same opportunity."

Marquesa's face stiffened. "You sure you want New York? How about its surrounding area and let's say, Miami and Atlanta?" She shook her head up and down like a bobblehead with a wide smile too scary to look at for long.

"New York, Marquesa." Ruby shifted in his seat. Her need to push the five boroughs out of the equation was unsettling.

"Marq, tell him," Glock urged her.

She zeroed in on the screen and the screen only. "You see, mi amigo, my family's looking to distance ourselves from your home. The city is too . . ." She searched for the correct word, and when she came up blank, she turned to her husband for assistance. "Mi esposo, what is the word your music friends use to describe when things have too much attention placed on them?"

"Hot. Listen, Ruby. Whoever's running Brooklyn is drawing attention, and not in a good way. You and I both know that's bad for business, and when business goes bad, people jump ship." Glock's shoulders lifted.

Marquesa rubbed the back of her husband's head and nodded. "Have you seen the news, seen the fires? And that's not mentioning the death and drug rate that's soured in the past six months and is talked about every day in the newspapers. It's a battlefield out there. Nothing that will go away easily."

"That is why you need me. I'll make this all go away before anything else gets deeper than it is and reinstate order. I'll protect your family, protect us. Let me help you keep your money flowing, and I can make you so much more."

Marquesa straightened the creases in her dress. Ruby noticed. Her chest rose and fell before she faced Glock. "What do you think, mi esposo? Should we give an old friend a chance?"

They spoke to one another like no one was around. The sexual tension and admiration for one another pushed through the video chat.

"I owe him, Marq."

Marquesa slapped her hands together. "The famous IOU. Then that has it! What mi esposo wants, mi esposo gets. I must speak with Bibiano and talk him into this new venture. Although I trust your promises, Bibiano is a man you must manipulate into believing he is in control and every good idea is his. Pack your belongings and make your way to Cuba within forty-eight hours. Don't be late. My brother has a thing about being late. This pet peeve of his has gotten us into plenty of situations."

"Marquesa, the light of beauty. Intelligent, delicate flower. The star in the sky. I need one more favor."

Her head rotated and lips poked out.

"Have Bibiano arrange a sit down with everyone he's currently doing business with in the areas I want, with me in attendance, and announce the change of business in person, in Brooklyn."

Marquesa wagged her finger from left to right. "You all come to us. The Roques don't go to the help."

Glock bounced her on his knee. "Marquesa, show some respect."

She leaned forward. Her hands waved at the screen. "No, no, you no help Ruby. You know I love you." She placed both hands over her heart. "But we go to no one. Never have."

"And that's why it needs to happen. You need to establish fear."

"Fear? Those do fear!" Marquesa insisted. Behind her back, Glock grinned.

"Not how you should be. If you were feared the right way, Brooklyn would have never fallen apart. Become unpredictable. Call a meeting, tell them you're coming, and I restore you. You'll feel their terror over the unknown. Bibiano wants a legacy of his own. Tell him to start hard and do something Daddy never has."

Marquesa used the tip of her nail to beat against Glock's nose. "I like the company you keep. He's a thinker. He's a manipulator." Slowly, her head moved his way.

"Okay, you win! But!" Marquesa yelled out. "I want that mink that actress wore on the red carpet with the matching mink clutch within one week! And if it's late, you'll owe me another in a different color! Mi esposo owes you, not me!"

"Why, Marquesa, I'm surprised you don't already have a closet full."

She sucked her teeth. "Mi esposo is anti-fur and refuses we buy. That's why you'll buy for me." Marquesa reached for the screen before everything went black.

Although Ruby was pleased with how the tables were turning, he knew that nothing concerning rebuilding Brooklyn would be easy. Recently, all he'd done was jump on and off his jet and play along with Straw and Miles in their sick game. He needed to rest because once he touched down in New York, there would be no rest until things changed for the better.

That night, he checked into a hotel, an unfamiliar place, a place he had no hands in creating memories in. Ruby needed to dull his mind and shut it off. And that's what he did. He gave himself such a needed break that Bibiano's text telling him where'd they meet within the next forty-eight hours didn't wake him. It only caused him to roll on his back and drool on the sheets.

Chapter 27

Manhattan, New York
2021

The large room was empty except for the twelve-foot-long table, boarded windows, and dishes of food laid out in front of each of the eleven men in attendance. The bright light brought down by the LED linear light fixtures made everyone in the room feel under investigation.

Word of Ruby making a comeback had Bibiano open to stripping territory from men in areas Ruby hadn't even asked for. Ruby considered it a bonus and a leap of faith on Bibiano's end, so he took on the added responsibility.

Bibiano inhaled the tightly rolled blunt. He could taste his girlfriend on the wrapping. If she wasn't the one to prep and roll his marijuana, Bibiano wasn't smoking. Smoke seeped out of the small opening between his lips.

"Who are we missing?"

Wearing professional attire accessorized with diamond studs and high heels, Bibiano's assistant Diana swiped through her tablet. She took the thin-framed glasses off the collar of her shirt and put them on. "Felix Brown, also known as Straw, took over Brooklyn no more than six months ago after his mentor, Bungee, willingly stepped down." She looked down at her boss, who sat at the head of the table and waited on further instructions.

"I haven't even met him, and already he's given me a headache." Smoke escaped out both nostrils. He put out what little was left of the weed and stood up. He undid the buttons to his suit jacket. "My apologies, gentlemen. I am not inclined to waste the time of others because my time is never wasted. Never. So, take note. If you want to piss me off and get on my bad side, be late. I dare you." He observed all the young men's reactions and skipped over Ruby when his glare fell upon him. He clapped, then rubbed his hands together. "However, Brooklyn's finest seems not to hold the same respect as we do, so we will start without him, and I will deal with him accordingly." He took his seat.

Bibiano was on the verge of starting their meeting when the wide metal six-foot doors banged against the tattered walls and brought in a gush of hot air that temporarily increased the room's temperature. Straw walked through the doors wearing baggy jeans, construction boots, and a baseball jersey. The same team that covered his hat covered his jersey.

"Now dude's a thug? Big switch-up compared to his everyday gear."

Ruby caught on to the comment made by the Asian man to his left.

He's a manipulator. He becomes whomever he has to be, whenever he has to be it, to get what he wants.

Straw sat in the only available seat. "My apologies. I lost track of time."

Bibiano rubbed the stubble growing on his cheek. "You lost track of time?" He looked around at all the men who were on time and repeated, "He lost track of time." He chuckled, which led to a few men nervously smiling.

Diana placed her tablet down next to the ashtray of weed and got behind her boss. She assisted with the removal of his jacket and laid it across her arm when he stood.

No longer sheltered by his jacket, Bibiano's vest equipped with one handgun on either side made its appearance on top of his gray button-down shirt. He walked over to the end of the table where Straw sat and asked his neighbor, "Did you hear what he said? This man right here," he pointed to Straw.

The guy with braided hair answered, "Yes."

"Do me a favor. Repeat for me what he said, because although I said it several times myself, I am still under the belief that I heard him wrong." Bibiano's hands were held out as if he were pleading for the man to help him.

"He said he was late because he lost track of time. You heard nothing wrong."

Bibiano patted the man on the shoulder. "Thank you for clearing it up for me."

At Straw's side, Bibiano fired out questions. "Do you feel you're the only man in this room, let alone this earth, who is busy?"

Straw tried to talk, but Bibiano held his finger up. "The richest men in the world do not let time get away from them, because they understand the concept of time is money. Therefore, they are when and where they say they would be. To be on time is a sign of business, maturity, and most importantly, respect for the party being met with. Do you not feel I am worthy of respect, Felix??

Straw refrained from answering right away. It was a conscious decision to avoid being shut down again. When Bibiano didn't continue speaking but only stared at him, he went on to fill the silence. "Not at all. I meant no disrespect at all. It was an honest mistake. Nothing more, nothing less."

Bibiano walked past Straw and along the other side of the table. "Nothing more, nothing less," he said to himself. His bottom lip stuck out slightly, and he nodded. After what felt like minutes of quiet, Bibiano finally silenced the voice in his head and went on with the meeting.

"A majority of you have done business with my father, and some with only me. In both cases, you've met with me and the old man when it was seen fit. That will no longer be. This will be the last time any of you connect with me. No in-person meetings, no calls, no text, nada. I no longer exist when it comes to you."

"Then how will we be in touch? Is this meeting to set up future orders or something?" asked the Asian whose head was shaved bald.

"This meeting is to introduce you to your link to me."

Every head looked around the setting they had already surveyed many times. When they canceled out familiar faces, each landed on the one foreign to them all.

Straw studied all of those who had come before him in the business. His head bopped from man to man; however, his search ended when it fell on Ruby. The lines in Straw's forehead deepened along with Ruby's, whose veins were on the verge of falling out of his neck.

Bibiano approached Ruby. He placed his hand on his shoulder. "A longtime business associate for my family will be the bridge between you and me. When issues arise, which they shouldn't,"—he locked glares with every stare—"you will report to him. Think of him as your fairy godfather." He beamed over his own joke.

"What's your name, OG?" the braided guy asked.

"Ruby."

"Resect, OG. I'm Heavy. I run Staten Island."

"Annnnnnnd, that is another thing," Bibiano comically slid in. "You all no longer run shit." His thumbs pointed Ruby's way. "He does."

The faces dropped, shoulders broadened, and chests poked out.

"Bibiano, you getting rid of us?" the tallest of the group inquired.

"No, mi amigo. You are all still in the business. You've just been demoted to number two." He held up two fingers and pointed at them. "You see. One, two."

"What's with the change? What can old man over here do that we can't?" the Asian disrespectfully asked.

Bibiano looked Ruby's way. "The floor is yours, old friend."

Ruby folded his hands on top of the table. "Whatever each of you is bringing in, I can double. I can start a new wave of shit the hood isn't up on and the white man overlooks. I can bring order and connections who otherwise would never look your way, so that none of you ever get caught up and see the inside of a cell or coffin. This so-called big-time shit y'all doing today, I was already doing in the eighties. Y'all some weak, ugly broads in need of a makeover."

Ruby eyed the Asian. "Call me old one more time, and motherfuckers down at the bowling alley will use your head as a ball."

Cornrows' shock of a question had broken Ruby out of his mean mug. "Ruby? Hold on." He stood up for a better look at him. "You the cat in the music videos back in the day. I heard stories about you. Word on the street was you were responsible for a string of murders in Brooklyn back in the nineties and never got charged."

One of the men with blond dyed hair waved him off. "Man, he ain't the first to not get caught."

"My dude, there were five neighborhood witnesses and camera footage from the traffic lights. All of the witnesses instead vouched for OG, and the footage magically disappeared. This is funny as fuck, because right after it happened, the mayor was seen out to lunch with the man. That's what the fuck he's talking about, having connects."

He threw his hands up and sat back down. "I'm good with whatever you want me to do, Bibiano." He gave his attention to Ruby. "Whatever you need, OG, the Bronx got you."

"I don't know, Bibiano. I'm not really feeling the idea of being second to no one," voiced the head of Long Island.

"I can understand your hesitation. Who else has reservations? Stand up, please."

Four out of the ten men stood.

"Okay, then. It was nice working with you, gentlemen. You may see yourselves out. Do know you will not do business in the areas I supply. If you do, well, I don't think I need to tell you the repercussions. Adios."

Three of the men made their exit, while the fourth balled his lips and swayed from side to side, which led him back to his seat. "On second thought, broke ain't my thing, and it takes too long to rebuild somewhere else. So, if you'll have me, Ruby, I'm all in," Connecticut confessed.

"Smart change of heart, young man."

He sat back down and whispered to Heavy, "Don't no motherfuckers let you out that easy. I'll take my chances with the old man."

"Facts," Heavy cosigned.

"Diana," Bibiano called.

Her face back in her tablet, Diana responded, "Taking care of it now. They will be disposed of within the hour."

"Thank you, my dear. Now that's taken care of, gentlemen, Ruby will be in touch with each of you. And yes, all forms of contact you've once had to me has been terminated."

Diana held up his jacket for him to get into. Dressed, Bibiano excused himself to the restroom. His security and Diana waited patiently.

The room quickly emptied, and other than Bibiano's people, only Ruby and Straw stood behind.

Straw walked up to Ruby. "I guess an apology is in order now that I'm working for you, Mr. Evans."

Ruby grabbed hold of Straw and slammed him against the wall. Straw's head cracked the plaster. "You guess you owe me an apology? I'm going to rip your insides out and feed it to the strays, you murdering son of a bitch." He banged his body into the wall again and watched as he went cross-eyed.

"You don't want to do that."

"Fuck you mean? You were in my home, around my family, and you destroyed everything I built because you don't have the balls to eat at a table catered by another man." He used one hand to keep him in place and the other to grip his face. "You killed my friends. I will make your death a slow, agonizing one. You'll be my special project." His saliva landed on Straw's face.

"If you kill me, how can I tell you who my partner is? You can't possibly believe I got this far without the help of someone close to you."

Ruby applied more pressure to his face. "I already know Miles was working with you. In exchange for fucking me over, he promised you the connect. Too bad that didn't work out."

Straw forced his words out through his fish-like lips. "Don't you want to know why your best friend turned on you? No one can walk away from those types of answers."

Ruby released him. "Talk."

"Not until you hear my offer." Straw felt the knot that grew on the back of his head. His hat was tilted to the right.

Ruby dove back at him. Straw jerked out of the way and yelled out, "I'll tell you where he is. I'll bring him to you if you grant me immunity."

"You're not on trial, motherfucker. Anything you say can and will be used against you. There is no way out!"

Bibiano stood beside Ruby. He dried his hands with brown, dark napkins. "Come on now, Ruby. Have a heart." He held the paper out, and Diana took it out of his hand.

"Bibiano, this doesn't concern you," Ruby seethed.

"I know. But you promised me I would have no worries when going into business with you. So, show me that I will have no worries. Let the man speak, then let the man go."

"Bibiano!" Ruby hollered.

"Mr. Brown, your request is granted. Speak."

"Your uncle killed Miles's aunt. That's why he's trying to destroy you."

Ruby grabbed Straw by the face and slammed him to the floor. His pointy-toed shoes met Straw's face again and again before Bibiano signaled for his men to pry Ruby off his enemy. Security pulled Ruby off and held him in place. On the floor, curled in the fetal position, Straw held on to his stomach and coughed repeatedly until blood was spit out along with saliva.

"Keep talking, Mr. Brown. I'm not sure how much longer my men can hold him."

"It's the truth," Straw said in between coughs. "The junkie was your uncle. JoJo covered it up because of you, Ruby. Protecting your family meant protecting you, which was protecting his business."

Intrigued by the admission, Bibiano asked, "How did this Miles find out?"

Straw stretched out and went right back to lying curled up when pain bolted through him. He sucked in air. "He found him strung out on the street. He was taking him home when his uncle confessed. He overdosed before Miles could get to him." He spit out a glob of blood. "He knew how much business meant to Ruby, so he made it his mission to allow him to build. The more he built, the more he would have to tear down. I happened to come in at the right time."

"Damn. You've been out of the game for how many years? And now he hit?" Bibiano questioned, followed by a grin. "Psycho."

"That's exactly what he is," Straw added. "But he did try long before now to take him down. Like putting the hit out on Ruby's father-in-law, the chief of police."

"Hold him!" Bibiano ordered his men. "Do not let him go. This is getting good!"

Although the aches and pains still throbbed, they became bearable. "He told me Ruby's father-in-law was his connection to the NYPD. So, he had some kid give him dirt, try to get the cop to turn on him, but it backfired. So, he had the kid take him out, and when he did, Miles killed him so he could look like a hero and shut the kid up."

No longer struggling against the security guard's hold, Ruby thought back to the night Asher was killed. He remembered Miles had offered to pick Sherry up and bring her to Glock's party.

"That did nothing to hurt me. I didn't lose Sherry, and I didn't lose my protection."

"Exactly. It only made you climb up the ladder of success faster and befriend the Mayor. It made you more powerful."

Ruby felt the hold from the large armed men lighten and snatched himself out their grasp. "Where is he?"

"Waiting out in the car for me. He's dying to know why Bibiano wanted to meet alone. He knows if I secure Bibiano on my own, there's no need for him, and I will no longer need to kill you, Ruby, for his vouch. So, he's out there shitting bricks." Straw sat himself up, his arm still wrapped around his torso.

"That's why you wanted back in." Bibiano's smile stretched from ear to ear. "You knew there was nothing Mr. Brown could do without a vouch. So, to get one up, you found a way to control his product and cash before he could be touched. You just left them both stagnant. Dammit, I love this shit!" Bibiano swung at the air and excitement. "Diana, do you hear this shit?"

"Yes, I hear."

"Wow. Mr. Brown, is there anything else Ruby should know?"

"Nope. Only that he killed Tony, not me. My man started the job, but Miles finished it."

The fury in Ruby's chest doubled.

"Ruby, is there anything else you need to know?"

When Ruby went without answering and eased for a gun that peeked out underneath his shirt, Straw spoke swiftly. "We're good, right? I'm in the clear, right? Brooklyn's yours. I'm sorry for everything. I'll help you get everything back into an order. I'll even—"

Straw's body fell back with a hard thump. The bullet to his head put him down; however, that wasn't enough for Bibiano, who put four slugs in his chest.

"Bibiano!" The anger that stampeded inside of Ruby took away his ability to verbally assault Bibiano outside of saying his name.

Bibiano tucked his weapon back in the holster. "What? You took too long. You didn't think I was going to let his tardiness go, did you?" He buttoned his jacket.

The silence from everyone in the room burned Bibiano's ears, especially when Ruby stepped away, his hands clasped behind his head.

"Okay, okay," Bibiano said. "He was one of your kills. Let me make it up to you and bring you Miles, free of charge."

Back still facing Bibiano, Ruby asked, "How are you going to do that?"

Bibiano nodded from Diana to Straw. Ladylike, she bent down and relieved Straw of his phone. She cleaned the bloody screen on her skirt and placed the device up to Straw's face. The phone unlocked, and she handed it over to her boss.

He went through Straw's texts and opened his messages with Miles. His fingers got to work, and within a matter of seconds, he got a reply. Bibiano read it and handed the cell back over to Diana for disposal.

"Ruby, one of my men will drive you over to a friend of mine's home. There, I will have Miles waiting."

"Bibiano, don't screw this up," Ruby mentioned, not caring who he was warning.

"My friend, trust me. You'll love your delivery."

Chapter 28

Thirty minutes outside of New York City
2021

Bibiano's way of thinking never seemed to fit inside of the same category as Ruby's. Back in the day, when houses were needed for kidnapping and dirt to take place in, it didn't happen thirty minutes out of the city, and even if it did, it never led down a mile-long driveway to a luxury villa. The longer they drove down the driveway, the more comical Ruby found it all.

"Yo, my man, what's all this?" Ruby picked the brain of Bibianio's security.

"This place belongs to a close associate of Mr. Roque. He's out of town for the week, and it's available for Mr. Roque to do as he please."

"A bit much, don't you think, for what needs to be done?" The lawn was impeccably green, bright, and full.

"Let me ask you, Mr. Ruby. If you were expecting a crime to be committed, which would you gravitate to initially? In the ghetto, low-income neighborhoods that people fear even in broad daylight, or the gated communities where folks leave their cars and front doors open, stay-at-home moms meet up for playdates, and no one dares to litter because homeowners pay their property taxes so they're not having it?"

"The hood. The unpleasant view of life."

"True story. With that being said, I'm surprised a man of stature will expect anything less than what you're being offered."

The sprinkler system came on, and the sprinklers turned the lawn into a water show.

"Cannot argue there. I guess you can teach a dog new tricks."

A text hit Ruby's phone. Attached to the message was the name Junior.

You good? I haven't heard from you Unc.

Ruby punched in the keys needed to make his response.

Handling some business. Hit me up tonight.

Junior replied almost instantly.

You've been ghost. I'm going to hit you up in thirty minutes after my meeting. If I don't hear from you, I'm coming your way.

Ruby stuffed his phone in his pocket and poked his head out the window as they parked in front of the fancy home. Ruby rid himself of his blazer and button down. Left in a wife beater and slacks, he slid a pair of brass knuckles on each hand. The security guard stood outside the car, his hands at his side and earpiece in his ear. Ruby stepped out of the vehicle, re-energized and focused.

Inside, Ruby's first welcome was the monstrous, boisterous laugh. Its coldness chilled Ruby's skin unexpectedly, paired with the fact the air conditioner pumped vigorously. Ruby followed the hyena laughter up into the second-floor dining area. The marble table and matching chairs had been pushed to the corner, and the animal rug it sat on was rolled up against a wall. The beauty and organic personality of the interior decorator had been rerouted and temporally pushed to the side.

In place of the detailed furniture sat a shivering Miles, tied down by sisal rope to an aged, worn wooden chair overrun by splinters. He was stark naked. The only material that covered him besides rope was a small white garbage bag.

Ruby made himself known. "You held true to your word, Bibiano. You've delivered."

"I've done better than deliver. I made a fucking statement!" he boasted. "Diana, would you do the honors?" The bass in his voice swam from the dining room down the stairs.

Diana snatched off the bag. Black and blue bruises and gashes plagued Miles's skin. His head sat low. A brown, thick, long object stuck out of his mouth. Its jagged base was stained with dried blood. Ruby fixated over the unknown.

"What is that sticking out of his mouth?" he asked no one specific.

"Tell him, D! Take me!" Bibiano shouted with joy.

"That is a penis. Mr. Brown's penis." Her voice went out, and she cleared her throat to restore it.

Bibiano's eyes were enormous and infiltrated with pride and energy. "Crazy, right? You ain't never seen no shit like that before. He wants to act like a dick, so I gave him one." He bit off his thumbnail, a grin stained on his face.

The contents of Ruby's stomach started to rise. He jolted to an empty part of the room and let out everything he had eaten throughout the day.

"That is some nasty shit," the security guard judged.

Next to the stairs, the back of her hand against her mouth, Diana said loudly and swiftly, "Excuse me," and took off.

"This is good. This is really good," Bibiano thought out loud. "Not the reaction I expected, but good nonetheless. I told you I deliver, mi amigo."

Ruby held his head high, only to drop it again and finish vomiting. Finally, at the end of emptying his stomach, Ruby yelled, "Shit's nasty, man!"

"Hey!" Bibiano shouted, his tone no longer amused. "You do bad shit, and it will come back to you! Now, it's your turn. You have the place for forty-eight hours. Do with it as you please." Bibiano waved his security over to leave.

"Hold on! Take that shit with you!" Ruby demanded without giving the severed penis another look.

Bibiano huffed and puffed. "Very well." He snapped his fingers for the security guard to get to work.

The man blinked fast several times. "No, no, no, I'm not touching anyone's john. Detached or not. I'm security, and from what I see, that shit is no threat."

Diana rejoined the men, paper towel clutched in her hand.

"D, bag the dick up, would you?"

She swallowed, covered her mouth, and ran off.

"If you want something done, you got to do it yourself." Barehanded, Bibiano snatched the penis out of Miles's mouth and dropped it in the garbage bag. He twirled the bag around and pretended to throw it at his guard.

"Don't play like that, man. What's wrong with you, throwing around dicks?"

Bibiano treated the bag like nunchucks and flung it over his shoulders and around his waist. He continued the action for the entire walk out the front door.

Ruby untied Miles's hands. The beating Bibiano had cast on him made him unable to defend himself, let alone attack Ruby now that he was free. His arms dropped.

When his hands regained feeling, he picked them up slowly and said, "Kill me because if you don't, I will kill you, then Sherry, and finally, Whitney. No more waiting."

To hear his family's names in the same sentence as the word *kill* made Ruby check out. He struck Miles in the face. The first punch crushed his nose, and the second busted open his lip. Miles's head swayed downward from side to side before he spit out blood and two teeth.

Ruby crouched down to Miles's level. He forced him to look at him. "You got a death wish or something, motherfucker? I bodied homies for less, so you would be a welcome change." Ruby's past self resurfaced more and more with every second spent around Miles. "You were my brother. We could have worked through this shit. You should have told me what Uncle Leon did."

"You knew Leon killed my aunt, and you said and did nothing," Miles's hands expressed. "We were never brothers. We were enemies from the beginning."

"Are you suffering from head trauma? I didn't know Leon was behind that. I just found out Uncle Leon did that shit."

"You're lying," Miles's vocals let out.

Ruby stepped back some. "You should be dead right now. We shouldn't even be talking. You're responsible for the murder of our brothers and the breakdown of my legacy, our legacy. But out of respect for Aunt Haddy, because of my uncle's sins, I'm going to hear you out and give you the chance to state your piece before you rest in peace."

Miles collected globs of saliva and blood. He cocked his head back, and with what little movement his tied legs allowed, he sat up and spit at Ruby. He crashed back down in the chair and held on to the sides of the seat when it started to rattle. The body fluids missed Ruby by inches.

Miles's hands simplified his earlier threat. "Kill me before I kill you."

Internally, Wesley fought for the life of Miles. When he looked at him, he saw the highlights of their friendship, or what he thought it to be. Yet here they were, at war over a sin neither was at fault for.

"You got soft. You're no king. You're a Ruby wannabe." Miles's chuckle caused his shoulders to bounce and bloody gums and teeth to show. "Do you really think you've done the real Ruby justice? You've done nothing but spit on his grave."

Ruby snatched off his brass knuckles and pulled out his gun. He jammed it into the side of Miles's head. What made the moment an out-of-body experience was Ruby's inability to recall when he had retrieved his weapon. One second, he was listening to his first best friend being spoken of, and the next, he was ready to take the life of the man he had labeled his brother. Outside of Sherry, Ruby kept the memory of his childhood best friend sacred and inside his heart. Miles was pulling his card. Now he was ready to show his hand.

"I tried, old friend. I tried," Ruby confessed. His finger pulled down on the trigger.

Miles looked Ruby in the eyes and smiled. He'd never admitted it, but the only way he'd ever come to peace with the actions of Uncle Leon and even himself, he'd have to die. There was no way of living if no type of revenge could be obtained. And if it had, he still questioned his ability to move on.

Ruby's phone sounded off. The jingling sound alerted Ruby of a text.

Junior, he remembered.

Ruby lowered his gun, and this time, it was his turn to smile. "On second thought, I got a better idea. A surprise for you. One you'll never forget."

Ruby did not wait for a response or reaction from Miles. He used the butt of the gun to knock him out. Deafness or not, Ruby needed silence during their travel back to the Bahamas.

Chapter 29

Paradise Island, Bahamas

One year later

The high heels sported by women invitees gave legs
length and firmness. The gentlemen were R&B singers
in the making, and combined, the wedding was an award
show full of style and finesse, sophistication, and envy.

Greenery and flower vines hung off the crystal-em-
bedded ceiling. The dark green and white flowers re-
flected off the mirrored chairs and added to the majestic,
magical aura. The green marble floors splashed with
silver matched the marble archway, where Whitney and
Terrance said their vows and became husband and wife.
The manmade waterfall beat down behind them, and its
stream of water circled the outside ceremony.

After kisses were exchanged and rings slid on fingers,
the knot had been tied, and cocktail hour dove into full
swing. Nosy guests, incapable of keeping their courtesy
at bay, peeked inside the reception room and gasped over
the ice sculptures carved into butlers whose serving trays
sat equipped with chilled champagne. A large terrace
outlined the room and gave a spectacular view of the
ocean. Rhinestones led the way to every seat, and soft
music hummed in the background.

"Look at that!"

"Do you think it'd be tacky to ask her for her wedding planner's contact info?"

"She had to spend at least a hundred K on all of this."

Opinions were given out loud by the threesome of women who pushed their noses and eyeballs inside the opening of the reception room's door.

"Do you smell that? Has to be lobster tails," the platinum blond, petite 1974 Miss America sniffed. "My kind of party."

"Gorgeous, isn't it?"

The three jumped in place and turned to a wide-smiled Ruby.

"Wesley, you, you—" Miss America threw up her arms. "You caught us!" Embarrassed, each woman let out a light chuckle to ease the tension.

"Yes, you are all caught." Ruby moved his finger down the line of women. "But I won't tell." His teeth showed more than before. "Please, call me Ruby."

Miss America took her back off the door and pushed her way past both women on either side. Within arm's length of Ruby, she spoke. "I heard you're getting a divorce. I'm so sorry." She pretended to remove imaginary lint off his dark green tie.

The wild, curly-head female to Miss America's right co-signed. "Oh, yes! Sherry mentioned it at the bridal shower a couple of weeks ago. We're all shocked."

The woman to the left nodded.

"There will be no divorce," Ruby confidently expressed.

Miss America's face stretched as much as the Botox and facelift would grant. "Sherry seemed pretty sure. The tune she sang left no room for assumptions."

Ruby invaded Miss America's personal space. "When my song releases, it will kick hers off the charts." He winked.

"Then that man she came here with is whom, her brother?"

"My favorite troublemakers. Casey, Esperanza, and Phyllis. As usual, you all look marvelous." Sherry stuck her hand to her hip. She gave off Vanna White, mother-of-the-bride vibes. Her floor-length dark silver sequined dress designed with a plunging neckline and attached chiffon capelet made her runner up to Whitney's custom gown. Her short-cut, honey- brown dyed hair was the perfect contrast against her diamonds.

"I'm so glad you're all here. I hope everything's to your liking." Her whitened teeth spoke louder than her words.

Casey stepped back into her friend's line. "It's gorgeous, Sherry. You all have certainly outdone yourselves." She smiled a closed-mouth smile.

Esperanza added her thoughts. "Wedding of the year is what I say. What a well-executed celebration."

Again, Phyllis's head bounced up and down.

"I'm glad to hear you all approve."

Casey looked past Sherry and her estranged husband. "Are those smoking cocktails the servers are passing around? I must have one. I fell head over heels for them at the engagement party."

Sherry stepped aside. "Be my guest. Have as many as you like."

The three quickly excused themselves and blended in with the more respectable guests.

Sherry struggled not to fold her arms and display her disapproval. So, she used her fingers to occasionally swipe her side bang back in place.

"Flirting with Casey. That's a new low."

Ruby waited for her fingers to relax, and he fixed her hair for her. "You know Casey. Always hunting for what she can't have."

Sherry sidestepped his touch.

"Do you find it respectful to bring a date with you to our daughter's wedding?" he asked.

"I don't see why not. We are getting divorced, Wesley. I wish you'd just sign the papers already, instead of forcing me to go another route."

"Separated, yes. Divorcing, no. I told you I'd give you your space, but when I feel I can trust New York to my protégé and oversee things away from the city, I'm coming home."

Sherry put her hand to her forehead and went back to fixing her hair when a guest walked by and spoke.

In a hushed tone, she replied, "I told you there's no coming back. I made a new life for myself in Texas, the place where you dumped us. That is where I will spend my golden years and focus on myself until Whitney gives me some grandbabies." She waved and blew kisses out to friends of the family.

"You made your choice, Wesley. My apologies, Ruby." She let the words marinate. "Now live with it." She walked away; however, her hand was pulled back.

"We are a family. You're my wife. We married for life. You met me when I was Ruby, and you're going to stay with me as Ruby."

"Or else what, Wesley?" Sherry searched Ruby's eyes.

"Nothing. You and Whitney are the only people I'd never hurt. But I will not live without you. Now, you have a few more months to play around with that sucka you brought here and have your hot girl summer. Because when my city is healed, I'm coming back, and we're going to work on us."

The eyes that looked into Sherry's were Wesley's. His look told her everything she needed and wanted to hear. Yet she knew Ruby was not going anywhere, and the life of happiness and peace she had pieced together in Texas would shatter if Ruby continued to tag along. Then there were the continuous thoughts that tormented her and had her wondering if she could really have peace and happiness without him. Without either of them.

Sherry could feel the tears threatening to weigh down her eyes. During the time spent away from Ruby, she told herself her need, yearning, and her obsession for him was canceled. It was a good fairy tale. What dumb thoughts, because true love is never turned off and surely never moves on.

"Why can't you let go? Please let go." She asked this to Ruby, when in actuality, it was a question for herself.

"Never."

"Okay, you two. We don't need no episode of the Old and the Restless at my wedding." Whitney approached her parents in her reception dress, a shorter version of her gown.

Together, her parents hollered, "Old?"

Whitney did a little two-step. "You heard me. The good old days are good and gone. Move on over for us young bucks."

She got in her mother's face and vogued. High off love and in the spirit of fun, Terrance danced on over to his wife. Not wanting to leave Ruby out of the fun, he planted himself in front of his father-in-law and began a sad, stiff attempt of doing the cabbage patch.

"You did this back in the day, right? What's it called, the green patch?" He moved his arms around harder.

"Terrance! Terrance! They used to do this! I saw it on tv!" Whitney kicked off her shoes and ran in place. At that moment, the battle of the eighties dance moves broke out.

"Oh, hell no!" Sherry let out. "Where is y'all rhythm? It goes like this." After tying the bottom of her dress in a knot, Sherry showed them how it was done.

Ruby moved his legs and hips. "Show 'em! Show 'em!"

Sherry was always a great dancer. It was the sole reason Ruby always took her to house parties and clubs.

"Watch this. Watch me now," Ruby insisted. The focus was on his legs as he skipped backward.

"Oh, no you didn't! Not the Roger Rabbit!"

Ruby kept up with the dance move and transitioned into the pendulum. Sherry took off her shoes and joined in on the antics. The venue's lobby, set up to give off class and beauty, consisted of high-end tables draped with silk cloths and a spread that could feed a small country. Now it had turned into a dance hall. Guest circled around the foursome, hands clapping and energy to the max, the bougie way of doing things went undone.

"Dang, y'all! For old folks, y'all could move!" Whitney moved into a new dance.

Sherry's eyes rolled. "There goes that word again."

"Oooh, man, it's going down! I want in on this! I can't remember much, but I can never forget this!" Linden ordered the room to give him space. When all attention was on him, he did the infamous moonwalk. The move was just as clean and slick as the day it was first televised.

Those with an appreciation for the eighties and nineties went crazy. The circle that surrounded the family tightened. Sherry had handed the floor to Linden and went on to hype the crowd when on the outskirts, she noticed her date pinned against a wall. He wore a pure smile, but Sherry had learned long ago how to see past the physical. Escaping the homemade Evans entertainment, Sherry headed over to Gary.

"I wish I had known you like to dance. I would have taken you dancing instead of to all those stuffy restaurants." His lips thinned as he scratched the light bags underneath his glasses. "You're getting back with your husband, aren't you?"

"Gary, I'm—"

Gary cut her off and took her soft hand into his. "It's okay. For me to fight to stay would only be selfish in my behavior. Besides . . ." His gaze drifted into the direction she had just come from. "How can I compete with that?"

Sherry looked behind her. Ruby and Whitney were now engaged in a one-on-one dancing battle. He was so energetic, so optimistic, so alive. Ruby stopped mid dance and grabbed a hold of his knees and started to shake his butt. The three-hundred-long guest list joined together in laughter.

He can't . . .

"I'm sorry."

Gary blinked one hard time. "I know." He kissed the back of her hand. "Thank you for the memories."

Gary had no audience to watch him walk out of the venue, even if he had only one person who mattered. Sherry gave him the respect of seeing; he disappeared from behind the door before she rejoined the festivities. She blended in with the cluster of people and looked on as Ruby and Linden joined in on the Kid 'n Play dance. Both old men struggled to link their feet, turn around, and keep their balance at the same time.

"Don't fall now!" Betty screamed over the laughter and spontaneous clapping.

If he can find me inside of this large mass of people, I'll give us a chance. I'm giving him ten seconds. One, two, three . . .

Sherry hadn't made it to pronounce the *o* in the word *four* before Ruby broke his ties with his dance buddy, looked around, and spotted Sherry amongst a world of family and friends. All bleached teeth and dimples, he waved her over.

She stepped out of the humongous human shield. Ruby held his married hand out for her, and she took it. Sherry squeezed him hard and long, and didn't let go for what she hoped was forever.

Two hours later

The legs and feet of all those Whitney and Terrance had declared old throbbed and sat tiredly at their assigned seats. Some waved their liquor glasses in the air while moving their upper bodies in their seats and enjoying the feel of the music. Then some continued to stuff their faces and popped their medications in hopes the foods their doctors spoke against would not do a number on their stomachs the next day. Ruby fiddled with the crystals that hung from the five-foot floral centerpiece.

"Where's your friend?" Ruby covered the crystal with his hand, then opened it back up immediately.

Sherry tapped the fork against the silver trim of her plate. "He left." She took some time, but she finally said it. "It was nothing serious. Just something to do while I tried to figure my life out." A server placed a champagne flute in front of Sherry. She didn't touch it, and Ruby didn't reply.

"Any offers on the house?"

Ruby plucked the crystal. "What? Oh, that? No, I never put it on the market. I only said that to fuck with you. I'm not staying there at the moment, but it's still there, waiting." He finished his drink. "I know what that house means to you."

"That's good to hear. Where are you staying?"

"I fly back and forth from here to New York. When I'm here, I stay in a condo a few streets down from our house."

"Why not just stay in the house?"

"Nah. It's not the same. Plus, I'm using it for storage until we"—Ruby pointed from himself to her—"figure this out."

"What if I want you to sell?"

The crystal Ruby toyed with rocked and slowed down. "Why would you want that?"

Sherry folded her hands. Her finger rubbed the tanned spot where her rings used to live. "To start over. To have a place we can call ours instead of mine."

"What are you saying?"

She touched the crystal Ruby had finished playing with. "I want to try again. See if we can make this work with a little compromising on both ends."

"Compromising. That's an interesting word to use. I wanted to tell you at a later time, but maybe now is the best time. While in New York, I'm in therapy. I'm trying to get a better understanding of this whole Wesley versus Ruby business."

Sherry slammed her back into her seat. "You're in therapy?"

"Yes. Losing my family brought on a certain clarity and made me want to explore it. I'm running away from a piece of myself, instead of trying to co-exist. And if I'm willing to lose you for that, there's something deeper going on inside of me that I need to know about. Because nothing is worth losing you." There sat a twinkle in Ruby's eyes.

"Wesley, that's very, very observant."

"See, told you I was in therapy." They grinned. "My therapist asked me what I'd do if you were willing to try again. He made me answer truthfully."

"What did you say?"

"I told him I'd give you what you want, because Ruby did not get and keep you by himself. Talking so much about Wesley had me see he's not so bad after all."

He took a shrimp off Sherry's plate and fed it to her. He knew she was hungry. She hadn't eaten all day as she kept close to her daughter and played hostess.

"You mean that, Wesley?"

"I do, but I need you to compromise and understand that Ruby is a part of who I am. Like it or not, it's true."

"You're right, and since you're willing to no longer hide from Wesley and allow all of who you are to co-exist, then I can learn to accept you, flaws and all. But, Wesley, having a hand in the drug game when we're in our sixties is just ridiculous. You have to let it go and move on to the next chapter of your life." Sherry's stare begged for Ruby to comprehend what she said.

Ruby took a deep, exaggerated breath. "I know that now. Sherry, shit done changed, from how guys wear their pants to this social media crap and the music these kids listen to. Really, Sherry, what the hell are these mumbling rappers saying?"

Sherry slapped her husband's leg while she let out a heavy chuckle.

"This generation is screwed up. They're all about posting pictures instead of doing what it takes to get money. I just don't get it. I want to say Straw did a number on Brooklyn, but now that I really think about it, he didn't do anything clowns out here aren't already doing."

"I know what you mean. Things aren't how they used to be. There's no order, no honor. I'm not saying things was all sugar and spice when we were growing up, but it was better than how it is today," she said.

"For real."

Sherry took a sip of her sitting champagne. "With that all being said, where does that leave you?"

Ruby took off his loosened tie and tossed it on the centerpiece. It hung next to the crystals. "I think I'd better let it go," he sang.

Sherry raised her glass. "Sing it, baby."

"I thought if I came back, things would fall back into place. Thought I was the missing link, but the world's not ready for how things used to be. These kids have a lot more stupidity they have to get out before they see what hustle is like. Give me a few more months. This kid I have studying me has potential. Maybe with a little more grooming, he can start something of his own, create the best of both worlds."

"I can do this. If you can do your part and not renege, then so can I."

Ruby held his hand out. "Then let's shake on it."

They did. When Sherry went to release her hold, Ruby held on.

"Your ring goes back on. There's no compromising on that." The tone of voice he used was all Ruby. And for the first time in a long time, she had to admit she enjoyed Ruby's presence.

"I wouldn't have it any other way." She leaned in for a kiss. Not ready to distance herself from him more than she already had, she cleaned her lipstick off him.

Then her facial expression went from bliss to confusion. "Wesley, why are you using the house for storage? What's in there?"

The look in his eyes changed. "That's a question for Ruby. At a later time."

"Dammit, Wesley. On second thought, I don't even want to know."

"Nah. It's not the same. Plus, I'm using it for storage until we"—Ruby pointed from himself to her—"figure this out."

"What if I want you to sell?"

The crystal Ruby toyed with rocked and slowed down. "Why would you want that?"

Sherry folded her hands. Her finger rubbed the tanned spot where her rings used to live. "To start over. To have a place we can call ours instead of mine."

"What are you saying?"

She touched the crystal Ruby had finished playing with. "I want to try again. See if we can make this work with a little compromising on both ends."

"Compromising. That's an interesting word to use. I wanted to tell you at a later time, but maybe now is the best time. While in New York, I'm in therapy. I'm trying to get a better understanding of this whole Wesley versus Ruby business."

Sherry slammed her back into her seat. "You're in therapy?"

"Yes. Losing my family brought on a certain clarity and made me want to explore it. I'm running away from a piece of myself, instead of trying to co-exist. And if I'm willing to lose you for that, there's something deeper going on inside of me that I need to know about. Because nothing is worth losing you." There sat a twinkle in Ruby's eyes.

"Wesley, that's very, very observant."

"See, told you I was in therapy." They grinned. "My therapist asked me what I'd do if you were willing to try again. He made me answer truthfully."

"What did you say?"

"I told him I'd give you what you want, because Ruby did not get and keep you by himself. Talking so much about Wesley had me see he's not so bad after all."

He took a shrimp off Sherry's plate and fed it to her. He knew she was hungry. She hadn't eaten all day as she kept close to her daughter and played hostess.

"You mean that, Wesley?"

"I do, but I need you to compromise and understand that Ruby is a part of who I am. Like it or not, it's true."

"You're right, and since you're willing to no longer hide from Wesley and allow all of who you are to co-exist, then I can learn to accept you, flaws and all. But, Wesley, having a hand in the drug game when we're in our sixties is just ridiculous. You have to let it go and move on to the next chapter of your life." Sherry's stare begged for Ruby to comprehend what she said.

Ruby took a deep, exaggerated breath. "I know that now. Sherry, shit done changed, from how guys wear their pants to this social media crap and the music these kids listen to. Really, Sherry, what the hell are these mumbling rappers saying?"

Sherry slapped her husband's leg while she let out a heavy chuckle.

"This generation is screwed up. They're all about posting pictures instead of doing what it takes to get money. I just don't get it. I want to say Straw did a number on Brooklyn, but now that I really think about it, he didn't do anything clowns out here aren't already doing."

"I know what you mean. Things aren't how they used to be. There's no order, no honor. I'm not saying things was all sugar and spice when we were growing up, but it was better than how it is today," she said.

"For real."

Sherry took a sip of her sitting champagne. "With that all being said, where does that leave you?"

Ruby took off his loosened tie and tossed it on the centerpiece. It hung next to the crystals. "I think I'd better let it go," he sang.

Sherry raised her glass. "Sing it, baby."

"I thought if I came back, things would fall back into place. Thought I was the missing link, but the world's not ready for how things used to be. These kids have a lot more stupidity they have to get out before they see what hustle is like. Give me a few more months. This kid I have studying me has potential. Maybe with a little more grooming, he can start something of his own, create the best of both worlds."

"I can do this. If you can do your part and not renege, then so can I."

Ruby held his hand out. "Then let's shake on it."

They did. When Sherry went to release her hold, Ruby held on.

"Your ring goes back on. There's no compromising on that." The tone of voice he used was all Ruby. And for the first time in a long time, she had to admit she enjoyed Ruby's presence.

"I wouldn't have it any other way." She leaned in for a kiss. Not ready to distance herself from him more than she already had, she cleaned her lipstick off him.

Then her facial expression went from bliss to confusion. "Wesley, why are you using the house for storage? What's in there?"

The look in his eyes changed. "That's a question for Ruby. At a later time."

"Dammit, Wesley. On second thought, I don't even want to know."

Chapter 30

Paradise Island, Bahamas
2021

Plastered all around the bulletproof glass to the extent where nothing from the outside was seen, Haddy's face stared at Miles from all angles, which included the floor and ceiling. Personal photos and articles from newspapers that followed the story of her murder had been photocopied and made into their own haunting wallpaper. Every week, the photos were taken down from the outside and replaced with new ones. Some were even edited to reenact what some pictured her last hours of life to have been like—her fight for her life, her loss, and ultimately her corpse at her funeral. Four flat screen televisions were bolted to the corner of the large glass box and showed slide shows of the prior week's photos and news broadcasts on her death. Over and over, the screens ran the same things. Only at 9 a.m. and 6 p.m. did a regularly scheduled sitcom play.

It was 1 p.m., lunchtime, and like every other day in Miles's cage, the food slot opened and his meal and drink appeared. You could set your clock by how on point things were run in that basement. The only mystery was who served the food. Miles always hoped for Betty. He knew when she delivered, because he caught glimpses of her manicured nails and knew her cooking due to the added spices. And from time to time, she gave him a large glass of liquor. She knew he was a lightweight, so it helped him through the day.

She never, not once, uttered a word. She did her job and kept it moving. If Linden was in town, he'd rip down two of the photos and stare at him from behind the glass. He treated him like the animals visited by families at the zoo. Linden could stand there for half the day if he wanted it.

There were a few times Miles found himself waking up from sleep he didn't recall falling into. Sleep was never grand. With a hand as your pillow, nothing was comfortable, especially when that hand was joined to a body that had lost over fifty pounds in the past year, starting from a 150-pound frame.

"Newly prescribed pills. Puts you on your ass, don't it?" Linden would tell him using sign language.

His worst visitor by far was Ruby. Had he delivered Miles's meal, he'd give him your historic prisoner's feast of bread and water. He, too, like Linden, would take away photos so he'd been seen. Ruby would sit outside of the cage for hours. No sitcoms were shown when Ruby came around, and Miles became sleep-deprived. Whenever he'd drift off, with the push of a button from Ruby's remote, electric shocks surged from the floor and zapped and woke him. Only when Ruby came down, there were the murder scene photos of Aunt Haddy displayed on the television. Ruby showed the explicit photos, the crime scene photos given to him years ago by Sherry's father.

Miles hadn't said a word to anyone in the year he was locked away. He could hardly remember the last time he signed. He'd move his long-nailed fingers and practice making words. His daily exercise.

The food slot opened. The hand that shoved in the meal tray was new. Miles didn't go for the food right away. From a distance, he stood and watched. The slot closed, and several photos that Miles favored, most of Haddy, were removed. On the other side, a light and bright husky young man, average in height and who donned fashionable eyeglasses watched him quietly. Miles walked to the glass that separated them.

His mouth ajar and voice a high pitch, he squealed, "Mayo?"

The young man allowed his hands to speak. "You're not dead yet, Miles, so you're not seeing my father."

Miles picked his chin and hands up. "Mayo has no kids."

"Not that he knew. My mother's name is Bethany. She found out she was pregnant with me after he died."

Miles stepped closer to the glass. He was a pure spitting image of his best friend. "What are you doing here?" his hands asked.

"I'm you!" Mayo Jr. held his arms out. "Let me explain. I'm Ruby's protégé. I'm going to help him get Brooklyn back where it needs to be. Repair you and Straw's fuck ups."

Seeing Mayo's son signing brought him back to his conversations with his old friend. Jr's. hand movements and sign language knowledge mimicked Mayo's.

"How do you know Ruby?"

"Ruby helped raised me. He said it was his duty to take on his friend's responsibility. Seeing how Ruby moved growing up and the respect he received made me want to walk in his shoes. But more so my father's, because I knew had he lived, he would have had the same image.

"Fast-forward to a few years back. I decided to get in the game. Begged Ruby to show me the ropes, but he refused." For a second, he got lost in the memories.

"And then, he started to miss it all himself, and when you and that bitch-ass Straw started some shit, Ruby thought it best to take me under his wing. You've been kept alive for the past year because of me. It would be, I guess, poetic if the one face you did care for following your aunt's death killed you. But the time was never right, and I concluded that I want to talk. Why resort to violence, you know? I mean, you do deserve it, but why not try a different route?"

"I knew nothing about you."

Mayo Jr. pulled over the seat used by Ruby when he was on his tormenting spree. "I'm glad you didn't." Junior cackled. "You probably would have killed me too."

Miles's eyebrows dropped.

"Yeah, OG, I know what you did. I know all about the jewel you dropped on Triggerz, but like I said, I'm here to talk. Hear your side of shit. You can't be that bad if my pops fucked with you hard, right?" He removed his glasses. Small tattoos sat on his eyelids and eyebrows. "Ruby's been straight with me about who my father was and how he died. He told me how Triggerz and his pops broke into Mayo's house and how he was supposed to have been at the movies that night. It's evident they were trying to rob my pops to pay off their debt, but there was always one thing that bothered me. Ruby told me the story of my father's death hundreds of times and every single time I heard it, I wondered. Out of all nights, how did they know when he wouldn't be home?"

Mayo Jr. looked Miles in the eye for a long time. "We all know how Ruby moves. He's not the type to announce his whereabouts, especially when he was out for leisure. And from what I was told, he and my pops were tight, so how Ruby moved, I'm sure that's how Mayo moved. So do me a favor, OG, and connect the dots. Who was close enough to know both Mayo's and Ruby's plans for that night and would have known about Triggerz' old man's debt?"

On the outside, Junior was all Mayo, but on the inside, he was pure Ruby.

"How did Triggerz know where my pops should have been that night, Miles? You're going to die in here, so set yourself free with the truth."

Miles sat on the cold metal chair. "He wasn't supposed to die. I thought he would leave right after us to head over to your grandmother. I only meant for them to rob him."

"Why? Why would you set him up?"

Miles walked up to the glass wall. "Mayo had changed. I didn't know who he was anymore. Ruby was a bad example. The longer we worked under Ruby, the more big-headed and untouchable he thought he was. He lost himself. It was an Evans that took away my aunt. I couldn't let another take away my friend. I wanted him to see that no good came from being Ruby's friend."

"You did a good thing, OG." Mayo Jr. stood at the door and punched in the code. The door automatically slid open. The feeling of fresh air outside of the cold air-conditioning in the box brought Miles back to life. "You brought me closure, told me what I needed to know. I guess there still is some good in you." He stepped aside for a skinny, long gray-haired Miles to make his exit. "Get out of here. I see no use in having you locked up now that I got what I wanted. I'm not Ruby."

Miles didn't move.

Junior held his hands up and took multiple steps back. "Better? Damn, you took the man out the hood, but you can't take the hood out the man, I see. I done told you, I only came for answers, and now I got it."

Eyes glued on his friend's offspring, Miles stepped out of the cage. Every step he took, he breathed a little easier. He made it to the elevator and called for it. Never once did he give his back to the bear-like a man.

He was inside the elevator when he signed, "I'm sorry." Behind the safety of the elevator doors, Miles felt his heart punch him from the inside and his bladder threaten to give out. He constantly banged his hand against the button to the upper level. His back to the door, he continued to press the button until the tip of his finger ached.

No, no, no.

Miles hit his answer to freedom one hard, angry time then the elevator jumped and moved up.

Yes! Yes! Yes!

He smiled so hard the corners of his mouth ripped into tiny cuts, his dry skin desperate for lubrication. The elevator hit the upper level. When nothing happened, Miles tried to pry the steel doors open himself. Both doors quickly opened halfway and slammed back shut.

Before Miles could fully comprehend the elevator's tantrum, it dropped him back down to the basement and flung its doors open. A monster of an arm wrapped itself around Miles's neck and pulled back into the basement. Miles pulled at the arm and growled.

Mayo Jr. whispered in his ear, "I'm nothing like Ruby. I'm worse." The icepick he had concealed inside his belt buckle penetrated Miles's spine from the bottom up. Mayo Jr. jerked Miles's head back by his scraggly hair. Blood trickled out his muzzle.

"You like stabbing people in the back, huh? How does it feel?" Junior swung his arm back with full force and stabbed Miles in the back of the neck. The tip of the icepick stuck out the front of his neck and the handle out the back.

Miles's grip on Junior's hold loosened, then released not long after. Once Miles's body had gone limp, Mayo Jr. granted him the freedom Miles had craved for the past year and let him fall out in front of him.

He used the back of his hand to wipe away the sweat accumulated on his face. Smears of blood ran across his cheeks. Hearing his phone ring, he dried his finger off on the thighs of his jeans and tapped down on the green circle.

"Is it done?"

"Yes. It is." Junior kicked at the body and smirked. "I needed to be the one to do him in. Needed to do it for Pops and Uncle Leon."

"Are you focused now? Are you ready to be king?" Ruby questioned from the other line.

"Did Uncle Leon like his drinks?"

"Like no other."

"Okay, then, let's get it."